Secret of the Songshell

Volume One of the Joel Suzuki Series

Brian Tashima

Text © 2011-2012, 2016 by Brian Tashima

Cover illustration © 2017 by Jill Colbert

Prism Valley Press logo by Purnima Prasad

ISBN: 0998775509
ISBN-13: 978-0998775500

To T & M

CONTENTS

ACKNOWLEDGMENTS

Mahalo to: Karen & John at Autism Empowerment;
The Nationwiders (Ann, Rolf, Steph); my Salon buddies (Jen,
Angela, Gail, Anita, and Ken); Leona; Roslyn; Mike; Charles;
Alice, Ron & Family; Brian & Family; James; Stacey; Gina;
Chris; SCBWI; Willamette Writers; and everyone else that had
a hand in making this book a reality.

CHAPTER 1: A BAD DAY

Why, why, why did I promise to do this?

Joel calculated in his head that he had three minutes and thirty-five seconds to pull this off. The next class started in six and a half minutes. He wanted to give himself a buffer.

Three minutes and thirty-five seconds—the exact same duration as "Hang on Darkness," the sixth song on Biledriver's first album.

Joel blinked a few times as he tried to refocus his thoughts.

WEEEoooWEEEoooWEEEooo

A high-pitched warbling sound squealed in his ears, accompanied by a brief, sharp pain that shot through his head from left to right. The sound lasted for two seconds, and then it was over. He looked around. No one else seemed to have heard it.

Joel rubbed his temples, closed his eyes and exhaled. It was the second time today that he had heard the strange noise, but there was no time to worry about it now.

He opened his eyes and caught a glimpse of his target: a head of long, shiny black hair cascading over a blood-red blouse. A cold, empty feeling gripped his stomach.

I can't do this. I can't even pass a stupid reading comprehension test. What makes me think I can do this?

Joel scanned the hall of his high school and saw that the other students were blocking off all possible avenues of exit. He replayed a vision of his sister in his mind.

"You promise, right?" Taylor's button-shaped ten-year-old face said to him.

With that, he took a deep breath and strode forward.

Three minutes exactly.

Sometimes, you just gotta say, what the heck.

And go with it.

The head of shiny black hair turned away from the locker it was facing, revealing a soft, pale face with deep brown eyes and bright red lips. The eyes regarded Joel with an air of bemused expectation.

"Um, hi," Joel whispered at his shoes.

"Sorry?" the lips said as the head leaned in a little closer.

Joel cleared his throat. He had only learned two weeks ago that "sorry" in this context meant that the other person did not hear you. "Hi, um, Suzi, right?"

"Right," Suzi said. "And you are—?"

Joel could almost feel his synapses firing. "Um, Joel—I'm Joel. Joel Suzuki. We're in, uh, the same chemistry class. Honors chemistry."

Suzi's eyes widened with recognition. "Oh yeah, second period, right? Sorry I didn't recognize you—don't you sit way in the back?"

Joel searched his brain for an appropriate response. The script was not going quite as he had planned. A large Junior Prom poster announcing a day of the week that was mismatched to the actual date distracted him for a moment. He shook his head to refocus once again. "No, I mean, yeah, I guess. It's not really way in the back, actually, it's the third desk from the back, and, uh..."

"Okay," Suzi chuckled. "Well, it's nice to meet you, Joel."

"Um, nice to meet you too," Joel replied. His mind started to drown in a pool of his own jumbled thoughts, one of which cried out *now what was I supposed to say next?* "Oh, well, the third desk from the back—in the second row on the right side of the room—if you're facing the class from the front, um, you know, from the teacher's perspective."

"Uh, okay," Suzi said.

Joel clenched his teeth. Faced with internal panic, he retreated to safer, familiar ground. "Um, speaking of chemistry, that's like science, right? And, um, did you know that Newton was the first person to come up with the theory of air resistance? It's like, for low flow speeds, drag is due to the dimensions of a body, the density of the fluid, and the—"

A hand with long red-painted nails closed a locker door. "Hey, um, Joel, I really have to get to class, but it's been nice talking to you, okay?"

"Oh—uh, yeah, okay," Joel stammered. He wanted to tell her that they had one hundred and thirty seconds left to get to class, but she had already turned to leave.

♫♫♫

Joel flung open the door to Art's Guitars and trudged inside. "Sorry I'm late," he muttered as he flipped his bangs out of his eyes.

"Hey, bud," Art said, looking up from the cherry-red five-string bass that he had been restringing. "Everything okay?"

"Well, no, not really." Joel walked behind the counter, dropped his backpack on the ground, and took the gig bag off of his shoulder. He placed the bag on top of the glass counter and unzipped it, revealing a Fender Stratocaster that had been smashed into pieces.

Art, a balding, middle-aged man in a rock concert T-shirt and faded black jeans, whistled and stroked his goatee. "Yikes, that doesn't look too good. What happened?"

"Mitch," Joel said with a sigh. "He, um, he saw me talking to Suzi this morning and said that she was his girlfriend. I didn't know."

"What?" Taylor exclaimed, putting down her handheld video game.

"Yeah, so he cornered me after school in the parking lot," Joel said without looking at Taylor. He was grateful that Art had agreed to watch his little sister while their mom was at work, but right now, he didn't feel like talking to her.

"Oh geez," she said.

Joel pulled out the remains of his guitar, which were held together by its strings like a fractured marionette. "He, um, he ran over it with his car—that stupid souped-up Mustang of his. Art, can you fix it?"

"Hmm, probably not even worth it at this point," Art said with a grim expression as he inspected the wreckage. "I'll look at it some more, though. Oh, I picked up your usual ham sandwich—it's by the computer."

Joel sighed again and sat down at the store's computer. "Well, at least I kept my promise," he muttered.

He took the sandwich out of its wrapper. *Art forgot the lettuce again.*

"So what did she say?" Taylor asked.

"About what?" Joel replied, navigating to his favorite Asperger's forum website to read the latest posts.

"Duh, about the prom," Taylor said. "You asked her, right?"

"Um, well, I—she's Mitch's girlfriend anyway. It, uh, it doesn't matter."

"Jooooel," Taylor whined.

"What?" Joel snapped while he read through a post titled "Dealing with Bullies." "Um, look, at least I talked to her, like you wanted me to. Why do you even care?"

"You're sixteen and you've never even been on one date."

"So? Um, have you been on a date?"

"Hello, I'm ten."

"Just—just forget it, okay?"

"I just want you to be happy." Taylor pouted, going back to her video game.

"Happiness is a state of mind," Art interjected in a gentle tone of voice. "You can simply choose to be happy with life the way it is rather than chasing after things you don't have."

Taylor shrugged the way she always did whenever Art spouted one of his philosophical sayings.

"I don't think she can understand most of the things you tell her," Joel said, now looking at his updated grades on the school's website. *Calculus: A. Language Arts: D.* He grimaced. *Ugh. Neither Nerd nor Normal.*

"Sure I can," Taylor huffed.

"She may be young, but she's wiser than you think," Art chuckled. "By the way, Joel, I'm almost finished mixing that awesome song you wrote. That was a killer solo you added to it yesterday. I'll burn a CD of it for you after I add the drum track. Really good stuff, I tell you."

"Um, okay." Joel felt himself blush as he kept his eyes glued to the computer monitor. Despite all the progress he had made in his social skills group, he was still working on the whole "accepting compliments" thing.

A car horn sounded from the street outside. "Gotta go," Taylor announced as she hopped off her stool.

"Uh—is that Mom already?" Joel asked. "I thought she was working."

"Nope, I guess she took the night off. Something about big news. She said to come home right after you're done here."

Big news? Joel wondered. *Hope it's something good. I could use some good news today.*

He navigated to the official Biledriver website, hoping to find that his favorite band had added a Seattle date to the North American leg of their tour. He couldn't afford a ticket, but he thought that maybe Art could give him one in exchange for a few extra hours of work at the store. Instead of a tour schedule, however, what he saw made him nearly choke on his lettuce-less sandwich.

Latest news—Marshall Byle thrown from tour bus in crash along Irish coast—body cannot be located— presumed dead.

Joel shivered as he continued reading.

Byle, 27, was evidently thrown from an open bunk window after the band's tour bus hydroplaned and tipped over while traveling through a torrential downpour. Search parties combed the area but were unable to find him. Band management is undecided at this time as to whether or not to continue the tour.

Continue the tour? Joel thought angrily. *How can they continue the tour without their lead singer and guitarist? I can't believe this. This is just—*

WEEEoooWEEEoooWEEEooo

Joel winced as the weird sound blared painfully in his ears once again. "Did you hear that?"

"Hear what?" Art asked as he tried to piece together two sections of Joel's broken guitar.

"Uh—nothing," Joel said. That was the fourth time today, and he was getting worried. He started a search for "hearing loss symptoms" on the computer when suddenly, out of the corner of his eye, he thought he saw movement on the far wall of the store. He looked around. His eyes gravitated toward an old Biledriver poster that showed all of the band members in full scowl. He blinked several times. Did Marshall just...smile?

Two minutes passed. Joel took another bite out of his sandwich as he continued staring at the poster. He could have sworn that he saw Marshall smile for a fraction of a second. *But that's crazy, right? It's just a poster...*

"Well, sorry, bud," Art said sympathetically as he set Joel's broken guitar aside. "It's pretty much totaled. That guy really did a number on it."

"Yeah," Joel sighed, finally looking away from the poster. *Stupid Mitch,* he thought. *What have I ever done to him? He owes me a new guitar. Rock stars don't have to worry about people breaking their guitars. In fact, they break them themselves, onstage. That is so cool. Must be nice to have endorsements and get stuff for free. After I make it big, who should I endorse? Fender, Gibson, PRS? Maybe I'll get to design my own model. That would be awesome. The Joel Suzuki Special. What would it look like? Maybe like a Jaguar, but more angular, or the Explorer—yeah, that would be cool, or maybe—*

"Oh, hey, I have an idea," Art said. "You know how sometimes I have to pay you in, like, strings or cables and stuff like that? When things are slow like this?"

"Um, yeah," Joel said, glancing around at the empty store. He was quite familiar with the dire financial condition of Art's business, but he loved working there anyway, surrounded by guitars and music. It was a good place to hide from his problems at school and at home. Plus, Art used to play in a band some twenty years ago, and Joel loved hearing the occasional story about those days, whenever Art took a break from giving him the usual boring philosophical sermons.

"Well, how 'bout this? I'll give you the back pay that I owe you for the last couple of months, and an advance on your next few paychecks, all in the form of—wait for it—a new guitar! Whaddya say?"

Joel's mood instantly perked up. "Um, wait, what? Are you serious?"

"Yup," Art said, walking over to where a black Epiphone Les Paul hung from the wall. "How 'bout this baby? I know you've been eyeing her up for a while now."

Okay, this totally makes up for the lousy day I've been having, Joel thought to himself with renewed enthusiasm as he stood up from his stool. He reached out his hand to receive the guitar. Just as his fingers closed around the neck, however, he paused.

"Are you—are you sure about this? Can, um, can the store afford it? I'm worried," he said.

"Don't worry," Art said in his usual reassuring tone. "After all, worrying is a waste of time."

"Um, who said that one—Lao Tzu?"

"No, Axl Rose."

Joel grinned and strummed an open G chord on his new instrument.

♪♪♪

Joel was so happy with his new guitar that he forgot about his mom's big news announcement until Art reminded him about it, twenty-five minutes past his usual quitting time. He raced down the four city blocks to his apartment building, his smile only interrupted by yet another strange warbling sound and the accompanying jolt of pain that shot through his head just as he reached the elevator. He shook it off and made a mental note to take some aspirin as he rode up to the nineteenth floor.

Ding went the elevator.

Joel got out and dashed down the hall to his apartment.

"Sorry I'm late," he panted as he opened the door. Something didn't feel quite right. He noticed the sad expressions on the faces of his mother and sister. "What's—what's the big news?"

"Joel, honey, why don't you have a seat?" his mother said, motioning to the small, round dinner table with the un-washable stains of many years of use. She was still wearing her waitress uniform with the name tag that read *Alison*.

I thought she took the night off, Joel thought. He shot a glance at Taylor, who just looked away. He put his guitar case on the floor and sat down at the table. "Um, is something wrong?"

Alison looked down at her hands and paused for a moment. She sighed before raising her head to look at Joel. "Honey, I lost my job at the restaurant today, and they raised the rent here again. We—we can't afford to stay here anymore."

Joel swallowed hard. Amidst the swirl of sad and angry thoughts that began to boil inside of his head, one in particular stood out: *What was that thing Dad always used to say before he left?* "Real men don't cry." Joel could feel the tears welling up in his eyes. *What did he know anyway.*

CHAPTER 2: A HOODED STRANGER

One thing that Joel had a problem with was letting things go. He wasn't quite sure where that issue came from, although he suspected that it might have had something to do with his parents' divorce. But even before that, he had always been a sentimental person anyway, probably to a fault. He had a classic Foo Fighters T-shirt that was four sizes too small for him still tucked away in his drawer; he kept it because it was his first-ever "rock tee" that he got as a ninth birthday present. When his mom had tried to donate it, he went into a genuine panic attack, and she relented.

Also, despite the difficulties he sometimes had in expressing his emotions, he had nevertheless always been an empathetic person. Even though he and Taylor had their usual share of brother-sister disagreements, he loved her, and her sadness made him sad as well, possibly even more so. When they had moved from Hawai'i to Seattle six years ago, he had no friends, but she had, and having to leave them behind broke both of their hearts.

So it wasn't so much that their little apartment was the greatest place in which to live, but Joel couldn't bear the thought of leaving it and all of its associated memories. It was the first and only place they'd lived in since they had moved. And to make things worse, Taylor's new best friend, Emma, lived two doors down the hall.

"Um, well, so," he said, trying hard to keep his emotions in check, "that's it? There isn't anything else we can do?"

Alison looked Joel in the eyes. "No, honey, I'm really sorry. We have ten days to move out."

"What? Why so fast?"

Alison sighed again. "I'm sorry, they actually told me earlier, but I thought I could scrape together enough to make it. I didn't want to make you kids worried. But then the restaurant had to cut back, and—"

"And now we don't even know where we're gonna live," Taylor interrupted.

Oh man, I hadn't even thought about that part, Joel realized. His stress level went up yet another notch.

"We'll figure something out," Alison said, although she didn't sound too convinced. "I applied for another job today, so hopefully that will work out."

"Um, when will you hear back about that?" Joel asked.

"Soon, I'm sure."

"So, uh, can't they give us an extension or whatever it was, like last time?"

Alison paused before replying. "I asked, but they won't give us another extension unless we can come up with about five hundred dollars, which we don't have, since I had to get the car fixed."

Having lived through a somewhat challenging childhood, Joel was good at latching on to glimmers of hope and mining them for all they were worth. "Wait," he said, "you mean, if we can get some money now, they'll give us some more time until you hear back about that new job?"

"I suppose, but I don't know how we would come up with enough."

Joel fidgeted as his mind raced around for ideas. *Money...where could we get...*

His foot hit the guitar case on the ground.

"Uh—how much money did you say we need?"

♪♪♪

Joel walked through the door to Art's store, guitar case in hand. It had taken a truckload of acting skills that he never knew he had to convince his mom that he was okay with this idea, and although he was dying a little inside, he knew that it was the right thing to do.

"Art?"

Art walked out of the back room. "Oh—hey, bud, what's up? Something wrong with the guitar?"

Joel's hands were shaking. "No—no, it's fine. I just— I just have to return it."

Art took a few steps forward, a worried expression on his face. "Why? What happened?"

"We—um, my family, we're getting kicked out of our, um, our apartment. We, uh, couldn't make the rent."

"Oh no, that's terrible."

"Yeah, so, um, I was wondering if—if I could, like, um, exchange the guitar, for, well, you know—"

"For cash?"

Joel felt his heart sink. "Yeah. I mean, I know the store doesn't have much money and all, but, um, this is like, an emergency and stuff...you know. I'll work extra hours, or whatever."

Art gave Joel a warm smile. "Say no more, bud. I'll help you out." He disappeared into the office.

Joel slumped onto a stool and looked at the guitar case. As he sat there, all of the bad events in his life, recent and past, started to drip into his thoughts, and slowly they began to coalesce into one giant overwhelming cloud of negativity.

Art came back out a minute later, holding a check in his hand. "Here you go. Don't worry about the store, okay? We'll be fine."

Joel just nodded. *Don't worry? All I do is worry. How can I not worry when everything just goes wrong all the time?*

"Joel? It'll be okay, trust me. Worrying is a waste of time, remember?"

Joel didn't hear the last thing Art said—his mind was becoming too overwhelmed with his own stressful thoughts. "I swear, when I become a rich and famous rock star, none of this will happen anymore," he said to no one in particular.

Art pulled up a stool next to Joel and sat down. "I know that things seem bad right now, but believe me, life will get better. Remember, 'this, too, shall pass.' You just need to be patient."

"All my problems will be solved when I make it," Joel continued, ignoring Art as he clenched his fists. "Money, school, girls, bullies, whatever—everything will be taken care of, and I'll finally be happy. I'll be the one in charge. Everyone will listen to me. I'll even be able to get my mom and dad to—"

Art put a hand on Joel's shoulder. "Joel—listen to me."

Art's words and the physical contact broke through the angry fog for a moment. Joel looked at him.

"It's okay to have dreams, but don't make your happiness dependent on them. We often think that if we get or achieve something, doing so will make us happy. But that's not always the case. Thoreau said that happiness is a butterfly—if you chase it, it flies away. But if you just sit there and wait, it'll land on you. You can be happy right here, right now—all you have to do is decide that you *will* be happy. Happiness is a state of mind."

Joel blinked as he tried to make sense of Art's words. But the angry fog was too thick. It rolled back in, stronger than ever. "You know what?" Joel snapped, grabbing the check from Art's hand, "I have no idea what you're talking about."

"Joel—"

Joel stood up and started for the door. "Or—or maybe I do. I think you only say these stupid things because you never made it in music yourself!"

"Joel, I—"

"That's it, isn't it? Your dream never came true, so you just—you just read and repeat all these nonsense sayings and quotes, to make yourself feel better about failing—failing as a musician, failing as a rock star. And now you're trying to destroy my dream, too!"

"Joel, please—"

"Well, you know what? I'm gonna be different. I'm gonna make it. You—you'll see! Everyone will see. You and Mitch and Suzi and everybody else!"

Joel shoved the check into his pants pocket and grabbed the door handle. Just as he was about to turn it, Art called to him.

"Joel," Art said as he held out a silver disc in his right hand. "Before you go, here, take this."

"What—what's that?" Joel snapped, his insides roiling.

"Your song. I finished mixing it. I think you'll like how it turned out."

Joel paused for a moment and looked at the ground. A part of him knew that he was going to regret this outburst later on, but when his emotions took over like this, it was basically impossible to just turn them back off.

"Look," Art said gently, "maybe after you've had a chance to calm down, come on by and we'll—"

Joel snatched the CD and stormed out, not bothering to listen to the rest of what Art had to say. He glanced at the disc and noticed that it had been preprinted with the store's name and phone number.

No problem, I'll just make copies of this at school and then send them out to every single record label. Then they'll all come calling, starting a bidding war, wanting to sign me to a record contract. It's gonna be awesome. First we'll buy our apartment, then we'll buy a mansion on Mercer Island, and then another one in Kahala. I'll have eight hundred and twenty-three, no, make that eight thousand, three hundred and fifty-two guitars. I'll have a huge finished basement, like, three thousand and five hundred square feet, just for my guitars.

Joel was so wound up that another occurrence of the strange warbling sound barely fazed him. He wandered around aimlessly for a while, losing track of time while thinking about all of the things that he would buy for himself and his family. He didn't feel like going back home, but he had no alternative destination in mind. The world felt like one big blur. He was so distracted by his own thoughts that he didn't notice the tall stranger wearing a gray hooded sweatshirt and a long black trench coat who sidled up next to him.

"Joel," the stranger whispered in a low, husky voice from within the confines of the hood.

Joel didn't hear the stranger. He continued to walk with his eyes fixed forward.

"Joel," the stranger whispered again, a little louder.

Joel heard him this time. "Huh—what?" he said as he jumped and looked around, startled out of his daze. "Whoa, you scared me—um, wait, who are you?"

"I'm Marshall Byle," the stranger said in a familiar British accent as he turned to look Joel in the eye.

Joel quickly looked away. "What? You can't be..."

For a second, Joel debated whether to turn and run or stand and yell at whoever this was for playing a lame joke on him, but then he turned his head back around and got a good look at the stranger's face. Although it appeared a bit older in person, Joel instantly recognized that the face's features and details—the light-green eyes, hooked nose, long sideburns, uneven jawline, the scar on the cheek from an on-stage accident—were exactly the same as the ones that he had been seeing on posters, album covers, and website photos all of these years.

Joel's jaw dropped. "Oh my g—"

"Shhh," Marshall hissed, his eyes darting around. "Don't blow my cover, mate. I'm supposed to be dead. Just keep walking."

"Your what? Cover? Um, why are you—what are you doing here? How—how do you know who I am?"

"Joel, listen to me. We don't have much time. I can make your dreams come true—your dreams of becoming a rock star. You just have to come with me."

"Um, go with you—where? And how do you know what I want to become?"

"It'll just be for a little while. You want to be a rock star, right?"

Joel's mind was reeling. Marshall Byle—his all-time favorite musician—was here, talking to him, offering to make him a star. Was this really happening? "Well, um, yeah, of course, but—"

Marshall stopped walking and grabbed Joel by the shoulders. "Joel, *trust me*," he said. "I know this all sounds very strange right now. But I assure you, you won't regret it."

"Regret what? Where are we going?"

Marshall's expression tightened. "We only have a few more minutes if you really want to do this. Are you in or not?"

"Um, I—well—"

Marshall sighed and raised his hands. "All right, if you don't want to be a rock star, fine with me." He turned around and started to walk away.

Joel stared at the back of his idol, a man who had somehow risen from the dead to appear next to him. He pushed aside the jumble of confused emotions filling his mind. As crazy as all of this seemed, he couldn't pass up what sounded like the opportunity he had been so fervently wishing for.

Sometimes, you just gotta say...

"Um, okay, what the heck, let's go."

Marshall looked over his shoulder at Joel, a wide smile on his face. "Excellent."

"So, uh, what do I have to—" Joel started to ask before Marshall gruffly ushered him into a side alleyway between two old buildings. Joel panicked for a brief moment, thinking that he was about to get mugged. "Hey! What—what are you doing?"

"Shh, don't worry. We just can't be seen," Marshall said as he reached into his trench coat.

Joel, half expecting Marshall to produce a knife or a gun, was quite perplexed by what he saw instead: a small-scale, odd-looking musical instrument that resembled a mandolin, with strings that glowed like the filaments of an incandescent light bulb and a teardrop-shaped body made of material that looked like it came from the inside of an oyster shell. "Wow—um, what is that?" he asked.

"I'll explain everything later," Marshall replied. "For now, just stay right there and try to relax."

I'm getting pulled into a dark alley by my dead musical idol who says that he'll turn me into a rock star while whipping out some crazy alien guitar—and he tells me to relax.

Marshall closed his eyes and seemed to enter into a state of intense concentration. He strummed the strange instrument, but Joel couldn't hear any sound coming from it. Joel was about to ask another question when a feeling of dizziness suddenly overcame him, not unlike when he first got seasick as a child. His vision became blurry, and the dizziness quickly gave way to a more intense sensation, which made him feel like he was being turned inside out. He wanted to scream, or perhaps throw up, but he found that he had lost all control of his own body. The CD that he had been carrying fell to the ground and rolled away, but that was the least of his concerns now. Tiny colored streams of light danced before his eyes before everything suddenly went dark.

CHAPTER 3: SPECTRALAND

Joel awoke with a headache that throbbed in time with the rhythmic bouncing of whatever it was he was sitting on. The realization that he was sitting, rather than lying down, made him recognize that he was not in his bed, but was instead tied to a person right in front of him, with his cheek and chest pressed into the person's back. His vision was still blurry, but he got the sense that he was in some sort of dimly lit tunnel. His first instinct was to try to struggle free of his bonds.

"Oh, good, you're awake," Marshall's voice said. "I must admit, this riding position was getting a bit uncomfortable."

As Joel's senses returned, he realized that the person in front of him was Marshall and that they had been riding double horseback-style on a creature that was definitely not a horse. Marshall had shed his hoodie and trench coat and was now wearing a sleeveless vest made of some soft, unrecognizable material, along with a pair of matching pants and boots. The mother-of-pearl mandolin hung from a strap at his side.

"Sorry about the rope there," Marshall said. "Had to keep you from falling off somehow. Probably best to keep it on for now until you regain your bearings—these beasts can be a bit unpredictable at times. You can sit up a bit more, though."

Joel sat up and placed his hands on the creature's sides, which, to his surprise, were not covered in hair or fur, but rather some tacky, glue-like substance. "Eww," he said, wiping his hands on his pants. "What is this thing?"

"The natives call it a slimeback," Marshall replied. "Pretty accurate description, if I do say so myself. You'll find that most things here are quite aptly named."

Joel looked around. From what he could tell, the creature was somewhat camel-like in appearance, with a long neck and a hump on its back, right behind where he was sitting. They were in a stone tunnel that was illuminated by what looked like faintly glowing patches of moss, spread out in irregular patterns across the walls. The air was warm and humid and had a musty odor to it.

"Uh, where is 'here'?" he asked.

"It's a place called Spectraland."

Joel never paid much attention in social studies class, but that didn't sound like the name of any place that he was aware of. Any real place, that is. "Spectraland? You mean, like the Minnow the Shark song?"

"Indeed!" Marshall laughed. "Brilliant band, they are. I had forgotten all about that track. Good observation, Joel."

"Um, okay," Joel said, realizing that his question had been answered but not in the way that he wanted. "But, really, where are we?"

"Ah, yes, where are we..." Marshall said in a wistful tone. "A beautiful, wondrous place...especially for people like us. You know, I never quite managed to figure out whether this was a different planet or an alternate dimension, or what have you. It's definitely not of Earth, though, I can tell you that much."

Joel felt his headache getting worse. "Not of Earth? Wait—you're dead, so...does that mean I—I'm dead, too?"

Marshall laughed again. "No, no, I assure you, we are both quite alive. And this is not a dream, either. I hope that covers all the bases, as you Yanks say."

Joel still felt disoriented. "Okay...so, um, it must be some kind of reality show, then, right? Like, uh, Home Makeover or whatever, but instead of getting a new house, I'm gonna get a record deal? Is that it?"

"Somewhat, I suppose—it's not a show, but it definitely is reality. Here we are, hang on, now," Marshall said as the slimeback slowed to a trot.

Joel saw that they were approaching a dead end, where a huge boulder with an ornate pattern carved into its center sealed off the tunnel. Marshall produced a primitive-looking stone knife from a sheath attached to his boot, turned around, and cleanly severed the rope holding him and Joel together. Despite Marshall's warning to hang on, Joel nearly fell backward, but the slimeback's hump propped him up. Marshall dismounted the creature and approached the boulder.

"What are you doing?" Joel asked.

"You'll see," Marshall said, pressing the front of his left forearm against the boulder's carving. There was a faint *whoomp* sound, like when a cork is pulled out of a bottle, and the boulder began to roll off to one side.

Joel noticed that among all of Marshall's many tattoos, there was one on his left forearm that was not in any of the previous pictures that Joel had seen of him. The tattoo matched the pattern on the boulder, but Joel wasn't sure if it had been there before or after Marshall had pressed his arm against the giant rock.

"Prepare to have your mind blown," Marshall said, hopping back aboard their mount. "Even more so, I mean."

They rode through the opening into a scene that was unlike anything Joel had been expecting. The environment, which was vaguely tropical, appeared to have been painted in vivid watercolors that kept shifting and shimmering in the warm breeze. Large trees that resembled a cross between palms and seaweed went from pale yellow to dark green and back again. Seemingly endless mountain ranges in the distance flickered between gray and black, at times invisible against the night sky. The sky itself contained the silhouettes of two moons, one crescent and one full, both much closer to the surface than Earth's own satellite. What Joel found most remarkable, however, were the faint waves of various colors that floated through the air, surrounding everything—including himself.

"Wow," was all he could say.

Marshall grinned. "You should see it in the daytime."

"What—what is all this?" Joel asked as he moved his hand back and forth in front of his face, parting the color waves like wisps of smoke.

"I believe that it's mostly electrical particles in the air—invisible to us back home, but very evident here. They're probably generated by light, sound, even our own bodies. I don't know. I've done some reading up on it, but I'm a musician, not a scientist, as you know," Marshall said with a smile. "The folks here call it the Aura."

"The folks? Um, you mean, like, aliens?"

Marshall chuckled. "Yes, I suppose so. Little green men, just like the old stories said. Rather funny. I guess some stereotypes really are based in truth. You'll meet them soon enough."

Joel's brain was going into sensory overload. "Um, meet them? Is that safe? Where are we going? And what does this have to do with becoming a rock star?"

"So many questions! Well, I suppose I felt the same way when I first arrived here. Don't worry, my friend, we'll—"

A piercing growl interrupted Marshall in mid-sentence. The slimeback reared its head, turned, and started to break into a faster pace while emitting a low, groaning sound rather like the croak of a toad. Turning to look toward the source of the growl, Joel saw a creature that resembled a reptilian kangaroo as it emerged from a nearby bush and began bounding toward them.

"Whoa!" Joel cried. "What is that?"

"Easy, now," Marshall said to their mount as he grabbed his alien mandolin and turned to face the creature. He held the instrument up and aimed the head of it at the creature, rifle-style, and began to strum in short, aggressive strokes.

This time, Joel not only heard sounds (something approximating a speed metal riff) emanating from the instrument but saw a stream of red light pour forth from its headstock that struck the creature square in the mid-section. The creature made a little grunting noise and collapsed.

"Holy cow," Joel said, "you got it! Whatever it is— was. Was it gonna eat us or something?"

"Probably not, it was just a scaletop. Those things are more bark than bite, really. But best not to take chances. That's one thing about this place—loads and loads of dangerous, indigenous wildlife. And they have this nasty habit of popping out at you any old bloody time they feel like it. So remember to stay on your toes. It's a beautiful place, but not exactly a relaxing tourist resort, if you know what I mean."

Joel glanced around, scanning for any other surprises, and noticed a slight change in the appearance of his surroundings. Rather than the watercolor painting vibe that he had gotten at first, he now noticed that the landscape had a more pixelated feel, like something out of an old-fashioned computer-generated cartoon.

"Whenever you manipulate the Aura, as I just did," Marshall said, anticipating Joel's next question, "it causes slight changes in our perception of the environment around us. It can be disorienting at first, but once you get used to it, it's rather quite entertaining, I should say."

"Um, manipulate the Aura?"

"Yes, with my wavebow."

"Wavebow? You mean that mandolin thing?"

"Yes, another quaint name the locals invented. You'll get used to all of the new terminology after a while. I prefer 'luxtar,' myself—because, you know, lux, for light, and guitar—but it hasn't quite caught on just yet. And I believe that there's some kind of Asian lighting company back home with that name. Oh well, such is life." Marshall chuckled.

Joel had tuned Marshall out three sentences ago, his mind still trying to wrap itself around the concept of Aura-manipulation. "Uh—am I—am I gonna get to try one of those things?"

"Oh, you most certainly are, in due time. There are many other matters for us to attend to first, though."

Joel had a lot of other questions, but for a moment, they all blended together and disappeared amongst the overwhelming sensory and informational input he was receiving. The slimeback continued to trot along on a path made up of a substance that resembled a mix of dirt and gravel, while the seaweed palms became fewer and farther between.

After meandering on for a bit through the trees, the path led up and over a small hill. A few football-field lengths in the distance, Joel saw a sprawling assortment of primitive mushroom-shaped hut-like structures nestled in the center of a large clearing, its perimeter surrounded by tall, imposing rock formations.

"Um, is that where we're going?" he asked.

"Indeed it is," Marshall replied. "That, my friend, is the village of Headsmouth. Sort of the capital of the island, I suppose you could say."

"Island?"

"Ah, yes, I forgot to mention, Spectraland is an island. Rather tiny, actually. And somewhat on the primitive side, technologically speaking. I'm afraid you won't find any Wi-Fi hotspots here," Marshall said with a wry grin.

As they drew closer to the village, Joel got his first glimpse of the "natives." Having been an avid fan of fantasy and science fiction throughout his life, he felt somewhat prepared for his first extraterrestrial (or extradimensional) contact, but it was still a bit unsettling to actually see them with his own eyes, rather than in his imagination or on the movie screen. They were basically humanoid in appearance but had pale-green complexions and sporadic leaf-like protrusions scattered about their skin. Most of them wore vests similar to Marshall's, or tunics made of a similar material, although a few were clad only in something akin to a loincloth.

"There they are," Marshall said. "Don't be afraid, they're quite friendly, really. Interesting little folks. Almost as if someone combined human and plant DNA."

"Like Poison Ivy," Joel observed, referring to the *Batman* character.

"Exactly!" Marshall laughed. "You certainly do know your pop culture references—I like that."

Joel smiled sheepishly. As they made their way to the village's outer edge, he saw that the huts were a bit more sophisticated than they had first appeared; most were built on raised platforms and had little stairways that led up to the primary entrance, and the outer walls were decorated with various drawings and markings. There were also tree houses—some simple, some with multiple levels that were connected by walkways that wrapped around the large trunks of their hosts.

The first native that they passed gave them a deferential nod. "Hello, Chief Byle, welcome back," it said in a low, guttural voice that had a metallic, processed edge to it, as if it were being run through an effects box.

"They speak English?" Joel whispered. "And what did he call you?"

"Hello, hello," Marshall greeted the native. Then, turning to Joel, he said, "They don't speak English *per se*, but I have managed to manipulate the Aura such that you hear the meanings of what the other person is trying to say, not what they are actually saying, for the most part. Sort of a translation spell, I suppose."

"Oh—so you say something in English, and they—they hear it in their own language?"

"Precisely. It is rather funny, as their mouth movements don't match the words you hear. It's like watching one of those old kung fu movies with the dubbed-in dialogue."

They rode the slimeback through the village, passing more natives along the way. There were male and female, young and old, all seeming to casually go about their business with a somewhat dazed look on their faces, almost as if they were sleepwalking. Some were accompanied by small animals that resembled anything from sheep with fish fins to spiny dachshunds. A group of native children played a game amongst themselves involving rocks and tree branches; at one point, a rock went whizzing by Joel's head and the children went scrambling in all directions. Any adult native that they crossed paths with greeted Marshall as "Chief Byle." Joel asked Marshall about this again, but Marshall simply told him that he would explain everything else in a few minutes.

After passing through an open area, Joel saw an impressive-looking hut that was much larger than all of the other ones. It sat atop a small hill and was flanked by a cluster of trees, which supported about a dozen different circular tree houses that seemed to be connected to the main structure by various sets of stairs, ladders, and walkways. Torches mounted to tall poles flanked either side of the primary entrance, which had a rather long stairway leading up to it and a taller, burly-looking native apparently standing guard. Joel could see waves of Aura dancing around the torches' flickering blue flames.

As Marshall and Joel approached the hut, the guard turned his head and made a whistling noise, as if calling out to someone. An older-looking native emerged from a low-hanging tree house and sauntered up to them.

"Greetings, Chief Byle," the native said in a voice that was smooth and pleasant, but with the same processed tone as the others. "And greetings to your companion as well. I will escort your mount to the stable at once."

"Hello, Suntooth," Marshall said as he dismounted the slimeback, motioning for Joel to do the same. "Our other guest is doing well, I trust?"

"Yes, Master. She has been resting comfortably."

Joel wondered what this exchange meant but decided not to ask for now.

"Excellent," Marshall said as he made an introductory gesture in Joel's direction. "Suntooth, this is Joel."

"Um, hello," Joel said while looking at the ground.

"Joel, this is Suntooth. He is one of my, uh, advisors."

"Greetings, young sir," Suntooth said in a sleepy, laid-back manner as he nodded at Joel. "Welcome to our home."

"Um, thanks."

"Please get Joel outfitted with some appropriate attire," Marshall said to Suntooth, "and bring him and our other guest to the main dining room in about, oh, twenty minutes or so."

"Of course, Master," Suntooth said with a slow nod.

"Wait, what? Where are you going?" Joel asked Marshall.

"Don't worry, just some minor business I have to attend to. Suntooth will fetch you some comfortable native clothes to wear, and I'll be right back."

"Please, sir, follow me," Suntooth said to Joel as Marshall walked away. Suntooth made a motion toward another native, who lazily walked up and then led the slimeback in another direction.

This is crazy, Joel thought for the hundredth time since he first woke up in this alien world. *It's totally like I'm in some kind of movie or something. If this is a different planet, I wonder how far away we are from Earth? A million light years? Two million? I guess all those people who said that extraterrestrial life exists were right. Or could it be a different dimension, or an alternate universe? What do these plant people eat, anyway? And how did they evolve?*

Suntooth led Joel up a walkway and into one of the tree houses. Remarkably roomy, it was illuminated by stones that were covered with the same kind of moss-like substance that Joel saw in the tunnel.

Suntooth reached into one of several baskets that sat against the wall and produced a vest-and-pants set similar to the one Marshall was wearing. "Here you are, sir. These should fit well."

There had been no time to think about it, but Joel suddenly realized that he had been sweating quite profusely in his long-sleeve T-shirt and sweater jacket. The humid tropical climate of this world felt similar to his former home in Hawai'i.

"What, you mean, change here?" Joel asked, glancing at the door-less entrance and open windows of the tree house.

"Yes, please," Suntooth said.

Feeling self-conscious, Joel stripped out of his earthly wardrobe and donned the native outfit, which was surprisingly light and airy. Suntooth tucked Joel's original clothes away in another basket.

"Is that comfortable, sir?" he asked.

"Um, yeah, totally," Joel replied.

"Very good. Now please, follow me."

It wasn't until they were halfway up another adjoining walkway that Joel remembered he was still wearing his terrestrial shoes. He decided not to say anything about it. *I guess Chuck Taylors work on any planet.* He shrugged.

They climbed a short rope ladder to a platform that supported another tree house. This one had a set of long vines hanging from the top of the doorway that blocked the view of whatever was inside, in a manner similar to a bead curtain.

Suntooth stopped in front of the doorway. "Miss Smith?" he called out. "Chief Byle requests your presence in the main dining room."

"Okay, okay, I'll be right there," a decidedly nonprocessed female voice replied from within the tree house.

Miss Smith?

Joel turned to Suntooth, ready to fire off a series of questions about the identity of their soon-to-be-companion, when suddenly a pale arm with no leafy protrusions parted the vines in the doorway. What he saw emerge from the tree house was more surprising than anything else he had seen up until this point: a teenage Earth girl.

CHAPTER 4: MARSHALL'S STORY

The girl looked at Joel with an expression that could be charitably described as annoyed surprise. "Who is *this*?" she asked Suntooth with irritation in her voice.

"This is Master Joel," Suntooth replied. "Chief Byle just returned with him."

"He didn't tell me there was gonna be someone else," she muttered mostly to herself.

Joel glanced at the girl but avoided making direct eye contact. She was dressed in similar native fashion and was about an inch and a half taller than him. She had a slim, athletic build, straight blond hair that came down to her shoulders, and matching scorpion tattoos on each shoulder. Joel's initial impression was that she was someone who could have been a cheerleader in high school but was just a little too off-kilter to fit in with that kind of crowd.

"Sir," Suntooth said to Joel, "this is Miss Felicity Smith—I believe she is also from your homeland."

"Uh, hello," Joel said, extending a hand while looking off to the side, keeping the girl in his peripheral vision.

SECRET OF THE SONGSHELL

Felicity ignored his handshake offer and rolled her eyes. "I can't believe there's someone else! That is so not cool. I was supposed to be the only one!"

"Um, sorry?" Joel said, trying to apologize for something that wasn't his fault.

"I said, *I was supposed to be the only one.* For the rock star training, or whatever."

Joel realized that she had interpreted his apology as an indicator that he had not heard or understood her. Words could be so confusing sometimes. "Oh," he offered as a reply.

"That's what you're here for, right? Isn't that what he told you?" she asked Joel.

"Um, yeah, I guess."

"Ugh, I knew it."

"We should get going," Suntooth cut in diplomatically. "Please, follow me."

Joel hadn't given any thought as to whether there would be any other "Earth people" here with him besides Marshall, as everything had been happening so fast, but he now found it comforting that he had some additional company, even if it was in the form of an obnoxious girl who didn't seem to like him very much. He decided not to say anything else to her for now.

They made their way back to the main structure, which was divided into several floors. They climbed down a ladder, past a couple of landing areas that had doorways covered by vine-ropes, and got off the ladder at the third landing. They passed through the doorway into a large, circular room that housed a wooden, surfboard-shaped table with intricately carved stools surrounding it. A round rock covered in luminescent moss hung from the ceiling, functioning as a simple but elegant chandelier. Marshall sat at the middle of one side of the table.

"Hello, hello," the Biledriver singer said as he turned to face them. "Ah, Joel, looking good. Much more comfortable, I presume? And Felicity, my dear, Suntooth assures me that you were well tended to while I was gone."

"While you were gone picking up this dork, you mean?" she snapped, glancing at Joel. "Yeah, sure."

"Such spirit," Marshall laughed. "Please, everyone, sit down, sit down. We have much to discuss. Oh, Greenseed?"

A young native girl with a sullen expression emerged from another doorway carrying a tray with four wooden cups. She began setting each cup down on the table. Joel noticed that her demeanor was a little different from the other natives—she appeared to act with a slightly greater sense of urgency, and she seemed a bit more deliberate in her movements. She noticed Joel observing her and reacted by shooting him a suspicious glance. He quickly looked down at his hands.

"Greenseed," Marshall said, "Dinner can be served now."

"Yes, Master," the native girl said in a soft voice before she disappeared back through the doorway.

Suntooth gestured for Felicity and Joel to sit, and they settled on stools on the opposite side of the table, facing Marshall. Joel made sure to keep an empty stool between himself and Felicity. Suntooth followed and took a seat next to Marshall.

"So," Marshall said, taking a drink from his cup, "as I've said, I've brought you here to become rock stars. Now, Miss Felicity has been here for a few days already, but I've wanted to save the whole grand story for when the both of you were here. Fortunately, she's not as persistently inquisitive as you, Joel." He grinned.

Joel gave a nervous half chuckle and peered into his cup. The liquid inside was a sickly green color and smelled like plumeria flowers. Suddenly, something Marshall had said hit Joel in the gut.

"Wait, a few days?" he asked. "Um, how long is this gonna take, anyway? I can't be gone long, my mom—"

"Will be worried, yes, I know," Marshall interrupted. "Don't fret. You see, time moves much faster here than it does back home. You know, interstellar physics and all that rot. We'll be done here in plenty of time for you to be back by supper."

"You didn't tell me you were bringing someone else," Felicity said to Marshall in an acidic tone.

"You didn't ask," Marshall replied coolly, taking another drink.

Joel glanced at Felicity, who continued to look sideways at Marshall with a petulant expression on her face.

"Ideally there would be more of you," Marshall continued, "but bringing people over through the Rift is quite taxing on the Aura, and it is only open for so long. But I digress. Let us start at the beginning, shall we?"

The native girl that Marshall called Greenseed returned, this time with four small wooden bowls, which she hastily set down on the table before dashing out once again. Joel inspected their contents and saw a murky brown fluid that didn't smell like anything familiar. He decided to ignore it. He wasn't feeling very hungry anyway.

"This particular story is best told with some visual aids," Marshall announced. He produced his wavebow and began to play a dreamy-sounding melody. The tone that the instrument produced was like a clean electric guitar being played through a flanger, with a touch of delay. Intertwining strands of purple light streamed out of the instrument and formed a swirling cloud right below the moss-rock chandelier.

"Years ago, our time," Marshall began, "before my band became successful, I was alone backstage after a show when suddenly I felt very dizzy and passed out. Turns out, I had been transported here, to Spectraland, by a couple of local shamans who called themselves Wavemakers—natives with a special ability to manipulate the Aura by combining the powers of their brain waves with music."

Joel saw images forming within the swirling purple cloud. Two natives carrying wavebows were talking to Marshall, who was clad in torn jeans and a Biledriver T-shirt.

"After working out the language issues by means of a special incantation that translates the sound waves of voices," Marshall continued, "they explained that they needed my help to defeat a rogue shaman warlord named Chief Fourfoot. Apparently, this nasty bloke wanted to unite the island's various villages under his rule and enslave all of the island's inhabitants."

In the cloud, Joel saw a tall and muscular native wearing a helmet adorned with what looked like enormous deer antlers with pointed ends. The native carried a large, dark-tinted wavebow and was dressed in flowing green robes woven out of vines.

"The other Wavemakers, who had always acted as the island's peacekeepers, tried to contain him, but he was too powerful for them. So, being desperate, they uncovered an ancient incantation that allowed them to search the universe for any kind of creature with similar—and hopefully stronger—abilities. Lo and behold, that 'creature' turned out to be yours truly. It seems that my particular brain waves, combined with my musical skills, gave me the ability to manipulate the Aura in amazing new ways that they had never seen before."

The image in the cloud was now one of Marshall standing with the native shamans, all of them carrying wavebows and conjuring up bursts of light in various different colors.

"Like the other shamans, I could perform feats that resembled magic spells—but in a more powerful fashion than they were capable of. In what you could call a crash course of sorts, they spent some time training me and honing my skills, and then it was off to confront Chief Fourfoot."

The purple cloud shifted to scenes of Marshall and the group of native Wavemakers all firing red streams of light from their wavebows at the tall and muscular native.

"We engaged in a series of intense battles, and sadly, all but one of the other shamans besides me were killed. In the end, however, I was victorious."

"Okay," Felicity interrupted, "this is *so* corny. I feel like I'm watching a video game cut scene or something. When do we get to the part about us becoming rock stars?"

"Patience." Marshall smirked. "After Fourfoot was defeated, the last remaining shaman, who was gravely injured, gave me instructions from his deathbed on how to travel back and forth between here and our world. The people of the island gave me their gratitude, and I returned home."

The cloud shifted again, and Joel saw a more familiar sight—Marshall with his signature Fender Stratocaster guitar, sitting in a recording studio.

"After I returned, hardly any time had passed by at all. My bandmates merely assumed that I had gone out for an after-show bite or something. Anyway, I soon discovered that although I could not replicate any of the magic-like abilities that I had learned, there was still one significant change in my *musical* abilities. I found that the Wavemaker training helped me to perceive sound and brain waves differently—I could actually *see* how certain melodies and chord progressions affected human emotions."

At this, Joel noticed Felicity's attention perk up ever so slightly.

"So," Marshall said with a smile, "how do you suppose that ability affected my career?"

Joel suddenly felt like he was in school and Marshall was the teacher. In typical fashion, he knew the answer but chose not to speak.

"That's how you were able to write such good songs," Felicity said, her tone a bit more reverent than it had been.

"Exactly!" Marshall said. "I realized that everything I had written up until then had been bollocks, and that's why my band had not gotten anywhere. But now things would be much different. Everything—everything!—I wrote after that was certifiably brilliant, as I'm sure the two of you can attest to, and I owed it all to this strange, wonderful alien land."

Joel saw Marshall looking at Felicity, and an odd feeling of competitiveness urged him to say something at that point. "So, uh, what was the deal with you dying and all that?"

"Ah, excellent question," Marshall said, turning to Joel. "After I made it, I felt that I now had everything I had always wanted—all the fame, money, and glory that one could ever hope for. Platinum records, the cover of *Rolling Stone*, what have you."

38

Both Joel and Felicity were now sitting straight up on their stone stools.

"But you know what?" Marshall continued. "Like the cliché goes, it wasn't all that it was cracked up to be. Not only did I feel suffocated by success—I couldn't even go out to the corner pub anymore without being mobbed—but I felt like there had to be more to life, a higher, nobler purpose."

The purple cloud then showed an image of the Biledriver tour bus, speeding along a road in a driving rain. It was a winding coastal highway with a short, makeshift stone wall running along the edge. On the other side of the wall was a steep drop, covered in rocks and vegetation, that led straight into the ocean some fifty feet or so below.

Marshall stared at the cloud with a reflective smile. "Then one day, fate chose to present me with an opportunity. As you know, our tour bus crashed in Ireland in an unfortunate accident. I was thrown from a bunk window and went rolling down the cliff. Amazingly, my fall was broken by a cluster of brush and I managed to escape major injury. But it was that near-death experience that made me decide it was time to make a significant change in my life."

"So, you faked your death," Felicity said.

"Indeed," Marshall said, no longer smiling. "Remember when I said that none of my Wavemaker abilities worked back home? Well, that's not entirely true—I had remembered that there was still one thing that I could do, and that was to return here, to Spectraland, using the instructions given to me by that final shaman before he died. As I laid there on the side of the road in the pouring rain, I knew that I had been given the perfect moment, the ideal opportunity."

Joel saw an image of several Spectraland natives greeting Marshall. A polychromatic Aura swirled in an energetic fashion around them.

"So yes, I did the Elvis thing," Marshall chuckled, "and escaped from the prison of my own stardom and came back here. Once I informed the natives that I was here to stay, they made me an honorary chief, due to my role in ridding them of Fourfoot's threat. Then the existing chief of Headsmouth suddenly passed away from natural causes, and I was nominated to take his place."

"We're getting to the part about us soon, right?" Felicity asked anxiously.

Marshall appeared to ignore her, seemingly lost in his own train of thought. "It was the perfect situation for me—I was still treated like a celebrity," he said, gesturing around the room, "but without all of the appendant rubbish that goes along with that back home."

Greenseed set a plate bearing something that looked like fuzzy roast beef down on the table in front of Joel before dashing off.

"Anyhow," Marshall continued, "I now had the time to peacefully reflect and consider what fulfilling cause I could dedicate my life toward. Because of the great feeling I received from saving these folks, I knew that helping people had to be involved. Then, one day as I rode through a lush, colorful jungle, it struck me: I would help young musicians achieve their dreams of rock stardom."

Joel felt a twinge of nervous excitement. His brain was beginning to anticipate what Marshall was going to say.

"It would be a simple process, really," Marshall said around a bite of food. "Using the same incantation that brought me here, I would locate those gifted individuals that evidenced similar brain wave patterns and musical talent, and then—with their permission, of course—bring them here to receive the same training that I had. Then they would return home and bless the world with their newfound skills, making multitudes of new fans happy with their glorious music. I'd be like an otherworldly Clive Davis."

"Sounds good to me," Felicity said. "When do we start?"

"Of course, I'd be less than honest if I didn't admit some sort of personal motive as well," Marshall said, ignoring her again. "Part of me hopes that among those that I do assist, there will be a few who discover the same awful truths about stardom that I did, and decide to join me here—in paradise."

"Wait, what?" Joel said.

"That is the only downside of living here," Marshall said. "It does get a bit lonely at times, being the only— well, *human*, I suppose."

"Hey, wait a minute now," Felicity snapped.

Marshall appeared to break out of a momentary daze. "Oh, forgive me—no, no, you misunderstand," he said, raising his hands in a defensive gesture. "That is only a selfish desire of mine, one that I wanted to be completely honest with you about."

"Are you sure that—" Felicity started to say before Marshall cut her off with a serious look.

"Please understand," he said, "I am in no way obligating either of you to return here. This is not some kind of Faustian bargain. Even if we never speak to one another again after you return, I shall merely be happy knowing that I helped spread some more joy to the world via music."

"You promise, right?" Joel said as he tried to remember what "Faustian bargain" meant. "Uh, 'cause my mom would freak if I told her I was going to move to some other alien world, or dimension, or whatever."

"Of course." Marshall smiled. "You have my word."

Joel decided to sample some of the fuzzy roast beef. It was quite tasty, actually.

CHAPTER 5: CASTING WAVES

Joel didn't sleep well that night. He always had trouble sleeping on the first night in a different place anyway, and the fact that he was in some crazy alternate dimension (or whatever this place was) with his musical idol—who, by the way, promised to make his dreams come true—certainly didn't help matters. He tossed and turned for what felt like hours on the surprisingly comfortable woven mat, and when he finally did fall asleep, he woke up every ten minutes or so, thinking that he was back in his Seattle apartment for a few seconds before the tree house interior reminded him otherwise.

It was only now—lying there alone in the dark—that the enormity of the day's events finally began to sink in. He had been chosen by Marshall Byle. *Marshall Byle!* Joel knew every song that Marshall had ever written—every lyric, every chord, every riff. Joel had read countless articles and interviews, studied pictures and videos, analyzed liner notes, and basically did everything he could to emulate this man. In more ways than one, Marshall was Joel's role model—his *hero*—and here he was, in person, ready to share his secrets.

And best of all, Joel thought, *he knows who I am. How cool is that? Also, now I'll get to ask him all kinds of questions, like which guitars he used to record which songs, why he decided to start endorsing Orange amps, how he got the ideas and inspiration for the artwork on the third album...*

It was at that moment that Joel realized how impolite he had been to Marshall up to this point. Really, though, there had been no time to be star struck—after all, it wasn't like they had met at some backstage autograph signing session. Swirling colored lights, wild hybrid animals, little green plant people...those kinds of things could be a bit, well, distracting. Joel resolved to make it up to Marshall in the morning.

After what seemed like an eternity of restlessness, Joel decided to get up and walk around. He passed through the vine curtain of his doorway and was shocked by what he saw: instead of the village, there was now a volcanic caldera with pools of bubbling silvery-white lava and columns of smoke emanating from the surface. Waves of red and orange light, denser than the ones he had seen before, whipped around through the air. He could see no one, although he thought that he heard faint screams coming from somewhere. He turned to find a pile of large rocks where his tree house had been. Feeling a sense of panic start to set in, he tried to run but found that his legs did not respond. He looked down and, to his horror, saw that his legs were gone, replaced by rapidly fading columns of white light. The screams started to grow louder as lava began shooting up out of the pools in dramatic explosions.

"Master Joel?" a voice called.

Joel sat up with a start as beads of sweat dripped down his forehead. A quick look around revealed that he was back in the tree house, with no white lava in sight. A bright beam of sunlight surrounded by little multicolored wisps shone through the single open window.

"Master Joel?" the voice called again. It was Suntooth. "Chief Byle says that your training is about to begin."

Joel took a deep breath. *Wow, okay, that was just a dream. And of course, the minute I finally fall asleep for real, it's time to get up.*

A few minutes later, Joel found himself walking into a grassy open area near Marshall's hut. As Marshall had said, the scenery in the daytime was spectacular—the air sparkled with waves and beads of color, and everything from the huts to the trees to the mountain ranges seemed to give off a radiant glow. The texture of the surreal landscape had shifted again from a grainy, pixelated appearance to a soft, abstract feel that could have been drawn with pastels.

Felicity was already there, standing with her arms crossed and an intense look on her face. Joel suddenly felt nervous for some reason.

"Morning, Joel!" Marshall said in a jovial tone, taking a bite out of a small, round blue fruit and handing one to Joel. "What did I tell you, eh? Such a beautiful place, this is."

Joel's thoughts from last night made him see Marshall in a different light, as if he only now realized just who he was talking to.

"Marshall, I—I mean, uh, Mr. Byle," Joel stammered, looking at his feet, "I just want to say thanks for giving me this opportunity. I mean, I've always totally looked up to you, and, uh—"

"Mr. Byle?" Marshall laughed. "Don't be ridiculous. I'll admit, I was a bit surprised at the lack of any fanboy pretense from you yesterday, but I respect that, actually. So, no need to start now. I'll give you my autograph after all this is through, deal?"

Joel gulped. "Um, sure."

"Now, have at some of that," Marshall nodded at the fruit. "Continental breakfast, Spectraland-style. Trust me, it's delicious. And quite filling as well."

Joel took a bite. It had a chewy texture and tasted like banana and watermelon, with a very slight minty aftertaste.

"Lifepods, they call 'em," Marshall explained. "One of these, and you won't feel hungry 'til dinner. Or perhaps longer. We've got a lot of work ahead of us, so I figured that eating one would be a good way to start the day, you know?"

Joel nodded in agreement as he took another bite.

"Now then," Marshall said as he gulped down the last of his fruit, "manipulating the Aura is a fairly simple concept to understand in theory but rather difficult to master in practice. As I alluded to last night, it requires a combination of sound waves—generated by a wavebow, of course—and brain waves, generated by, well, your brain."

Greenseed came walking into the area, carrying a couple of wavebows similar to Marshall's. She handed one to Felicity and one to Joel. It was surprisingly light. The neck was thin and fretless. The mother-of-pearl body had several brown streaks across its surface that looked like burn marks. Joel ran his fingers over the six glowing strings and noticed that they felt very soft and silky, almost like a spider's thread. He didn't pluck or strum them out of fear that they would break.

Marshall picked up his own wavebow. "The simplest way that I can explain this, as it was explained to me, is that you need to visualize what you want to happen at the same time you play the appropriate note or chord. For example, say I wanted to levitate one of those lifepods over there."

Joel turned in the direction that Marshall was facing, toward a small wooden table where several of the blue fruits were resting.

"I create a picture in my mind of the lifepod rising in the air," Marshall continued, raising his wavebow, "while simultaneously playing what basically amounts to a G chord."

Joel heard the familiar basic chord and then saw a thin bolt of green light burst forth from Marshall's instrument. The bolt grabbed the fruit and lifted it about a foot in the air, where it remained. All of this happened in less than a second. "Wow," Joel whispered.

"So the notes and fingerings are the same as on a regular guitar?" Felicity asked, inspecting her instrument.

"For the most part, yes," Marshall replied as the fruit fell back down on the tabletop. "Apparently, music is as universal as people had long thought. Now, why don't you try it."

Felicity raised her wavebow, stared in the direction of the lifepods for a moment, and then confidently strummed out a full G chord. At first, nothing happened, but then a faint green light slowly began to trickle out of the instrument's headstock. She furrowed her brow in concentration as the light made its way over to the fruits, surrounded one of them in a spiraling motion, and then lifted it several inches. After hovering there for a few seconds, the fruit fell and Felicity exhaled loudly.

"Brilliant!" Marshall exclaimed. "A wonderful start. Now Joel, why don't you have a go."

Okay, just relax. How hard can this be? Joel thought as he lifted his instrument into position. He fixed his gaze on a fruit and tried to picture it rising up in the air, higher and higher. He placed his fingers into the correct positions on the smooth strings, which were much stronger than he had expected. Everything seemed simple enough.

Only, it wasn't. Nothing happened, even after he waited longer than it took for Felicity. He tried repeating the process, but to no avail.

"Focus," Marshall said. "See the fruit rising as if it were actually happening."

How many times had Joel's teachers in school told him to focus? It was easier said than done when there were so many other interesting details to think about and be distracted by.

Joel tried a third time, then a fourth. Finally, on the fifth try, little specks of green light scattered out from his wavebow, but that was it. Joel suddenly felt exhausted, as if he had just run a sprint. He glanced over at Felicity, who was snickering.

"All right, all right," Marshall said. "Take a little break, and we'll come back to it."

"Why," Joel said in between gasps, "do I feel so—so tired?"

"Manipulating the Aura is a draining exercise," Marshall explained. "Your brain has a limited capacity as to how much energy it can expend in this fashion. Too much at once, and you won't be able to try again until it has a chance to recover."

"So, it's like a gas tank that you need to refill after it's empty?" Felicity asked, looking for confirmation.

"Something like that, yes. It will refill by itself, but it takes time. Once you get more experience, you'll be able to retain and use more energy."

"This keeps sounding more and more like a video game," Felicity muttered to herself.

"Don't worry, mate, you'll get it," Marshall said to Joel. "Like anything, it just takes practice."

And practice they did. The remainder of the day was spent levitating fruits and other small objects. Driven by his competitive nature and a desire to impress Marshall, Joel would occasionally overdo his attempts, necessitating a fair number of breaks to restore his Aura energy. By nightfall Joel was able to keep a lifepod suspended in mid-air for several minutes. Felicity, meanwhile, was making rocks three feet in diameter do little dances and twirl around like granite ballerinas. Exhausted and frustrated, Joel declined an invitation to join Marshall and the others for dinner and retired to his tree house, where he promptly fell sound asleep.

Over the course of the following days, Marshall taught them the twelve basic effects that each individual note produced, from creating light (an F note or chord) to inducing sleep (an A note or chord). The louder you played, the more intense the effect. They also learned that notes could be combined into short riffs or melodies called casts that generated entirely different results, although these were harder to master. And harder still were the longer songlike casts known as incantations, which were reserved for the most complex of effects—and the most draining.

Although Joel's wandering thoughts still caused him to lose focus at times, he slowly began to catch on more and more as time went by. Felicity, however, continued to learn at a much faster pace, fueling Joel's jealousy and providing him with another source of unwanted distraction.

One night during dinner, yet another question popped into Joel's head.

"Um, how did you decide to pick the two of us, anyway?" he asked. This seemed an obvious thing to wonder about in retrospect, but like many of his other thoughts, it had been lost in the whirlwind of activity.

"Brilliant question," Marshall replied with his mouth full. "Using a very complicated incantation that the previous Wavemakers had taught me, I scanned the Earth for the proper patterns of brain waves that would indicate the necessary aptitude and ability."

"The same process that they used to find you," Felicity said as more of a statement than a question.

"Precisely. Do you recall hearing a strange warbling noise? One that gave you a bit of a headache?"

"Uh, yeah," Joel replied.

"That was you?" Felicity grumbled to Marshall. "Thanks a lot for that. You almost made me get into an accident the first time it happened."

"Oh—so, um, that was you scanning for us," Joel said. "And, uh, did you know that I was a big fan of yours?"

"Happy coincidence," Marshall chuckled. "I suppose I could have been drawn to you by virtue of your feelings toward me. Felicity here is also a huge fan—I don't think she's admitted that to you yet."

Joel glanced in Felicity's direction, but she merely rolled her eyes in response.

"So you see," Marshall continued, "it was basically like fishing—I just cast my pole into the water and caught the first thing that came up. As far as you two being from the same area..."

Joel glanced again at Felicity, who said nothing.

"You don't talk to each other at all, do you?" Marshall laughed. "My dear, you really should communicate with your training partner here beyond the taunts and insults I hear at practice. He's not a bad guy, you know."

"Why should I?" Felicity said. "We didn't know each other before this, and I don't see why we'll need to know each other afterward."

Joel felt his ears getting hot.

"Anyway," Marshall said, turning back to face Joel, "once I found her, I just searched the surrounding area until I found you. Are you familiar with the game Battleship?"

Joel nodded. He remembered playing that game on a classic compilation on the school's computer.

"It's like that—get one hit, then try again right next to it. A surprisingly successful strategy. Saves energy, as well. Then I just basically followed you—learned your names, and all that—until a good opportunity to talk to you arose. A rock star stalking his fans. How's that for role reversal, eh?"

Joel felt a bit less special now, knowing that he had been selected at random, but still, he was grateful for his good luck. After everything he had been through in his life, he felt that he deserved a bit of a break. He let out a little sigh as he reflected on his positive fortune.

Marshall washed down his last bite with a long drink from his cup. "Well, on to other matters. I have an announcement to make."

Joel looked at Marshall blankly, savoring the contented feeling he had at that moment.

"In two Spectraland weeks, you will be done with your training. I will have taught you most of what you need to know. However, there is one final test that you must pass before I am confident that you will have the necessary skills when you return home."

"Um—what kind of test?" Joel asked.

"You will need to perform a particular series of casts in a public exhibition—a concert, if you will—where you will demonstrate your new talents to an adoring crowd of natives."

Joel's feeling of contentment quickly changed into one of sheer terror.

CHAPTER 6: THE CONCERT

Though Joel had accomplished many things in his musical life, playing live was not yet one of them. He could still recall the preschool holiday songfest where, frightened out of his mind by the glaring lights and interminable sea of faceless parents in the audience, he had attempted to run off the stage, only to be ushered back by a frantic teacher's aide. Having no other means of escape, he spent the rest of the evening hiding behind a taller classmate and not singing a word. This became his standard *modus operandi* throughout elementary school, where similar performance functions were deemed mandatory every December. Once he reached middle school, he was interested in band class until he found out that the band was required to put on concerts.

So Joel became a private virtuoso, practicing his guitar and playing along to (mostly Biledriver) recordings in his room at home. He knew that if he were to eventually fulfill his wish of becoming a successful musician, he would have to perform shows for thousands of people, but he reconciled this dissonance by convincing himself that becoming a star first would give him the confidence to overcome his childhood fears.

But now he would be thrown into the fire. That it was to be in front of little green alien plant-people instead of preschool parents made absolutely no difference. He wished that Marshall had saved the announcement until the last minute, because the distraction of his dread interfered with his focus during their training. A week went by, and both he and Marshall were becoming frustrated with his apparent lack of progress.

"This isn't supposed to be that difficult," Marshall said with irritation in his voice as they practiced one morning. "As I've said before, you need to block everything else out, just for that moment. Can you do that?"

Joel started to feel an angry response coming on, but he kept his mouth shut and channeled the feeling into a heavy speed-picked riff. A red wave of light flowed out and struck his target, a man-sized straw-and-vine dummy that resembled a scarecrow.

"Better, better," Marshall said.

"Why are we practicing stunning casts, anyway?" Felicity asked. "Seems a little unnecessary, since we're not going to be fighting a so-called warlord like you did."

"My dear, I thought you wanted to be a rock star. Or was I mistaken?" Marshall smirked. "We need to at least cover all of the basics to make sure that your mind is properly primed when you return home."

Felicity shrugged and fired off a red stream of light that knocked the head off of one of the scarecrows.

Marshall walked over and placed a hand on Joel's shoulder. "Keep your eyes on the prize, all right? Remember what you told me a few nights ago—this is the key to your happiness. This will solve all of your problems."

Joel nodded as he tried to catch his breath.

"Don't worry," Felicity sneered. "I'll put you on the guest list for my sold-out show at the arena. I don't know about a backstage pass, though. I'll have to think about that one."

Joel shot her a dirty look as he gathered up more Aura power for another attempt, which ended up sailing wide of the straw man.

♪♪♪

Later that evening Joel wandered through the village, his path as aimless as his train of thought. Natives scurried to and fro with their usual glazed expressions, looking rather like people who had just walked into a room and then forgot their purpose for doing so. Joel took notice of this and felt that he certainly could relate.

This is the hardest thing I've ever done. Playing guitar is easy, so why is this so difficult? Maybe I should just quit. I'll tell Marshall I don't have what it takes. That way, I won't have to do the exhibition. But then I'll go home, and I'll be nobody, with no friends, and I'll still have to deal with school, and our money problems, and Mitch, and...look at these people. Such a simple life, living in their little village. It's totally just like a primitive culture or something. Maybe I should just live here. Get Mom and Taylor and move here. That'll take care of our house problem. Taylor wouldn't want to live here, though; she'll miss her friends and everything. Wow, look at that! That section of Aura is shaped like a bowling pin. That's pretty cool. I wonder if—

He had nearly run over a native who was emerging from a hut.

"Oh, I am sorry, Master Joel," Suntooth said, picking himself up. "I should have been more careful."

"Oh, uh, what? Oh, no, sorry, Suntooth, I wasn't watching where I was going."

Greenseed followed Suntooth out of the hut, carrying several wooden boxes. She looked at Joel with a solemn expression and then quickly looked away.

"Um, what are you guys doing out here? I thought you were still back at Marshall, um, I mean, Chief Byle's place."

"Just running some errands," Suntooth replied. "How is your training going?"

"Ugh," Joel said. "Not so good. This stuff is really, really hard. I—I dunno, I'm, uh, I'm thinking of quitting, maybe."

"Oh—I am sorry to hear that, sir."

"It's okay, it's just—it's just that, I feel, I dunno, I feel—"

"Overwhelmed?"

"Yeah." Joel nodded. "Pretty much. Like, I try my best, and I feel like I know what I have to do, but I just can't do it."

"Hmm," Suntooth mused. "If I may say so, I think that you just need to relax. Enjoy what you are doing for its own sake and do not be so concerned with the re-sults."

Joel looked at Suntooth. It felt a little odd to be hear-ing advice from the elderly-looking native, whose speech up until now had consisted mostly of brief wake-up calls and polite greetings. "Relax?"

"Yes, lose yourself in the moment," Suntooth said in a fatherly tone. "Take what you are doing seriously, but not to the point where it works against you. Let go of your fears and concerns, and you will see that everything is usually fine in the end."

"Um, okay," Joel said. For a moment, he felt like he was back in the music store, listening to Art and his half-baked beliefs.

"We must be going," Greenseed said curtly to Suntooth. That was about two more words than Joel had ever heard her say at one time.

"Yes, yes, of course," Suntooth replied. Then, turning back to Joel once more, he added, "Remember, relax. Your personal Aura is very powerful. You will do fine." And with that, he followed Greenseed away from Joel and out of sight.

That was weird, Joel mused to himself. *Seems like a pretty wise dude—for a butler.*

♩♩♩

Suntooth's words definitely had a positive effect on Joel during the last few days of their practice leading up to the exhibition. He tried very hard to relax, which seemed to him to be somewhat of a paradox but was effective nonetheless. At times, he even felt like he was actually having fun—and the resulting incremental improvement in his performance was readily apparent.

"Yes, yes, that's it! Now you're starting to get it," Marshall exclaimed as a thin, piercing reddish-yellow beam leaped out of Joel's wavebow and shattered a rock some twenty feet away. "Just in time too, I'd say. Two more days 'til the big show, and then you get to go home and embark on your grand career. I must say, I'm very proud of the improvements that you've made."

Joel grinned. He had always responded better to positive reinforcement, and hearing praise from his hero filled him with the additional confidence that allowed him to relax even further.

"Felicity, my dear," Marshall said in what seemed like an obvious attempt to bait her, "you've been awfully quiet today. Aren't you proud of your colleague here?"

"Yeah, whatever," she muttered, blowing up two rocks in quick succession.

Marshall chuckled. "All right, let's take a short break, and then we'll go over the entire choreographed routine once more. Don't go anywhere. I'll be right back."

Flushed with an unfamiliar sense of bravado, Joel felt an urge to talk to Felicity at that moment, to try to at least engage her on friendly terms, seeing as they were only going to be around each other for two more days. Although they had spent almost every waking moment of a Spectraland month together, they were yet to have an actual conversation. He walked up to her as she took a swig from a wooden cup.

"Um, hey," he improvised.

"Seriously?" she said, regarding him like a fly that had just landed on her lunch. "You're talking to me?"

"Uh, yeah, I—I am. I just wanted to say that, well, it's been pretty cool, uh, having someone else around to do this stuff with."

"Pfft," she spat. "I'm shocked you didn't ask him to send you back home after the first day, when it was obvious that I was so much better at this than you."

Every word she said felt like a sharp projectile that eroded the wall of Joel's confidence. "Um, well, I—I think that—"

"Listen," she interrupted, "once we're done here, don't bother trying to contact me, or track me down, or anything like that. We'll go our own separate ways and have our careers, but I'm not interested in being friends. Understand?"

Joel was stunned into silence. After Mitch, Felicity was definitely the most unlikeable person he had ever met. Fortunately, Marshall returned at that moment, sparing Joel from further abuse.

"All right, kids, let's get back to it, shall we?"

They launched into the first of a series of wavecasts, but Joel was so rattled from his non-conversation with Felicity that his initial attempt spiraled out of control and headed straight toward Marshall.

"Whoa, there!" Marshall shouted, ducking out of the way.

♪♪♪

Two days passed by. Joel did not make any more attempts to talk to Felicity. As night fell and the twin moons loomed large on the horizon, Joel stood in their training field, nervously fingering his wavebow. He had recovered nicely from his little mishap and finished his training smoothly enough that he felt reasonably prepared, although his stomach was still churning quite a bit. Anxious thoughts about his mom and sister kept creeping into his mind, threatening to cloud his focus, but he just kept reminding himself about what Marshall had said regarding the time difference. He would be going home tomorrow, and only a few hours would have passed by. Everything would be fine.

He wanted badly to practice a bit more before the exhibition, but Marshall had explicitly instructed him not to—that he needed to save all of his Aura energy for the performance. He glanced around at the now-familiar-but-still-odd scenery one more time and wondered if he would miss this place. He closed his eyes and started to go over his routine in his mind.

"Not thinking of practicing a bit more, are you?" Marshall grinned as he approached Joel, seemingly appearing out of nowhere.

"Huh? Oh—um, no, of course not. Just—just making sure I remember what I'm supposed to do."

"The stage area is ready. We'll meet in the village center in fifteen minutes."

"Okay."

"Don't worry, I'm sure you'll do fine."

"Thanks, Marshall. For, um, for everything."

Marshall gave Joel a warm smile. "My pleasure. Remember, this is my joy in life as well now—giving talented youngsters such as yourself the break they deserve. But there'll be time for sentimentality tomorrow. Just have fun tonight, all right?"

Joel nodded as Marshall turned and strolled away. After mentally calculating that nine Spectraland minutes had passed by, Joel walked down into the heart of the small village and saw that a rather large crowd of natives had gathered—certainly more than he had ever seen at one time prior to this. He scanned the area and did a quick head count that revealed a hundred and twelve of the green-tinted beings milling about, quietly buzzing amongst themselves. The number of butterflies in his stomach instantly doubled.

In the normally empty area of the village that usually served as a sort of central courtyard was a rectangular wooden stage. About twelve by twenty feet and built on risers that put it three feet above the ground, it was constructed with the same attention to detail as the village's huts, and on top of it were various small statues, rocks, and other assorted items. It had a latticed backdrop covered in colorful vines and flowers and was surrounded by circling wisps of Aura. Joel saw Felicity and Marshall standing behind it and made his way over to them.

"Almost looks as if you're about to get married," Marshall chortled as he inspected the floral arrangements.

"Oh, shut up," Felicity snapped. "Let's get this over with."

Even after a month, Joel still marveled at the cavalier manner in which Felicity spoke to someone she supposedly admired as much as he did. He wondered, not for the first time, what kind of parents she had.

"Um, why are there so many of them?" Joel asked, nodding at the mass of aliens.

"Oh, did I forget to mention?" Marshall replied. "There are visitors from the other villages here. It's a rather big deal, but don't let that faze you. You're going to be a rock star, remember?"

With that, Marshall leaped up onto the stage and raised his arms.

"Everyone! Thank you all for gathering here tonight. As you know, this is a very special occasion—two extremely gifted and talented individuals from my homeworld are going to be putting on a wonderful show for you, demonstrating the skills they have learned as brand new Wavemakers."

Joel felt his anxiety level ratchet up yet another notch.

"Now, I know that we all miss the master shamans that heroically gave their lives in the battle against Chief Fourfoot, and this performance will be dedicated to their memory. It will be a ceremony to honor their sacrifice and to celebrate the eternal freedom of the people of Spectraland!"

A cheer rose up from the crowd that sounded a bit subdued given the inspirational nature of Marshall's introduction, but that seemed to be par for the course with the island's natives, whom Joel had observed to be quite laid-back and low-key. He glanced peripherally at Felicity, who radiated the air of a Michael Jordan-level player about to tip-off against a team of middle schoolers.

"Please welcome—Joel and Felicity!"

The fact that Marshall had said Joel's name first did not go unnoticed by either of them. Felicity shot Joel an angry look, as if to say *I'm the headliner!* And Joel returned her look with a sorry shrug by which he meant *Um, hey, that wasn't my idea* and *I'm sure he didn't mean anything by that* and *I know you're better at this than I am, so don't get mad at me, and besides, it just sounds better with the monosyllabic name first anyway.*

They took the stage amidst a swirling cloud of Aura energy. Joel's heart was pounding and his hands were shaking as he tried to recall the first part of their carefully choreographed routine, but his mind was drawing an inopportune blank. An urge to flee started to crawl up his throat, and it took all of his willpower to push it back down. It felt like a billion eyes were on him at that moment. He turned his face away from the crowd and saw Felicity effortlessly produce a wave of green light that lifted a small carved stone statue several feet off the ground. Seeing this, the steps to their routine snapped into his memory like puzzle pieces coming together, and he too brought forth a green stream of light that found its target.

Relax, he told himself.

The performance moved along without a hitch after that as brilliant flashes of light lit up the night sky like a laser show. Rocks and statues and fruits went flying this way and that, forming circular patterns and figure eights in the air before being launched high up above the stage, where they exploded into showers of harmless, sparkling dust. The music from their wavebows created a strange yet beautiful soundtrack that was at once modern and primitive, melodic and dissonant, harmonious and cacophonous.

Joel occasionally afforded himself a glance out into the audience, which he could see very clearly given all of the light surrounding the area. Marshall wasn't among them, but that was just as well; seeing one's idol standing in a crowd, watching him perform, was possibly one of those surreal moments (amongst the hundreds of other surreal moments happening at the time) that could derail Joel's burgeoning confidence. The natives were mostly folks that he did not know, and would not see again after tomorrow, and this thought gave him a measure of comfort as he scanned their awestruck faces. He felt safe, secure, and most of all, he was having fun.

I've done it, he thought. *I've conquered my fears. Now nothing can stop me from achieving my goals. Marshall was right. I* am *going to be a star.*

Joel's self-esteem swelled to new heights as they approached the finale. He felt the Aura's energy coursing through him, felt the secrets of the power of music being unlocked within his mind. He and Felicity played a dramatic, complex succession of riffs in unison, conjuring up a billowing rainbow tide that pulsed with every note and bathed the village in light and color and sound, like a spectacular larger-than-life combination of fireworks and computerized media player visualizations. Victory was only moments away.

Then, just as they were about to complete their final note, the air around them went cold. Joel could feel the momentum abruptly slipping away, despite knowing that he and Felicity were doing everything right. A small, dark circle of Aura energy, or antienergy, appeared in the middle of their display. Like a black hole, it began to suck in the surrounding waves of colored light, muting their music and growing larger in the process.

"What are you doing?" Felicity screamed at him.

"Uh, nothing—nothing! It's not me!" Joel yelled back at her.

The dark circle expanded until it dominated the space above the stage and all of the other Aura energy had been swallowed up. It throbbed along with a low, loud droning beat that sounded like the deepest bass drum Joel had ever heard, and black streaks of nonlight leaked from its edges like watery ink. Joel could see Felicity frantically trying to cast something, anything at it, but nothing emanated from her instrument.

Then a shape began to coalesce in the middle of the circle. It slowly took on a humanoid form, and although its features were muddled, Joel instantly recognized the helmet with the giant deer antlers.

"Chief Byle!" the form roared in a deep, guttural, distorted voice. "You thought that I was dead. You thought that you and the traitors were victorious. Well, as you can see, you were wrong. My spirit lived on in the Aura, and thanks to your pitiful little show here tonight, it has been restored!"

Joel desperately looked around for Marshall, but he could not see him among the crush of panicking natives.

"And now you and your otherworldly *apprentices*," the voice said scornfully, "will pay for what you have done to me."

Three black tentacles snaked out from the circle, one reaching for Joel, one reaching for Felicity, and one apparently reaching behind the stage area.

"We need to do something!" Felicity yelled at Joel.

Joel tried to perform an exploding cast, but no sound came out of his wavebow. The tentacle wrapped itself tightly around him. It was very cold, and it shot tiny electric jolts all throughout Joel's body. The tentacle began to squeeze, and Joel suddenly felt woozy. Through his blurred vision, he could see Felicity in a similar predicament on the other side of the stage.

"My vengeance will be complete," the voice growled.

Just as Joel felt he would pass out, he heard a loud *crack!* and saw the third tentacle that was reaching behind the stage dissolve into wisps of gray smoke. With additional cracking sounds, bright orange bolts of light shot through the lattice, striking the other tentacles and causing them to dissipate as well. Joel gasped for breath as a final bolt hit the figure in the center of the circle, which exploded in a shower of black spots.

Marshall came running onto the stage, breathing heavily, wavebow in hand. "Joel! Felicity! Are you all right?"

"Yeah," they said in unison. Felicity sharply added, "Where were you? And what was that?"

"Fourfoot," Marshall muttered, a grim look on his face. "I should have known."

CHAPTER 7: THE TEMPLE

Whaat?" Felicity shouted. "I thought you said you killed him!"

"Didn't you hear what he said?" Marshall snapped. "*His spirit lived on in the Aura.* We killed his physical body, but somehow he was able to prevent the energies that make up one's spirit, soul, whatever, from dissipating."

"But—so, he's gone now, though, right? Didn't you just get rid of him?" Joel asked.

"Hard to say. I broke up this particular manifestation, but he still may be lurking out there somewhere."

Felicity looked at Marshall with an expression of incredulous anger. "Whoa, whoa—he's still alive? We almost just got killed! So what do we do now?"

"I'll probably just send you back home tonight, before he gets a chance to—"

"Chief Byle! Chief Byle, please come quickly!" a young native yelled as she rushed up to the stage.

"What is it?" Marshall asked her.

"It's—it's Suntooth, sir, he's—he's—"

Marshall jumped off the stage and followed the young native girl into the crowd, which was in a state of confused chaos, apparently unsure of where to go or what to do. Joel and Felicity glanced at each other and then followed as well.

The native led them into a nearby hut that Joel had visited several times during his training to receive treatment for some minor cuts and bruises. The doctor, named Brownstump (Joel thought this was a particularly humorous translation for some reason), was a squat, stocky native with more leafy protrusions than the others and thin purple striped patterns on his skin. He was normally on the jovial side, but now he was standing over Suntooth's prone form with a very serious look on his face.

"What happened?" Marshall asked.

"He was struck by some of Chief Fourfoot's dark Aura energy," Brownstump replied. "This is beyond my ability to heal. I was hoping that you might be able to do something."

Marshall, Joel, and Felicity gathered around the table that Suntooth was lying on. Vibrating patches of black light dotted his skin, and his body was giving off faint traces of smoke that felt cold, like vapor rising up from dry ice.

"Um, Suntooth?" Joel said, but there was no response.

"He is not conscious," Brownstump said. "He might even already be dead, but I cannot tell for sure. It is very strange."

"Can you do something?" Joel pleaded with Marshall.

"We'll see," Marshall replied. He took a step back, raised his wavebow, and began playing a soft, somber melody. A purple stream of light poured out and formed a cloud that enveloped Suntooth's body. The black spots remained, but after a minute or so, the native's eyes fluttered open.

"Suntooth?" Joel tried again. "Are you okay?"

"Songshell..." Suntooth whispered. Although his eyes were open, they had a very empty look to them.

"What did he say?" Felicity asked.

"Shh," Marshall hushed her as he leaned in closer.

"You must find it...the Songshell. It is the only way," Suntooth continued, barely audible, his eyes struggling to stay open.

"Suntooth, it's Chief Byle. The only way to what? What is the Songshell?"

"The only way...to defeat...defeat Fourfoot. Go to the temple. All of you...must go."

"All of who?" Felicity asked. "Does he mean us too?"

Joel leaned in closer as well. At that moment, the black spots abruptly grew larger, until they covered most of Suntooth's body, which jerked in response. His eyes turned deep black, and his voice became harsh and distorted. Felicity shrieked as all of them jumped back.

"Byle," Suntooth said in the new, guttural voice. "You will pay for what you've done." The old native tried to sit up, arms reaching out in menacing fashion. Marshall fired a green wave that wrapped itself around Suntooth like a rope. Brownstump and the young native girl retreated to a corner of the hut.

"Don't!" Marshall yelled as Joel and Felicity raised their wavebows. "I think he's possessed—we don't want to hurt him!"

"How nice of you," the voice hissed. "But you will find that I am not as merciful."

"You won't win, Fourfoot," Marshall said as the green wave began to turn yellow, then red. "We'll find a way to destroy you for good."

"We?" Fourfoot scoffed as Suntooth's possessed body struggled against its bonds. "You mean you and your little friends here? Don't make me laugh. Your feeble skills cannot compare to my infinite power."

Joel and Felicity looked at each other, unsure of what to do.

"If you're so powerful," Marshall said as the black spots on Suntooth's body began to recede, "then why am I defeating you as we speak?"

"You may have the upper hand for now, but I will continue to regain strength until I cannot be stopped."

"Stopped from what?" Marshall asked.

"Reclaiming what is mine—namely, this island. Then I will take over *your* homeland as well."

Joel felt a twinge of panic shoot through his body.

"We'll see," Marshall said through a grimace, his body shaking with effort. Finally, with a flash of yellow light, all of the black spots vanished, and Suntooth's body slumped back down on the table.

"Fourfoot? Suntooth—is that you? Can you hear me?" Marshall said, obviously shaken.

Suntooth's voice was back to normal, although even softer and weaker than before. "Yes...he is gone."

"Gone? Completely?" Marshall asked.

"No...just from me. He has sealed the Rift...I saw it."

"Sealed the—but how?"

"He is...with the Aura. At the next Nadir...he will return."

"What?" Marshall exclaimed with shock in his voice.

"I am sorry...I could not...stop him...."

With that, Suntooth's eyes closed again, and his body went completely limp.

"Suntooth? What happened?" Joel asked. "Is he...?"

"He's gone," Marshall said softly. "I couldn't save him."

When Joel was around seven years old, before his dad left, he had a pet dog, a beagle, named Sammy. Sammy was still a young pup when a car hit him in a street near their house. Even though Joel didn't feel exactly the same way about Suntooth as he did about Sammy, he was still struck with the same overwhelming feeling of grief and powerlessness, that emptiness in the bottom of his stomach. He had become rather attached to the elderly native and felt grateful for the advice that Suntooth had given him.

"What is going on here?" Greenseed said as she rushed into the hut. She saw Suntooth lying on the table and made a sound that was probably a gasp.

"Fourfoot," Marshall said to her. "He possessed Suntooth and then killed him before I could drive all of his energy away."

Joel stood in silence, fighting back tears.

"That is terrible," Greenseed said with a stunned look on her face. "Is he—Fourfoot—is he gone now?"

Marshall shook his head. "Afraid not. He's still loose, free within the Aura."

"So what's gonna happen now?" Felicity asked, seemingly unmoved by Suntooth's passing. "What was all that he said about a temple, and the whatever-shell, and whatnot?"

Joel's mind snapped back to the conversation at hand. "And, um, after that—didn't Fourfoot say something about taking over our homeland? Did he mean Earth?"

"We need to sit down and discuss all of this," Marshall said with a sigh. "Let's go back to my hut. Brownstump, please see to Suntooth's body."

♫♫♫

A few minutes later, Marshall, Felicity, and Joel were back in the dining room where Marshall had first told them his story. Greenseed brought out cups filled with an aromatic hot liquid.

"All right," Marshall said, taking a sip from his cup, "the first big problem here is that I cannot send you back home."

"What?" Felicity spat. For some reason, Joel did not feel surprised by this announcement.

"Suntooth said that he saw Fourfoot sealing the Rift," Marshall said. "And as long as Fourfoot is part of the Aura, it would be way too dangerous to even open it, much less try to send anyone through. He'd sense your presence and destroy your life energy the moment you tried to pass."

"Great," Felicity huffed. "So we're stuck here, with a ghost who wants to kill us."

Joel took a small sip of his drink. It scalded his tongue and tasted like mushrooms. He wrinkled his face.

"Indeed," Marshall said. "The second problem is that in a Spectraland month—twenty-two days, to be precise—he will be able to gain enough power to reconstitute his physical form."

"Suntooth said that?" Felicity asked.

"Yes—'*at the next Nadir, he will return.*' You need to learn how to pay better attention."

"Hey, I don't even know what that means," Felicity sputtered.

"The Nadir is a phase of the twin moons where neither of them are visible—sort of a lunar eclipse. The Aura energy is very strong during that time. Anyway, once he does that, I don't think I'll be able to keep him from carrying out his threats. I had the help of a dozen other shamans the last time."

"I thought you were so *awesome,* Mr. Rock Star," Felicity said with a good dose of vindictive sarcasm.

Despite the funny taste, Joel found himself craving another sip of the odd brew, which he took.

"The good news," Marshall continued, sidestepping Felicity's verbal jab, "is that before Fourfoot possessed him, Suntooth gave us a possible solution to our problems."

"The, um, Songshell?" Joel said.

"Precisely," Marshall said.

"Okay, so what is that, anyway?" Felicity asked.

"I don't know for sure," Marshall answered, "but he said that it's our only hope for defeating Fourfoot."

"How would he even know about something like that?" Felicity said. "I thought he was just a servant."

"Um, he seemed kinda smart to me, actually," Joel cut in as he took another sip. "He—uh, he gave me some good advice that helped with my training."

"Did he now?" Marshall said. "Hmm, perhaps there was more to the bloke than even I was aware of."

Out of the corner of his eye, Joel saw Greenseed looking intently at them from the doorway leading to the food preparation area. He turned in her direction and she quickly stepped away.

"So, what, we have to go to some temple now or something?" Felicity said, sipping her drink.

"Yes," Marshall replied. "I believe that he was referring to the Wavemaker Temple, which lies a bit east of here. I suppose that it may hold some answers for us."

"So if we get that shell thingy and kill Fourfoot tomorrow, we can still go home?" Felicity asked.

Marshall laughed. "We can only hope it's that easy, my dear. We're already running out of time as we speak."

"I, uh, I guess we should get going, then," Joel said.

"Master," Greenseed said as she suddenly appeared in the room. "I think that I should accompany you. You will need someone a bit more...familiar...with the trails leading toward the temple. As you know, traveling over-night can be a bit disorienting."

Joel stared at her. That was *way* more than he had ever heard her say before.

"Hmm," Marshall said, fingering the scar on his cheek. "Yes, yes, I suppose you're right. I have only been there once, and in the daytime at that. Very well. Please get the slimebacks ready. We should leave as soon as we can."

"Yes, Chief Byle," Greenseed said before hurrying out.

♪♪♪

The slimebacks stood around in what Joel figured was a stable, quietly grazing on piles of green plants that looked like seaweed. While they all had the same camel-frog appearance, they varied in size and color; some were green, some yellow (with orange spots), some blood red, some with large humps, some with small humps. He rec-ognized Marshall's uniquely white mount and saw that it was a bit larger than the others.

"Hello, girl," Marshall said to it as he patted the side of its long neck. "Yes, we're off again. A bit longer ride this time."

"Um, so, we have to ride one of these things by our-selves?" Joel asked. He had never ridden a horse before. He had a bicycle that was stolen a few years ago (and was never replaced), but that was the extent of his experience with controlling a mobile mount of any type.

"Of course." Marshall smiled. "Riding tandem is fine for short distances, but it tires them out after a while. Don't worry, mate. You'll be fine."

"Ugh, they're sticky," Felicity said after touching a red one.

"Their skin secretes a viscous fluid that makes it easier to stay seated on them," Marshall explained. "It's like they were made for this purpose. Quite brilliant, I must say."

"Quite gross, if you ask me," she muttered, wiping her hand on her tunic.

Joel started to walk over to the nearest slimeback, a tall green creature with a large hump. It saw him approaching and made a loud, derisive-sounding snort. *Hmm, not too friendly,* Joel thought, when suddenly a smaller pale yellow one peeked out from behind its green stablemate. Feeling strangely drawn to it, Joel walked over, carefully avoiding the larger one, and patted it on the neck. It made a soft, purring-croaking noise and closed its amphibian-like eyes.

"I think she likes you," Marshall said, noticing the interaction. "Your Auras seem compatible."

"Uh, okay," Joel said.

"You got the runt," Felicity sniffed as she hopped on the red one that she had touched. "Figures."

"Do they have names?" Joel asked Marshall.

"I believe that one is called Destiny," Marshall replied.

"You gotta be kidding me," Felicity chortled.

"Yours is named Dreamer," Marshall told her with a smirk.

"Ugh. This place is so corny."

Greenseed came trotting out on her slimeback, a brawny-looking green one with little horns. She handed a backpack-sized brown sack to everyone. "This should last us for the journey to the temple. It is a few hours each way."

Joel looked into the sack and saw that it contained a couple of lifepods, a flask of liquid, and a spare vest-and-leggings set. He slung the sack over his shoulder, where it hung on the opposite side of his wavebow, and climbed onto Destiny's back.

"Ready?" Marshall asked, already halfway out of the stable.

"Sure, why not—whoa!" Felicity said, nearly falling as her mount lunged forward.

♪♪♪

Joel was pleasantly surprised to discover that he seemed to have a knack for slimeback riding. Destiny was very mild-tempered and responded easily—almost telepathically—to Joel's directions. Felicity, on the other hand, struggled with Dreamer, and she was constantly chastising the animal and muttering under her breath. After playing catch-up to Felicity for the past month, Joel found this development a bit amusing.

They traveled briskly (or as briskly as possible with Felicity and Dreamer occasionally stopping and/or wandering off course) over an orange dirt trail as the surrounding vegetation grew increasingly dense. The air was still warm, even in the dead of night. On occasion, their surroundings appeared to shift and distort when the wind blew, making Joel feel a little dizzy. After a short break about two hours into the journey, Greenseed led them off the trail directly into a dense forest of thin, luminescent trees that swayed back and forth like metronomes.

"Are you sure this will take us in the right direction?" Marshall asked her.

"Yes, Master, I have traveled this path before, when I went to visit my sister," Greenseed replied, her voice trembling.

"Sister?" Joel asked.

Greenseed lowered her head and rode on.

"Greenseed's sister was a Wavemaker," Marshall said quietly to Joel, "killed in our battle against Fourfoot. I wouldn't bring her up again in front of her." He nodded in Greenseed's direction.

"Oh—um, sorry," Joel said.

After about another hour, the trees became sparser and sparser until the party finally rode into a tree-less clearing that was bisected by a narrow river. About two hundred yards away, Joel could make out a large structure that consisted of several interconnected huts constructed out of plants and rocks, in a manner similar to Marshall's residence. Tall stone humanoid statues, four of them, surrounded the small hill that the structure rested on. A thick cloud of purple Aura hovered over the area, giving it a dark, foreboding feel.

"That was much faster than the established trail," Marshall said to no one in particular. "Wish I had known about that sooner."

"So, uh, that's the temple?" Joel asked. "It looks kinda—I dunno, evil, I guess."

"It wasn't always so," Marshall replied. "The temple fell after one of our battles with Fourfoot. The dark Aura that you see is left over from that encounter."

"Is anyone still in there?" Felicity asked.

"No," Marshall said. "Although some of the native beasts may have taken up shelter in it, now that it's abandoned. So stay alert."

The slimebacks trotted up to the edge of the river, where they stopped and sipped at its clear, flowing water.

"Um, is this thing pretty shallow?" Joel asked.

"It is about fifty feet deep," Greenseed said.

Joel looked at her with a shocked expression. "What? How—how are we going to get across? These things can't jump that far, can they?"

"No," Marshall said, "but they can do something else." He urged his mount into the water, where it flattened its body, splayed its legs apart, and began doing something akin to a frog-like breaststroke. It glided effortlessly across the fifteen feet or so to the bank on the other side, where it climbed out and did a little shimmy, shaking off drops of water from its legs and lower body.

"Oh, cool," Joel said.

After the rest of them crossed the river (which Felicity seemed the most nervous about doing, given the unpredictable nature of her mount), they rode up to the front of the structure, where a set of wood-and-vine stairs led up to the main entrance. Up close, Joel observed broken supports, holes in the walls, and other obvious signs of a conflict. Aura streams drifted listlessly through the air, and Joel thought that he could actually hear the streams make a low, groaning noise as they passed by.

"The slimebacks will need to stay here," Marshall said. "Greenseed, please remain with them until we return."

"Yes, Master," Greenseed said softly.

They walked up the stairs, whose weight support seemed rather precarious, and entered the main hall of the temple. Tall tree-trunk pillars with intricate drawings and carvings on them lined the sides of the hall, which ended in an altar-like area that was decorated with stone statues and colorful masks. In the center of the area was a dais, upon which stood a circular stone basin. To either side of the area was an open doorway.

"Looks like a church," Felicity whispered.

"This is where the Wavemakers meditated, to gain additional connection with the Aura," Marshall said, stepping up onto the dais.

"So, uh, the shell we're looking for is supposed to be in here?" Joel asked.

"Possibly," Marshall said, peering into the basin. "This altar was the source of much power, as the shamans would often pool their energies together here, in this fountain. Doesn't seem like there's anything now, however."

"So, now what?" Felicity asked.

"Let's check the library," Marshall said, moving toward the doorway on the right.

The doorway led into a dark hall. The three of them played a single shimmering note that illuminated their wavebows as they entered.

"What, the Wavemakers didn't believe in light?" Felicity asked.

"When they were here, their Auras lit up the entire temple, so there was no need for torches or glowmoss," Marshall explained.

The passage exited the main hall and led to an open walkway. Keeping their wavebows lit, they crossed over the walkway into an adjoining hut that seemed much larger on the inside. A stale odor filled the air. Rows and rows of parchments—rolled up, bound, and stacked on top of each other on wooden shelves—lined the walls up to the ceiling, which Joel figured was exactly fifteen feet high. A faint crackling noise murmured in the background.

"Wow—um, you think the shell is in here?" Joel asked.

"I don't think so," Marshall said. "Surely an object powerful enough to defeat Fourfoot would have a strong Aura imprint, and I'm not sensing anything of the sort within the area. Perhaps we should peruse the archives here for some information."

"Are you serious?" Felicity groaned. "Guess we can forget about getting home any time soon."

Joel pulled out a parchment and inspected it. Strange characters written in green ink covered both sides. *Guess the translation spell or whatever doesn't apply to written words*, he thought. *Of course, why would it? Marshall said that the translation is due to modifications in the sound waves of our speech. And is Felicity right? Could we be stuck here? 'Cause that would...that would be a problem. Mom is going to be totally worried, and—*

The crackling noise, which was growing louder by the second, interrupted his train of thought. It sounded almost like somebody was chewing or crunching on something...something crispy. "Do you guys hear that?"

"Hear what?" Marshall said as he sifted through some papers.

"Hey, check this out," Felicity said, pointing out a softly glowing basket that was tucked away in a corner of the hut, hidden behind a small stone statue of a bear-fish-like animal.

"Interesting," Marshall said. He walked over and carefully lifted the lid off of the basket, revealing a single rolled-up scroll that radiated a faint yellow light. "Odd that a document would be infused with Aura energy."

"Well, c'mon, read it," Felicity urged.

Marshall picked up the scroll and unfurled it. Joel saw that it was covered with the same strange writing that was on the other parchment.

"Hmm," Marshall said as he studied the writing, "I've learned a bit of their written language during my time here, but not enough to read something of this complexity, I'm afraid."

"Ugh, that's bloody fantastic," Felicity said mockingly in a terrible faux-British accent.

"Ever so charming." Marshall smiled. "Fortunately, I do have some other tricks up my sleeve."

He set the parchment down and played a short lick on his wavebow. A yellow stream of light jumped out and covered the parchment, which began to take on a blurred appearance. Joel calculated in his head that thirty-seven seconds had passed before the alien characters morphed into tiny English letters that shifted in and out of focus.

"Cool," Joel said, now ignoring the gradual crescendo of the crunching sound. He figured that since Marshall didn't seem alarmed, it must not be anything to worry about.

Marshall picked up the document. With Joel and Felicity on either side looking over his shoulder, the three of them read silently together:

Secret of the Songshell

In ancient times, long before the splitting of the light, a maker of the waves discovered a special artifact unlike anything anyone else had ever seen. This artifact, an otherwise ordinary-looking shell, not only attracted the power of the Aura, but was able to absorb it, store it, and transport it as well. The Wavemaker discovered that this artifact bestowed upon him tremendous power, such that his own abilities were magnified by many orders. Also, he was able to use his powers without becoming weary or fatigued. He named the special artifact the Songshell.

At first, he applied the Songshell toward the good of all, and all were grateful. But soon, the temptations of its powers proved to be too great. He became corrupt, using the artifact for selfish and evil purposes instead. The other makers of the waves, aided by the element of surprise and the willingness to accept great sacrifice, were miraculously able to overcome him. The Songshell was now in their possession.

After much discussion, it was decided that the artifact's potential for abuse outweighed its potential for good, and thus, it must be destroyed. However, it refused to be vanquished so easily. Ordinary means were ineffective. Finally, the most powerful incantations by all of the Wavemakers working in unison were successful, but only to the point of nullifying its abilities, not the total destruction of the shell itself. The shell was then hidden, to shield future generations from its dangerous allure.

One night, however, an elder Wavemaker was visited upon by the Aura during his sleep. He had a prophetic vision, one of a day when the services of the Songshell would be necessary to overcome an even greater threat to the people of the land. On that fateful day, travel to *the Caves of Wrath will be required. And as both a means to overcome the protections as well as a shield against corruption, no less than three makers of the waves will need to do so.*

The words ended there. Joel thought that it seemed to lack a conclusion of some sort, and he didn't quite understand the last paragraph. "So, what does this mean?" he asked.

"It means," Marshall said with a strange look on his face, "that we have to travel to the Caves of Wrath."

"I sure hope that they're, like, right next door to this place," Felicity grumbled.

Little bits of straw and wood fell from the ceiling. "Do you hear that?" Marshall said, eyes looking upward.

"The crunching noise, right?" Joel said, happy that someone else had finally heard the same sound.

"Yes...I think we should—"

At that, the entire roof of the hut caved in, and what were probably hundreds, or maybe thousands, of thin, foot-long furry snakes came crashing down in one big, writhing, hissing mass.

CHAPTER 8: COAST OF FANG

Joel had seen pictures of furry caterpillars before, in science class. At the time, they seemed like cute, interesting creatures that you might even want to keep around as pets. What he found himself buried up to his neck in, while still furry, were definitely not such creatures.

While thrashing around in a frantic attempt to shake the snakes off, Joel saw that Felicity was in an even more precarious position. Her screams were muffled by the pile of black-and-white-striped snakes that had covered her head as well as her entire body.

"Felicity! Marshall!" Joel yelled as he began to feel the bites of many tiny teeth on his skin.

After a few long seconds, a bright orange burst of light accompanied by the ring of a single chord exploded out from under a swirling reptilian mass, sending a bunch of the creatures flying in a multitude of different directions. Marshall played the chord twice more, clearing away most of the remainder.

"Are you two all right?" Marshall asked in a casual tone of voice.

Felicity simply stared at him with an open-mouthed look of shock.

"Um, yeah, I think so," Joel said as a single snake skittered away between his feet. "What—what were those things?"

"Ratworms," Marshall said. "Herbivorous, fortunately for us. Pretty common pests around these parts."

"That—was—so gross," Felicity said, still gasping for air.

"The two of you are going to have to learn how to use your abilities under actual duress," Marshall said as he dusted himself off. "Those things were fairly harmless. But the island is full of far more dangerous creatures—not to mention Fourfoot possibly lurking about."

"Okay, we get that," Felicity said. "But how much longer are we gonna have to stay here, anyway?"

"Well, based on this new information we just discovered—a week, perhaps? Maybe more."

"A week?" Felicity shrieked.

"I'm not really sure, actually," Marshall said. "All I know is that the Caves of Wrath are quite a ways from here, if what I have heard is true."

Felicity let out a long, angry sigh as she bowed her head.

"The good news," Marshall continued, raising the scroll that he clutched in his right hand, "is that we apparently have the power of prophecy on our side. Or, in more realistic terms, the power of Aura-assisted clairvoyance."

"You mean, that—that vision it talked about?" Joel asked, nodding at the scroll.

"Yes. Sometimes the Aura spontaneously warps time within a shaman's subconscious mind, essentially showing him images of the future. Only the most trained and experienced can tell the difference between that and a normal dream. It would seem, based on this legend, that we are destined to locate this so-called Songshell."

The gears in Joel's mind turned. "Because—so—is that what it meant by 'no less than three makers of the waves'? That line was referring to us?"

"Precisely! Or, at least, I strongly believe so."

"Well, let's get going, then," Felicity muttered resignedly as she started walking back toward the main hall, kicking aside a stray ratworm.

Marshall chuckled. "Don't fret, my dear. Another week is a pittance in terms of elapsed time back home."

Joel exhaled, feeling relief at hearing those words.

"I just want to get my career started," Felicity said in a barely audible voice.

They retraced their path back through the temple and exited the way they'd come, via the main entrance. Joel saw the slimebacks huddled together on the ground, apparently sleeping, while Greenseed stood near them, keeping watch. The sky was starting to brighten with the advent of dawn, and Joel realized that they had been up all night. He suddenly felt very tired.

"Is everything all right, Master?" Greenseed asked Marshall in her soft, reserved tone. "I heard a loud noise and saw the Aura shift."

"Yes, yes, quite all right, thank you," Marshall said. "Just a minor ratworm encounter is all."

"Ah, good. Did you find what you were looking for?"

"Not exactly, but close. Do you know how to get to the Caves of Wrath?"

Greenseed tilted her head ever so slightly. "Master?"

"The Caves of Wrath—you *have* heard of them, I presume?"

Greenseed's expression changed subtly, but what emotion it reflected, Joel couldn't tell. "Yes, of course, but—"

"Brilliant!" Marshall exclaimed, sounding like a kid who just got what he wanted for his birthday. "We must journey there at once."

"Master, the way there is perilous, as are the caves themselves."

"Understood. I'm sure it's nothing that three trained Wavemakers can't handle."

Joel gulped. As Marshall himself had pointed out in the temple, duress is one thing when you're practicing against straw dummies, but something totally different when you're faced with wild, living creatures.

"Very well," Greenseed said. "The fastest way there is probably along the Coast of Fang."

"Then the Coast of Fang it is," Marshall announced.

Joel yawned conspicuously. "Um—can we, uh—"

Marshall looked at him and snickered. "Ah, of course. I almost forgot that we've been traveling all night."

"I'm tired too," Felicity said, "but is it safe to sleep? What about, like, wild animals? Or rain? Or Fourfoot?"

"My dear, have you not seen any adventure movies?" Marshall winked at her. "We sleep in shifts, of course. Also, I know some handy shelter casts, as well as ones to reduce fatigue, so that we won't have to sleep as long. That should make our journey faster, which I *know* you like."

The left corner of Felicity's mouth turned upward, making an expression that Joel didn't realize was a half smile of grudging acceptance. Sometimes facial expressions were just as confusing as words.

Twenty-one days until the Nadir

After a quick nap in the clearing outside the temple, during which Marshall had volunteered to keep watch ("I stayed up four days in a row on tour once, so this is nothing," he said), Joel felt quite refreshed. The morning sun shone a brilliant bright orange, and tiny specks of Aura glittered in the air like snowflakes. As Joel looked into the shifting colors of the sky while munching on a lifepod, something dawned on him.

"Um, Marshall?" he asked.

"Yes?" Marshall said as he filled his flask in the river.

"Why—why are there no, you know, birds? Or anything that flies, like insects, or whatever."

"Brilliant observation," Marshall replied.

"Um, because I was wondering," Joel said before Marshall could continue, "couldn't we just fly to the caves? I—I figure you would be able to do something like that."

Marshall laughed. "That would be great, wouldn't it? I like the way you think. But alas, it appears that in a world where all seems possible, flying is the one thing that is not. Not with Aura powers, and not even the old-fashioned way, with wings."

Joel made a puzzled face. "That just seems, I dunno, weird."

"It certainly does," Marshall said, looking into the sky. "I suspect it has something to do with aerodynamics and gravity and how they are affected by the Aura, or something like that. As I've said before, I'm no scientist."

Joel actually knew quite a bit about aerodynamics. After a visit to the Seattle Museum of Flight four years ago, he'd become obsessed with learning everything he possibly could about how things flew, to the point where his regular schoolwork suffered. His mom decided not to take him back there again, but that didn't deter him from continuing his relentless research. At first, he shared details about everything he learned with anyone who would listen (and some who would not), until eventually his interest waned. He still retained the knowledge, but he decided not to say anything about it to Marshall.

Of all the crazy fantasy alien worlds to land in, I have to get the one where you can't fly. Now I really know that this isn't a dream. Not that I wasn't convinced already, but if my imagination were to think up an alternate universe, it would definitely have flying in it. There's so much to choose from—dragons, starships, brooms, pterodactyls, carpets, anything! But no, no flying, not even a mosquito.

"And no, there's no way to teleport or anything like that, either." Marshall grinned, trying to preempt Joel's next question.

♪♪♪

They set off again, with Greenseed leading the way. Joel took in the sights of the lush, tropical landscape (whose lack of birds, now that he had noticed it, kind of bothered him) as they traversed a seaweed-palm jungle and approached an enormous, jagged mountain range not too far off in the distance. The mountains were covered in vegetation that shimmered pale green or purple, depending on how you tilted your head when you looked at them.

"This is the Dragonspine Range," Greenseed announced. "The fastest way to the coast will be through Roughrock Pass." She pointed at what looked like the faint beginnings of a trail, at the bottom of the range where two of the mountains intersected.

"Splendid," Marshall said.

Minutes later, Joel decided that it was not so splendid after all. Like most things on Spectraland, Roughrock Pass certainly lived up to its name, and the slimebacks occasionally grunted their displeasure at having to navigate such challenging terrain. Dreamer in particular seemed like she was ready to call it a day, and Felicity had to soothe her with more bits of lifepod than was probably prudent, given their dwindling supplies. After they traveled for what Joel calculated was about six and three-quarter miles, the trail began to make a slight incline, which definitely did not help matters.

"Um, I think Destiny's getting tired," Joel said as he patted his mount's sticky, panting head.

"There is an area of flat ground at the top," Greenseed said. "We can rest there—if that is all right with you, Master," she added, turning to Marshall.

"Yes, of course," Marshall said.

The incline got steeper and steeper (and the slimebacks crankier and crankier) until finally, it leveled out into a plateau from which there was a magnificent view of the beach and coastline below. The breeze blew warmer and saltier here, and Joel got his first glimpse of the ocean of this world: a deep green body of rolling water that hummed with the energy of the surrounding Aura.

"Beautiful, innit?" Marshall whistled, stopping to admire the scene.

"Whatever gets us there faster," Felicity said, obviously unimpressed.

"She is right, Master. We should not linger here long," Greenseed said, a bit anxiously.

"Relax, ladies, we—"

Seemingly out of nowhere (but, really, from behind the brush and scrub that lined the edges of the plateau), several scraggly-looking natives had emerged, carrying odd spiral-shaped bows loaded with spiky projectiles that were aimed directly at the traveling party. Joel counted six of them at first, but then, as he looked around, he saw that their number had doubled, then tripled. They were a bit taller and broader than the village natives, and they formed an intimidating circle around Joel and the others.

"Hnnddzz inn thee errr," one of the natives said as he stepped forward. His voice sounded like one of those electronically-distorted telephone voices that criminals use to disguise themselves.

"Pardon me?" Marshall snorted.

"Ay sddd, hnnddzz inn thee errr," the native repeated.

"We are unarmed, my friend," Marshall said, reaching for his wavebow. "These are merely...musical instruments."

The native raised his spiral bow in an aggressive fashion. "Wwee nno whttt yoo arrr," he hissed. "Annd wwee doo nttt tallk too othrrwrrdlee ssliime lliike yoo."

"Greenseed...?" Marshall said through the side of his mouth.

"A vagabond tribe, Master," Greenseed answered. "Known for ambushing travelers of the pass. They speak an odd dialect, which is why—"

"I meant," Marshall said through clenched teeth, "please talk to them and tell them to let us pass."

"Oh, of course," she said. Then, turning to the leader of the vagabonds, she announced in a diplomatic tone: "Friends, this is Chief Byle. He, um, he defeated Chief

Fourfoot of Nightshore and saved our island. He is now on a quest to make sure that—"

"Wwee dnnt crrr abboutt yrr polliticss, vvillage-dwellerr," the native spat. "Ourr ttriibe tkkes crrr of itssllff."

Although he was scared, something about their predicament felt familiar to Joel—almost comfortably so.

"That may be true," Greenseed said, "but I do not think you understand the extent of the danger that we face."

"Dnnt tll uss whtt wwee dnnt unnrrstnnd!"

Joel felt a strange impulse making its way from his gut to his head. He could almost see a door opening in his mind, beckoning him to walk through, while a disembodied voice that was his own—but yet not—said something like, *This is your moment. You are the one that can handle this. It's you or nobody.*

In that same split second, he argued with himself: *Me? What can I do? Arrows are pointed at me and I'm scared out of my mind.*

Don't be scared. You can do this. This is your solo.

My what? What am I supposed to—

Stop thinking so much. Sometimes, you just gotta say, what the heck.

And go with it? Um—

His mouth opened, seemingly of its own volition. "Um, excuse me, but you need to let us pass, please."

No one said anything as all eyes turned toward him.

"We are on a mission to save all of you," he proclaimed, adrenaline surging through his body, his mind suddenly feeling strangely clear and connected. "If we succeed, you'll continue to live in freedom. If we fail, you'll be enslaved by an evil chief who doesn't care whether you are part of a village or not."

"Wwee dnnt—"

"You must let us pass!" Joel said in a firm voice, without shouting, while blurred images of websites saying odd things like *stand up for yourself* and *don't bully back* danced across his memory.

The leader looked at his companions and lowered his spiral bow, just a bit. Joel took a deep breath in through his nose, raised his chin slightly, and urged Destiny toward the perimeter of the vagabond circle. He made sure that she walked at a pace that seemed neither too slow nor too fast. The two natives that he approached glanced at each other, then back at their leader, and then parted just enough to let Joel and Destiny pass through. Marshall made a nodding gesture to the others that said *quick, follow him,* which they did. No one said a word until they had descended about two hundred yards down the trail leading away from the plateau and the vagabond natives were out of sight.

"Blimey, that was brilliant!" Marshall effused. "Good quick thinking there, Joel. I was about to blow them away with a repulsing cast. You saved us a lot of mess."

"Um, thanks," Joel said with a modest grin, the adrenaline rush now fully abated. "I, uh, have some experience with bullies."

"I bet you do. You know, you lucked out," Felicity mumbled grudgingly. "We could've gotten killed there, for all you know."

Joel felt a little pool of anger bubbling up, which he tried hard to rein in. "You know, why are you so mean?" he snapped.

Felicity furrowed her brow at him, apparently surprised by this first-ever attempt at verbal fight-back from her training companion. She opened her mouth to retaliate but instead opted to urge Dreamer into a faster gait that put her several yards in front of their pack as they headed down the trail toward the sandy landing below.

"Women," Marshall chuckled as he sidled up to Joel. "Don't take her too seriously, lad. She'll drive you crazy if you do."

Joel always hated conflict. And tension. Especially of the lingering variety. He suspected it had something to do with his less-than-tranquil upbringing, with the way his father would erupt in bursts of volcanic temper, often for seemingly random reasons, and then stew in chilly silence for hours afterward.

Or perhaps it was just the way he was wired. Either way, the discomfort that underlined his relationship with Felicity gnawed at him even harder now. He wasn't sure why he cared, actually—only that he did. The good feelings that his success with the vagabonds gave him were already a distant memory. Since they were going to be around each other longer than expected, why couldn't they just be friends? Why couldn't she say nice things for a change?

With his thoughts occupied by questions of a similar nature, the trek down the trail seemed to go by much faster than their ascent up the other side. They reached the warm sands below, which were granular and pale orange, with flecks of bright red occasionally scattered throughout. The shoreline continued for miles, with sparse vegetation lining the side opposite the ocean, until it ended in another mountain range off in the distance.

The slimebacks could only walk or run through the sand for short stretches before wearing out, so in between, they swam along the shallow edge of the calm ocean. For Joel, the smell of the seawater brought back childhood memories of going to the beach—an activity that he wasn't overly fond of, beyond the fact that it seemed to at least make his parents happy for a little while.

They traveled the rest of the day and well into the evening without much in the way of breaks or conversation. Finally, Greenseed broke the silence.

"Master, the animals are tiring. We should probably set camp for the night."

"Agreed. Let's stop over there," Marshall said, pointing to a small cluster of seaweed palms.

They dismounted, and Marshall started playing the various melodies that created a weblike tent of Aura energy that would serve as their shelter.

"I will venture a bit inward to look for possible food and water sources," Greenseed declared. "That is, if you approve, Master."

"Yes, yes, that's fine," Marshall said, still focused on his casting.

"Um, could we maybe learn how to do that too?" Joel asked, trying his best to be unobtrusive. Although he said "we," Felicity was actually still down by the water's edge, petting Dreamer on the neck.

"That's a splendid idea," Marshall replied as he put the finishing touches on their fluorescent pavilion. "It is a rather draining cast, however, so probably best to practice it later. Don't want to have all three of us out of ammo at the same time."

"Oh, okay."

♪♪♪

About an hour (actually fifty minutes, by Joel's count) later, Marshall had fallen fast asleep in the light-tent, and Greenseed still had not returned. The slimebacks were resting peacefully a few yards from the tent on a patch of soft yellow grass. Felicity sat alone on the beach with her chin on her knees, looking out toward the horizon, while Joel stood outside the tent, eating the last few bites of a lifepod. He spotted her and realized that this was the first time, in all of their time here, that they were basically alone together. His stomach knotted up at the thought.

Okay, what the heck, here we go, he sighed to himself. He walked out toward Felicity as carefully and casually as he could, as if she would bolt away like a scared animal at the very sight of him.

"Um, hey," he said, clearing his throat. "Want a— want a bite?"

Felicity glanced at the remaining piece of fruit in his outstretched hand and grimaced. "Ugh, no."

Feeling embarrassed, but determined to carry on, Joel sat down on the sand about three feet away from her. He waited a few seconds to see if there were any further declarations of disgust forthcoming. There were none, so he pressed forward.

"So—um, this is all pretty crazy, huh?"

No response.

"Are you...are you mad about something?" he ventured.

After nine more painful seconds of silence, he was about to stand up and walk away when suddenly, Felicity let out an exasperated sigh.

"I'm just always mad," she said, her gaze still fixed on the ocean, which was now starting to roll small, gentle waves up onto the shore.

"About what?"

"I dunno. Life, I guess."

Joel's brain tried to process this broad declaration and ferret out whatever specifics it could boil it down to, but eventually he just gave up and settled on asking, "Why?"

"Why what? Why am I mad about life?"

"Yeah."

"'Cause it sucks, basically. At least mine does."

At that moment, Joel felt a wave of empathy along with a small jolt of excitement over finding what seemed to be a kindred spirit in angst and misery. "Really? Like how?"

"Anyone ever tell you that you ask a lot of questions?" she said with mild irritation as she looked at him out of the corner of her eye.

Joel could feel his face turning warm. "Oh—um, sorry."

After a few more seconds, she sighed again. "I don't know, I've just always been like this. When I was, like, three, or whatever, my older sister fell off her bike and broke her arm, and I just laughed at her. A couple of years later, our cat died, and I didn't feel sad, or anything."

Joel was so stunned by her actually speaking to him in a civil manner that the content of what she just said didn't really register with him. "Um, wow," he muttered.

"Yeah...and I always just say whatever I feel, whatever pops into my head. I have no filter. Never did. No matter how hard I tried, I just couldn't relate to what other people were feeling or thinking."

It was Joel's turn to sit in silence as a few stronger waves crashed up onto the sand. His mind was starting to drift as Felicity related her story to him. *She's actually talking to me normally! That's such a relief. I wonder where Greenseed went? She's been gone for, like, sixty-two minutes.*

"And so anyway," Felicity continued, "this didn't make me very popular in school, as you can imagine. Any friends I made, I chased away after a while. I was so stressed out about it that I always got bad grades and stuff. They even put me in these special classes for 'developmental issues,' or whatever."

That got Joel's attention. "Um, hey, I was in those kinds of classes too!" he said.

"I'm not surprised," she snorted.

"What, uh, what did they diagnose you with? They said that I had—"

"I really don't want to talk about that," she interrupted. "At any rate, I was the only girl in there. That was pretty rough. Eventually I just kinda decided, if people think I'm a witch, I'm just gonna go with that and actually *be* a witch. Good thing I had music, otherwise I dunno what I would've done."

"You know," Joel said, as bunches of brightly glowing pink and purple flowers suddenly started washing up with the tide, "I—I totally know how you feel."

"Yeah, I bet you do," she muttered.

By Joel's count, about forty-nine seconds of silence passed by.

"So—um, are you still mad?" he asked, hoping for some closure.

After a pause, she sighed again, heavier this time. "Why do you keep asking me that? What is your problem, anyway?"

That wasn't the response that he was looking for. "Oh—uh, sorry, I—um—"

Felicity stood up and starting walking toward the water. "Just leave me alone, okay? I don't even know why I told you all that stuff."

Unable to come up with anything else to say, Joel just stared in no particular direction as Felicity bent down to pick up a cluster of purple flowers. As a kind of defense mechanism, he could feel his thoughts defaulting to things that made him feel comfortable: chord progressions of Biledriver songs, model names of import cars, episode names from season three of *Spongebob Squarepants*. While hiding under these mental security blankets, he noticed something odd about the light emanating from the flowers. He couldn't quite understand it; he only knew that there was reason to be concerned.

"Miss Felicity! No!" Greenseed yelled as she came running onto the beach.

Joel jumped up as the flowers in Felicity's hands exploded into a cloud of tiny spores. She screamed and recoiled. Joel rushed forward to help her, but Greenseed called out to him, stopping him in his tracks.

"Master Joel, get your wavebow, quickly! And please wake Master Byle!"

Joel turned around and dashed up to the light-tent while Greenseed hurried past him in the opposite direction. Just as Joel reached the tent, Marshall emerged from it, looking rather groggy.

"What in blazes is going—oh, bloody hell," he said, and turned back into the tent.

Joel glanced back, and his eyes widened in shock. The small flower clusters had grown and mutated into man-sized, jellyfish-like creatures, with the only remaining vestiges of their previous forms being the little pink and purple blossoms scattered about their translucent bodies. Joel counted six of them in all. One of them had

Felicity in the grips of its numerous tentacles, while the others were lashing furiously at Greenseed as she darted about, stabbing at Felicity's captor with an eight-inch knife.

"Here!" Marshall yelled as he came back out, thrusting a wavebow at Joel while carrying another in his other hand. "Use a stunning cast—go!"

Joel frantically aimed his instrument and speed-picked a heavy riff while running back down toward the melee. For one absurd micro-second, his actions reminded him of Steve Harris from Iron Maiden dashing across the stage with his Fender P-Bass held up like a rifle. That momentary distraction, combined with his frazzled emotional state, disrupted Joel's focus just enough that rather than a precise wave of red light, a harmless burst of sparks emerged from his wavebow.

"Concentrate!" Marshall yelled as he fired off a red bolt that knocked one of the jellyfishes over. "My energy's not fully back yet—we need you to step up here!"

Joel struggled to relax and clear his mind. As he formed an image of a giant jellyfish being pushed back into the ocean, a real one quickly scurried up to him, flailing its tentacles like a dozen angry bullwhips. Joel managed to produce a short, swirling burst of light that pushed it back a few feet. But before he could do it again, the surprisingly fast creature was back in front of him, and this time, it managed to slap the wavebow out of his grasp, sending it flying some ten feet away.

Joel wanted to look around for help, but he found his attention monopolized by the hulking gelatinous mass that evidently wanted to hug him in a decidedly non-friendly way. Without room or time to run, he resorted to a series of wild kicks and punches in an attempt to fend off the undulating appendages.

He was successful for a second, but more because of the jellyfish's surprise than anything else. It quickly realized that its opponent's limbs were no match for its own, and it started to close in once again. Joel fell to the ground and shielded his face with his arms.

Suddenly, there was a bellowing croaking noise, followed immediately by a loud *thud* as a pale yellow slimeback head rammed into the side of the jellyfish, knocking it off balance.

"Destiny?" Joel said, uncovering his eyes.

Then, Joel heard the flange-y sound of a wavebow riff (*hey, that's the bridge to "Stay Away," the fourth song on Biledriver's third album*), and a red wave of light struck the jellyfish, sending it tumbling down onto the sand.

"Yah!" Marshall shouted. "Go on, get out of here, you bloody maggots!" He raised his wavebow in a threatening fashion, and the creature scuttled away toward the water. Marshall followed it for a bit as Joel got to his feet.

"Where—where's Felicity?" Joel asked as he looked around, trying to regain his bearings. "Is she okay?"

"Over here," Marshall called out.

Joel turned. He saw Marshall jogging over to where Greenseed was kneeling on the sand next to Felicity's prone figure. Joel quickly followed, panic rising in his throat.

"What happened?" Marshall asked.

"She is alive," Greenseed said, much to Joel's relief. "But the bloomfish—it stung her."

"Um, what—is that bad?" Joel asked.

Greenseed paused a moment before replying. "If we do not get the correct medicine for her within the next hour, she will die."

CHAPTER 9: SPEARWIND

Joel always had a hard time dealing with guilt. Not that he didn't want to accept responsibility when things went wrong—quite the opposite, actually. He had a tendency to blame himself for everything that, in his mind, he was even peripherally at fault for. For instance, if he walked into a room and then his mom spilled a glass of juice, he would wonder if he had somehow distracted or startled her. After that, he would feel bad about it and apologize repeatedly for the rest of the day.

So Felicity's condition weighed on him heavily as they raced off the beach, her limp and barely conscious body strapped to Marshall's slimeback.

Oh man, if only I hadn't talked to her and made her mad then she wouldn't have picked up that flower and none of this would have happened and she'd be okay and, oh man, it's all my fault.

Fortunately, Greenseed knew that they were relatively close to a village called Spearwind, a place that Marshall said he had traveled to before but from a different direction. It would mean backtracking a bit, setting them back on their time-sensitive quest, but this problem was more important right now.

"Is—is she gonna be okay?" Joel asked as they urged their mounts through some dense underbrush.

"I told you," Marshall said, apparently trying to rein in his impatience, "she should be, as long as we can get to the village in time. I know someone there who should be able to provide the antidote."

Joel still didn't feel better, despite Marshall's repeated assurances. *Should* just sounded a bit too uncertain.

Why wasn't I able to help her? I freaked out, and I got distracted. Again. He wanted to beat himself up, to punish himself for his failure, but he knew that doing so wouldn't help matters.

After thirty-two excruciatingly long minutes, the village finally came into view. Huts and tree houses similar to Headsmouth's were clustered closely together on a ridge that was nestled in the center of a small valley. The settlement was dotted with torches and glowmoss-covered stones mounted on poles, making the place resemble an arena rock show during a power ballad. The breeze picked up considerably as they moved closer, and little orange shards of Aura swirled around the night sky like fireflies.

Marshall stopped abruptly and picked up his wavebow.

"Um, what—why are we stopping?" Joel asked, glancing over at Felicity and noticing that she looked extremely pale.

"What? Oh, well, I can't cure the poison," Marshall said as he wove a complex little arpeggio that spread a blue blanket of light around them, "but I can make an adjustment to her body temperature—keep her a bit more comfortable while we hunt down the antidote."

That seemed to make sense. "Oh, okay," Joel said. "So, uh, who—or what—are we looking for? Is there a doctor, like Brownstump?"

"Actually," Marshall replied as he finished up the cast, "there's a seedy little potion vendor who deals in all manner of strange concoctions. The other villagers used to trade food and whatnot for his so-called elixirs. If I recall correctly, he claimed to possess a cure for bloom-fish venom."

"Great," Joel said with a measure of relief. "Does—does it work?"

"You know, I'm not sure. I never saw anyone use it before."

As Joel's anxiety level ratcheted up another notch, they rode to the edge of the village, where Marshall was instantly recognized by the first native they encountered. A portly specimen, he appeared to have been standing there alone, seemingly awaiting their arrival.

"Chief Byle?" the native said in a slightly incredulous tone. His tunic was colorfully decorated with carefully painted symbols, and on his head he wore what looked like an upside-down wooden bowl with various flora attached to it in a haphazard manner. Joel would have laughed if the situation at hand wasn't so serious. "What brings you to Spearwind?"

"Hello, Chief Raintree. We have," Marshall said, nodding at Felicity, "a bit of a medical emergency here. Is the potion man still around?"

"Darkeye? Yes, he is. In the same place, by the statue. I am not sure he has even moved from that spot since the last time you were here," Raintree said, making a sound that Joel interpreted as a chuckle.

"Excellent," Marshall said. "Once we have matters in hand, we will stop to chat. For now, however, we must be off."

"Understood. I would like to meet your new other-worldly friends—as well as your charming little assistant here," Raintree said as he looked at Greenseed, who remained silent and expressionless.

"Indeed," Marshall snickered.

After ascending a series of steps that had been carved out of the side of the rocky ridge, they entered the main portion of the village, with Marshall briskly leading the way. There were many resident natives walking about, which Joel found unusual for this time of night. All of the natives stared intently at them as they passed, making Joel feel a bit uneasy.

"Um, why are they looking at us like that?" he asked Marshall.

"They're not used to seeing offworlders—us," Marshall replied. "Before you two arrived, I was the only one, and I live in a different village, remember?"

"Oh, right," Joel said, still feeling unsettled.

They entered what Joel figured was Spearwind's equivalent of a central plaza. It was much smaller than the one in Headsmouth, and a large wood-and-stone statue of a weird-looking tree with spiral branches took up a lot of the room in the middle.

At the base of the statue sat a disheveled native wearing a silky gray hooded robe. He was surrounded by dozens of jars and pots (fifty-four, actually, by Joel's count), each of them a different size and shape. A few of them were overturned, with their contents spilled carelessly out onto the ground. Joel fervently hoped that Felicity's antidote wasn't one of them.

Marshall dismounted and walked over to the native. "Darkeye," he said.

The native looked up. His face was wrinkled and scarred, and where his nose should have been was instead just a flat, greenish-black spot. He had an empty eye socket that looked like an endless cavern, and his one remaining eye had a crazy, vacant look to it. "Ah, Chief Byle, what a—*hic*—pleasant surprise," he said in a soft, serpentine voice.

"The antidote for bloomfish venom," Marshall said matter-of-factly. "You have it, I presume?"

"Bloomfish, eh?" Darkeye said, his long, thin lips forming what Joel figured to be a smile. "Very—*hic*—rare creatures. Even rarer, the cure for their—*hic*—sting."

Marshall idly fingered the headstock of his wavebow. "We don't have time for this. I know you boasted of possessing some not very long ago."

Darkeye looked at Felicity, who was still slumped over on the slimeback. "The—*hic*—victim, I assume. She looks...not well. Is she—*hic*—your mate?"

"That's none of your concern," Marshall said. (Joel found himself wishing that Marshall had said "no" instead, although he wasn't quite sure why.) "Do you have the antidote or not?"

"I may," Darkeye said, looking over his array of jars. "But—*hic*—such a precious fluid is not parted with so easily, you—*hic*—understand."

Joel began to feel angry and impatient as he jumped off of Destiny and stood next to Marshall. *The nerve of this rotten native, not giving Marshall—Chief Byle— what he wants! Can't he see that our friend is dying?*

As Joel glared at Darkeye, he noticed an unusual Aura pattern surrounding the native—instead of the usual corona-like waves, tiny dark blue and purple spots flitted about his hooded head like flies.

"Fine," Marshall sighed. "We'll give you the remainder of our supplies. My assistant recently managed to obtain a fresh batch of lifepods—several weeks' worth."

"A nice—*hic*—start," Darkeye said as he picked up a small white jar. "But the cure for bloomfish venom must be obtained from the beast—*hic*—itself, from its eggs. A very hazardous undertaking, to be sure. As your—*hic*—unfortunate companion has discovered, they are highly protective of their young."

Marshall gritted his teeth. "Listen, you slimy git, don't play games with me, I—"

"You...what?" Darkeye said with an amused air.

Joel looked at Greenseed with an urgent expression of *can you help?* To which Greenseed replied with a little sideways head motion that Joel had come to learn was a Spectraland native's version of a shrug.

Marshall paused for a moment, apparently to collect himself, and then said in a soft, steely voice, "Very well. What else do you want?"

Darkeye adopted the look of a child set loose on a toy-store shopping spree. "See? I knew we could be—*hic*—reasonable about this. I am not greedy, I am only interested in—*hic*—fairness. And as such, I believe... your mounts—all of them—shall make for—*hic*—sufficient compensation."

At this point, Joel decided to try and replicate his earlier victory at the pass. "Um, sorry, but we can't give those to you. We're on a very urgent mission to—"

"Ah—er, never mind," Marshall said, holding up a hand to Joel. "It's quite all right, mate." Then, turning back to Darkeye, he continued: "You make a painful demand, potion-maker, but one that I'm afraid we cannot refuse. Our mounts it is. But I say, this antidote had best work."

"Have I ever failed you—*hic*—before?" Darkeye hissed through his toothless grin.

"What are—why—" Joel stammered, looking back and forth between Marshall and the native sitting in front of them.

"Don't worry," Marshall said, and then he silently mouthed the words *trust me*.

With both hands, Darkeye held the white jar in front of his face. His pale single eye rolled upwards in its socket, and a horrible gurgling noise could be heard originating from his throat. Joel saw the dark Aura spots begin to move faster, in a more uniform elliptical orbit around the native's head. After thirteen seconds of gradual crescendo, the gurgling noise escalated into a loud hum that Joel thought for sure would attract the attention of the entire village. When he looked around, however, he saw that all of the natives in the immediate area were ignoring them and going about their business as if nothing was happening.

Then, with a sudden *snap* like a single firecracker going off, Darkeye opened his mouth, and a thick, purple liquid began to pour out, rolling off of his tongue and into the jar.

Joel felt disgusted and fascinated at the same time.

As a trail of hazy blue smoke wafted out of the jar, Darkeye picked up a thin stick and proceeded to stir the contents. "This should be effective, but she—*hic*—will need some time to fully recover."

"How long?" Marshall asked.

Darkeye made the Spectraland shrugging motion. "Two—*hic*—days, perhaps three."

"That's unfortunate," Marshall muttered.

"Here you go," Darkeye said, handing the jar to Marshall. "She should be—*hic*—lying down in a more comfortable spot when you administer this. And now, my—*hic*—payment, please."

Joel looked back at Destiny, who somehow seemed to be aware of what was going on. Her head was slumped, and her frog-like eyes were downcast. Joel walked over to her and stroked her neck. He noticed that her skin didn't seem to be secreting as much sticky fluid as usual, and her near-constant purr-croak was absent.

"It's okay," he said sadly. "We need to do this, to, you know, save Felicity. Like how you saved me on the beach. Oh, and uh, thanks for that, by the way. Maybe—maybe Marshall can figure something out. I dunno. I'll talk to him later, okay?"

With that, Joel turned and followed Marshall, who had lifted Felicity off of his slimeback and was now carrying her like a small child out of the plaza. Greenseed trailed close behind.

"Are we really going to let him keep them? Isn't there something you can do?" Joel asked.

"I don't know," Marshall sighed. "I'll figure something out. We may just be able to get to the caves on foot."

Joel grimaced. Transportation wasn't the foremost concern on his mind—it was more the sentimental aspect of having to part with an animal that he considered a pet, or a friend, even. The sadness over this loss wrestled with his relief at having procured Felicity's antidote, leaving him in a state of acute emotional confusion.

"Over here," Marshall said as he ducked into a small hut that was built on a platform overhanging the ridge. The inside of the hut was empty, save for a couple of woven sleeping mats and a handful of bowls strewn about.

"Is this somebody's house?" Joel asked.

"Looks like a bachelor apartment," Marshall said as he laid Felicity down on one of the mats. "They're probably out partying or whatever, I'm sure they won't mind us borrowing it for a bit."

Felicity's face was completely drained of color now, and even though she was unconscious, her body appeared to be shivering. The Aura surrounding her was very faint. Joel figured that they had about six minutes of the one-hour window left, although he realized that Greenseed was probably just giving them a general time frame. He wondered, with a renewed sense of panic, if that one-hour time frame was applicable to humans as well as to the more plant-based native populace.

Marshall carefully turned Felicity's head to the side and opened her mouth so that her lips were parted by about a centimeter. He slowly poured the contents of the small white jar over her lips, letting most of it spill onto the mat.

"Um, are you sure you're doing that correctly?" Joel asked.

"Let's hope so," Marshall replied.

A minute went by, and nothing happened. Marshall put a hand to Felicity's forehead. "Hmm, still cold."

"Should we ask that Darkeye guy for help?"

"Are you serious? He's already asked for our slimebacks. Who knows what he'll want next? I don't think he included a warranty with the initial purchase."

Joel anxiously studied Felicity's Aura, which had started to flicker. As he stared at it, his focus began to shift, as if he were looking at one of those optical illusion stereograms where you have to find the 3-D image.

"Oh...I—I think it's working, but since she's human, um—hold on," he said, feeling a sudden inspiration.

"What are you doing?" Marshall asked.

Joel picked up his wavebow and began to play. He saw that circular gaps had formed in the Aura around Felicity, and following some unknown instinct, he envisioned them being filled in, like water flowing into cups. A soft green wave of light streamed out of his instrument and did exactly what he was thinking.

Marshall's look of curiosity turned into one of amazement as Felicity's eyes started to flutter. She coughed and convulsed violently a few times. Joel stopped playing.

"All right, here we go now," Marshall said, helping Felicity to sit up. "How are you feeling?"

"Terrible," she whispered, her voice hoarse. "Geez, that stuff is disgusting. You try drinking it next time."

Marshall grinned at Joel. "I think she's back, mate."

♫♫

Twenty-four minutes later, Marshall had managed to secure some relatively comfortable resting quarters in Chief Raintree's tree house complex. Felicity had gone back to sleep, but her color and warmth had returned.

"Another brilliant maneuver back there," Marshall said to Joel. "We'll make a right proper shaman out of you yet, we will."

"Um, okay," Joel said sheepishly.

"Now, we just need to figure out what we're going to do for transportation."

Joel felt sad at the reminder of Destiny's absence. "Yeah," was all he could think to say.

Marshall rubbed the scar on his face for a few moments, and then turned and started to head out the doorway. "I'm going to go check some things out. You get some rest; it's late."

Their tree house suite was comparatively luxurious: a circular interior twenty-two feet in diameter, its woven vine-and-wood walls were adorned with colorful abstract paintings depicting various scenes of nature, including the spiral tree whose representative statue Joel had seen in the courtyard. The four sleeping mats in the suite each lay atop a thick wooden slab, presenting a rough approximation of an actual bed, and were positioned at the main compass points of the room.

Joel lay down on the south mat, opposite from where Greenseed was sleeping. He had long since gotten used to the absence of a routine (something that had bothered him quite a bit at first) and quickly felt himself start to drift off, when suddenly he heard a soft voice coming from the west mat.

"Joel?" the voice whispered. It was Felicity.

"What—me?" he whispered back. That was the first time she had addressed him by his name, so he wanted to be sure.

"Is anyone else here named Joel? Yes, you," she said.

"Sorry," he said. *Yup, she's definitely feeling better.*

"No, don't be. Look, I—I just wanted to say... thanks for saving me back there."

Well, that was different. "Oh—um, well, it wasn't really me, Marshall was the one that got the potion, and, um, you know—"

"Yeah, after giving away our rides," she said dismissively. "And that gross potion wouldn't have even worked if it weren't for you."

"Oh—yeah, well, I dunno, I—wait, how do you know about all that stuff? I thought you were unconscious."

"Almost, but not quite. It was pretty bad, though. Thought for sure I was gonna die."

"Yeah, um, you know, I'm really sorry about that. It was totally my fault that you got stung in the first place."

"What are you talking about?"

"If I hadn't made you mad, on the beach, you wouldn't have went over and picked up those flowers."

"Pfft, I was gonna do that anyways. They looked nice."

"What—seriously?"

"Yeah, of course. No worries, okay?"

"Oh—um, okay."

In the two-and-a-half minutes that followed, Joel replayed the previous conversation over in his head while the sound of Greenseed's light snoring seemed to fill up the room.

Aliens snore? Joel found this rather funny. Bright moonlight began to shine through one of the open windows.

"I gotta say, though," Felicity said with a quiet laugh, "You looked pretty stupid trying to fight off that jellyfish with your bare hands."

"What—you saw that?"

"Yeah. You totally need to learn some karate."

"Um, it's not *kuh-rah-dee,* it's *kah-dah-tay,*" he corrected her, trying to sound as diplomatic as possible. He was afraid of upsetting her, but mispronunciation of Japanese words was one of his pet peeves, despite the fact that he hardly knew the language himself.

Fortunately, she didn't seem to take offense. "Whatever. You're not the one with the black belt."

"You—you have a black belt?"

"Yup. When I was a kid, my parents forced me to take lessons. They said it might help with my 'anger issues.'"

"Um, why didn't you beat up those guys back on the pass?"

"Really? Hello, there were, like, twenty of them, pointing those funky arrows at us. I'm not Bruce Lee, you know."

There were eighteen of them, actually, Joel wanted to say, but he didn't want to press his luck. "Well, that's—that's still pretty cool."

"I know. That's why it's kind of lame, having been the 'damsel in distress' this whole time. That's totally not me, I hope you know."

"Um, okay." Joel wasn't completely sure what she meant, but he decided not to ask.

"I'll show you some time. You can learn some basic moves. That way, maybe next time we're getting attacked by giant clams or whatever and you drop your wavebow, you won't look so ridiculous."

Joel thought that sounded like a great idea.

Twenty days until the Nadir

The next morning arrived, and with it, the first genuinely bad mood that Joel had ever seen Marshall in. Apparently, his excursion to "check some things out" the night before had not yielded any discernible results in the way of securing some mode of transportation, be it their old mounts or anything else.

Anxious to resume their journey, Marshall sullenly suggested heading out on foot, but it became quickly evident that Felicity was not yet fit enough to travel in that manner, as she could only stay awake for anywhere between ten and fifteen minutes at a time before she required an hour-long nap that she could not be roused from.

"I'm going to investigate some other options," Marshall said, visibly frustrated after Felicity had passed out yet again.

"Um, for what?" Joel inquired nervously.

"Transport, of course," Marshall snapped.

"Oh, right. Sorry."

"It's all right, mate," Marshall sighed. "It's just that Fourfoot could show up again any time now. The faster we find that shell, the better."

"Do—do you want me to come with you?" Joel asked.

"Eh—no, best you stay here and look after these two," Marshall replied, nodding toward Felicity and Greenseed, the latter of whom was preparing a tea made from various roots and leaves. "If anything really serious happens, just fire up a signal cast. I won't be far."

Joel was actually happy to hear this, as he wanted a chance to follow up on the connection he seemed to have made with Felicity the night before. He spent the next hour and nine minutes occupying himself with his own thoughts (interrupted once by Chief Raintree, who claimed to be checking up on them, but really only talked to Greenseed, who ignored the portly native) before Felicity woke up again.

"Ugh, my head really hurts," she mumbled.

"Here, drink this," Greenseed said, offering her a cup of the freshly made tea.

"Where's Marshall?" Felicity asked, taking a small sip.

"Uh, he went to investigate some other options," Joel said.

"For what?"

"Transport."

"What? We need to get moving," Felicity groaned.

"You are not yet in the proper condition," Greenseed reminded her.

"I know, I know. Man, I really thought I'd be feeling better by now."

"The potion guy said that it could take two or three days," Joel said.

"Are you kidding?" Felicity said, nearly spitting out her tea. "I didn't hear that part. Wow, that's a bummer."

In the fraction of a second after Felicity finished speaking, a thought process ran through Joel's mind that went as follows: *I need to distract her from this subject of being unable to continue our quest before she gets too angry. As she regains her strength, she also seems to be regaining her attitude. Before she forgets, I should try to take her up on her offer to teach me some martial arts. This is also a good time for it, seeing as how we can't go anywhere anyway, and Marshall isn't here to make things awkward.*

The thought process complete, Joel said, "Hey, uh, maybe you can teach me some of that karate stuff in the meantime?"

"What, now?"

"Um, sure, yeah. Why not?" Joel shrugged, Earth-style.

Over the next nineteen minutes, Joel learned some basic ideas about stance and blocking before Felicity had to go back to sleep. They continued in this fashion, with the lengths of her naps gradually growing shorter, until well past nightfall. Felicity seemed to enjoy her role as an instructor, and Joel welcomed the chance to finally be on some kind of friendly terms with her.

They were in the middle of a kicking exercise when Marshall burst in, short of breath and appearing some- what anxious.

"I'm afraid we've got a little situation on our hands," he announced.

"Um, what kind of—" Joel started to ask.

"The good news is," Marshall continued, not waiting for Joel to finish, "I've managed to recover our slime- backs. They're all waiting out back."

Joel smiled, feeling very happy at this news.

"What's the bad—" Felicity started to ask.

"The bad news is, Fourfoot's found us. He somehow managed to possess an entire bloody mob of villagers, and they're coming after us right now."

Joel felt a little less happy at this news.

CHAPTER 10: FLAMING FIELDS

Joel always found the whole idea of an "angry mob" to be somewhat humorous, although he wasn't quite sure why. Something about a rioting group of people, all carrying torches and pitchforks and marching along a street, unified in some abstract purpose of destruction, just seemed patently absurd.

Now that one was after him, however, all the humor was gone.

"Why can't you just un-possess them, or whatever?" Felicity shrieked as they ran out toward the clearing behind the tree houses.

"Too risky," Marshall said breathlessly. "I don't want to kill off an entire innocent village by accident. Best we just get out of here as quickly as possible. They won't be able to keep up on foot."

Joel looked over his shoulder and saw waves of dark Aura rising up from the village paths like black smoke. He could hear unsettled murmuring and the clattering of what was probably weaponry.

The four of them entered the clearing, where their slimebacks stood around, absently chewing on the orange grass. The animals didn't seem to be any worse for wear. Destiny looked up and let out a small croak of recognition.

"Um, yeah, good to see you too," Joel said as he quickly hopped on.

"This way," Marshall said, guiding his mount through a thick set of trees in the back of the clearing.

After thirty-seven minutes of urgent, nonstop riding, they came to rest in an area filled with tall purple and gold grasses, right at the edge of a sharp cliff. The familiar sight of the Dragonspine Range lay off in the distance.

"I think we've lost them," Marshall said.

"But why would he give up chasing us?" Felicity asked in an exhausted voice, obviously in need of yet another nap.

"My guess is that possessing that many others diluted his energy enough that he couldn't maintain it," Marshall mused. "Probably was hoping to surprise us. Good thing I sensed what was going on."

"Okay, so, uh, now what?" Joel asked.

"Well, I believe that if we circle around the edge of this cliff, it should take us back to our original path. Greenseed, what do you think?"

"Yes, Master, that is correct. We just need to follow the mountain."

They rode in the dark for several hours, with Felicity slumped on Marshall's slimeback during her intermittent naps. Finally, they emerged at a spot in front of a large, rolling hillside that appeared to be at the edge of the Coast of Fang. Joel saw the miles of sand that stretched all the way back to Dragonspine Range.

"Back on track." Marshall grinned.

"There is one more obstacle between us and the caves," Greenseed said. "Over this hill lies the Flaming Fields, within which lives the Heatwraith."

"Uh, the what?" Joel said.

"You gotta be kidding me," Felicity grumbled, having just woken up.

"Wraiths are sentient accumulations of Aura, or at least that's what I was taught. Kind of like ghosts, I guess," Marshall said. Then, turning to Greenseed, he asked, "So, they're real, then?"

Greenseed nodded. "Very much so. The Heatwraith in particular is not known for its hospitality. Like I said, the path to the caves is a dangerous one."

"Nevertheless, it's one we must follow," Marshall declared.

They scaled the lower part of the hill and decided to set up camp on the first plateau. After a brief sleep, they awoke at dawn and continued upward, passing several herds of grazing squid-goats along the way. As they ascended the hill, Joel noticed that the temperature was getting progressively warmer, although oddly, it did not feel any more uncomfortable.

Nineteen days until the Nadir

Once they reached the top of the hill, the view drew an audible gasp from Felicity. The landscape abruptly shifted from grass and vegetation to barren rock, and before them lay a deep, sprawling canyon dotted with tall stone obelisks. Even more remarkably, the entire canyon floor appeared to be burning with licks of white flame. Yellow and red Aura energy fields swirled ferociously but silently in the air, like a quiet, colorful hurricane.

"Um, how are we gonna get past this?" Joel asked.

"I know a fireproofing cast, but it would take a lot of energy to maintain it through the entire canyon," Marshall said.

"Can't we just wait until it rains?" Felicity muttered.

"The fire itself is not harmful, for the most part," Greenseed explained. "It is unlike regular fire in that it contains heat but does not burn."

"Oh—then no problem, right?" Joel said.

"The problem—or problems, as it were," Greenseed continued, "are the flamefeeders."

"Of course," Felicity said. "There's always something."

Greenseed pointed at several dark spots near the middle of the valley floor. "They gather in clusters—you can see them there, there, and there. We will need to be careful to avoid them. If they notice us, they will attack. They are very territorial."

"And what about the Heatwraith?" Marshall asked.

"It is at the other end of the fields. That will be an entirely separate challenge."

"Great," Felicity said. "Because we know we don't have enough of those."

Joel chuckled softly as Greenseed gave Felicity a confused look. *Hey, at least I learned what sarcasm is,* he congratulated himself.

Wavebows at the ready, they carefully guided the slimebacks down the treacherous path leading to the bottom of the canyon. None of the animals seemed very anxious to take the first step into the foot-high flames, but once Greenseed coaxed hers in, the others cautiously followed suit.

After they had walked about five yards, the white fire started to rise up around the travelers, as if they were wading into the deeper end of a pool. Dreamer let out a loud croak of alarm and attempted to turn around, but Felicity managed to calm her down.

"Try not to make a lot of noise," Greenseed warned in a low voice. "Doing so may attract the 'feeders."

"Could've told us a little sooner," Felicity grumbled under her breath as she stroked Dreamer's neck.

Just as Greenseed had said, the fire was hot, but so far, no one had felt any pain or burning sensations. The flames quickly grew to be nearly six feet high as the party made its way along the desolate terrain.

"Um, if we see any of those flamefeeder things, what should we cast at it?" Joel said in a voice a few ticks above a whisper.

"You should—I—I do not know," Greenseed replied.

"Hey, I'm the mentor here, remember?" Marshall said. Joel looked at him, expecting to see the familiar grin, but it was oddly absent, and in its place was more of a scowl.

"If they feed on heat," Marshall continued, "I say we try a freezing cast. Just like the one we practiced for the show."

Joel mentally prepared himself, envisioning an object encased in a layer of ice. *Hope I can do it better this time. I just have to remember to relax...*

After they had marched along without incident for another several hundred yards, all the while trying to remain as quiet as possible, Joel suddenly noticed something odd on the ground up ahead. For a moment, he thought that he saw thin blue lines of light arranged in an organized, almost weblike pattern lying flat on the surface. He blinked once and they were gone, but then he blinked again, and they returned.

Since no one else seemed concerned, he waited until they were almost at the edge of where the lines began before he decided to say something. "Um, hold on," he whispered as he drew Destiny to a stop.

"What?" Marshall turned his head but continued moving forward on his mount.

"There's, uh, there's something—something strange on the ground. Don't you guys see it?"

"Yeah, there's white fire coming up to our necks," Felicity said, also not stopping. "Thanks for the scoop."

"No, no, it's—it's a—wait," Joel stammered, unable to verbalize his thoughts quickly enough.

Marshall's slimeback took a step directly onto the blue line. A high pitched squealing sound began to register in their ears.

It's a trap? An alarm? Okay, yeah, an alarm.

Immediately, a pack of creatures that looked like wolves with eight long, gangly arachnid legs emerged from behind a nearby obelisk and surrounded the party. The creatures were covered in wild fur that was black as pitch, and their eyes glowed an eerie green. As they growled, they bared a set of serrated fangs that were highlighted by an impressive pair of striped insect mandibles that jutted out from their lower jaws.

Joel tried to count them. *Twenty-three, twenty-nine, thirty-six—aw, forget it.*

"Freezing casts! Now!" Marshall shouted.

Waves of dark blue light flew as the three otherworldly shamans formed a protective circle around Greenseed and her mount. The air around them started to get cooler, and tiny particles of ice formed on the fur of the flamefeeders.

Joel was pleased that he seemed to be producing the cast correctly, but he quickly noticed that it didn't appear to slow the beasts down very much, if at all. They merely shook the ice bits off like dogs after a bath and continued to close in.

"Um, I don't think this is working!" he yelled over the din being generated by their wavebows.

"Oh really? What gives you that idea?" Felicity shouted back as she sprayed more blue light in every possible direction. Joel started to formulate a response, but then remembered: *oh, right—sarcasm.*

"Try anything!" Marshall yelled as the color of his waves shifted from blue to yellow to red.

Joel tried a stunning cast, but it merely halted a few flamefeeders in their tracks for a second or two before they resumed their approach. The innermost circle of spider-wolves started to tense and coil, as if preparing to jump.

"The bottom of their feet—hit the bottom of their feet," Greenseed said.

As soon as she finished speaking those words, seven 'feeders pounced, leaping through the air with their fangs bared. Just in time, Marshall shot out a yellow burst of light that formed a half-circular shield around him and the others.

The beasts landed on the barrier, growling ferociously. One of them crawled right up above Joel, its pointed claws mere inches in front of his face. Several steaming drips of drool leaked out of its mouth and passed through the criss-crossing waves of the light shield onto Joel's arm; he let out a cry of pain as the drops sizzled on his exposed skin.

"A flame cast—bottom of their feet," Greenseed said, struggling to keep her panicking slimeback under control.

Still grimacing from his burns, Joel took aim at the fleshy green pads on the bottom of the flamefeeders' paws and fired out several laser-like bursts of red light. The creature yelped, slid off of the shield, and then retreated behind his companions.

Eyes wide with pleasant surprise, Joel looked over at Felicity, who caught his glance and began firing off her own casts with expert precision.

"Ha-*ha*! Brilliant!" Marshall exclaimed as he continued to fuel the waves that formed their protective bunker. "Keep going, keep going!"

Joel and Felicity continued to steadily knock off the flamefeeders one by one, but for each one they repulsed, two others lunged forward to take its place. Joel tried to look beyond the immediate group of creatures surrounding them to get an idea of exactly what they were still facing, but all he could see was an ocean of black fur in all directions.

"There's too many of them!" Joel yelled at Marshall. "They just keep on coming!"

"I can keep this shield going for a while," Marshall said. "But how are you two holding up?"

"Fine, great, thanks for asking," Felicity said as she struck another flamefeeder.

"Um, I—okay, I guess," Joel replied. He was feeling a bit tired, but he wasn't sure if that was due to Aura drainage or just plain fatigue.

After repelling another hundred or so of the beasts, however, Joel was definitely feeling the effects. He looked at Felicity and saw that she was also visibly straining to summon enough strength to continue their defense.

"Um, I—I don't know how much longer we can keep this up," Joel said to Marshall as the flamefeeders maintained their relentless attack.

"All right," Marshall said. "That's going to be a problem, then, because I certainly can't do everything at once. I was hoping these buggers would have given up by now. Any suggestions?"

"Uh, well, I dunno, I guess—"

"STOP," a booming, yet distant voice sounded.

The flamefeeders immediately backed off. Everyone looked around for the source of the voice, but there was nothing evident.

"OTHERWORLDERS," the voice said, echoing throughout the valley, "WHY ARE YOU HERE?"

"Who wants to know?" Marshall said as his eyes scanned the area. "Show yourself."

"The Heatwraith," Greenseed said under her breath. "Be careful."

"I GUARD THE PASSAGE TO THE CAVES. NO ONE MAY CROSS WITHOUT MY CONSENT."

"Ah, the Caves of Wrath, you mean?" Marshall said in a casual tone of voice. "That's perfect, because that's where we happen to be headed. So, if you'll kindly let us go, we'll just be on our w—"

"ONLY THOSE WITH THE SIGHT MAY PASS," the voice boomed, a little louder.

Marshall looked questioningly at Greenseed, who warily gave him a Spectraland shrug.

"We need to pass," Marshall said, taking down the shield and pulling the Songshell scroll out of his pack. "It was written right here, in this prophecy: '*greater threat...Caves of Wrath...three makers of the waves...*' and so forth. See, jolly good, it's all here. Now if you please—"

"HOW DO YOU KNOW YOU ARE THE ONES THE VISION SPEAKS OF?"

"Well, it's obvious, innit?" Marshall said as he waved the scroll around. "Spectraland is in great danger, and as it happens, there are three of us, and, well, we made it this far, didn't we?"

After a pause that seemed to last forever, the voice spoke again. "YOU MUST TAKE MY TESTS."

"All right, what kinds of tests?" Marshall asked.

"THE TESTS THAT PROVE YOU HAVE THE SIGHT," the Heatwraith replied. "IF YOU PASS, YOU MAY PROCEED."

Marshall looked at the others with a satisfied expression on his face. "Very well, sounds fair to me."

Felicity then asked the question that was on Joel's mind. "And if we fail?"

"YOU WILL DIE."

"I knew he was gonna say that," Felicity grumbled.

"Look, you two," Marshall said, "we can do this. Have a little confidence, all right? Whatever it throws at us, just—whoa!"

Marshall, Joel, and Felicity were swept off of their slimebacks by a surge of Aura waves, as if they had been caught up in a miniature tornado. The waves carried them up and dropped them off on a small ledge that was jutting out from one of the rocky canyon walls.

Joel looked down at Greenseed and the slimebacks, who were now about a hundred feet below them. "Um, yeah—I'm a little afraid of heights, so can we—"

The ledge started to shake. The three of them flattened out in an attempt to keep from falling. The ledge shook some more before it broke off from the canyon wall. Then it floated out into mid-air, where it stopped some fifty feet away from its original position.

"Is this really necessary?" Felicity yelled.

"THE FIRST TEST IS SIMPLE. YOU MUST LOCATE ME AND TELL ME WHAT SHAPE I AM CURRENTLY ASSUMING."

"Great. I'm on an alien planet, playing hide-and-seek," Felicity mumbled to herself.

"Um, assuming?" Joel asked anyone within earshot. "Does he mean what he's thinking of?"

"No," Marshall shook his head, "I believe he means what shape, or what form he is, like if he's a circle, or a fish, or whatever."

Stupid words—still confusing even through a translation spell that—

Suddenly everything went dark. It was neither the normal nighttime kind of dark, nor was it a total blindness—rather, it was some murky state in between the two, as if everything had been submerged in a bottle of ink.

"Whoa, okay, this is not cool," Felicity said.

"YOU MAY BEGIN," the Heatwraith intoned.

"Uh, begin what?" Joel asked. "What are we supposed to do?"

"Find him, I suppose," Marshall replied. "I think—just fire some reflective casts out there and start looking. At least we have some time to—"

"YOU HAVE FIVE MINUTES."

"All righty, then," Marshall said.

Joel started to feel panicky. He hated time pressure. He played an urgent riff on his wavebow, but all that emerged was a tiny shower of silvery sparks.

"Remember," Marshall said, clearing his throat, "stay calm. Stay focused. We can do this."

Joel took a deep breath and tried again. The three of them each generated a bright yellow wave that resembled a spotlight reaching out into the darkness.

"What are we even looking for?" Felicity asked.

"I'm not sure," Marshall replied as he moved his spotlight around, scanning the area. "Something out of the ordinary, I suppose."

Exactly three minutes passed, but they saw nothing. Joel started to feel extremely nervous, and the light from his wavebow began to flicker.

"Relax," Marshall said through clenched teeth.

Relax? Yeah, sure, why not, since we're all gonna die anyway in a hundred and fifteen, fourteen, thirteen, twelve—wait, what's that—

"Oh—um, hey, I think—I think I see something," Joel said, squinting his eyes.

"What? Where?" Marshall asked.

"In—in Felicity's wave. Over there. See?" Joel said, lowering his wavebow and pointing at a red spot that was intermittently blinking in and out of view.

"I don't see anything," Marshall said. "Felicity, hold that still!"

"What do you think I'm trying to do?" Felicity snapped.

"Where is it?" Marshall yelled.

"It's—it's right—right there!" Joel yelled back. "But—but how can I tell—"

Battleship—it's like that.

"Felicity—um, move the wave down," Joel urged.

She did, but there was nothing there.

"Okay, okay—um, no—up, up," Joel said.

Felicity shot him an irritated glance but did as he asked. He saw that the red spot extended into a thin red line that continued upward.

Ninety-eight, ninety-seven, ninety-six...

"Okay—uh, still go up, and, uh, a little more—"

"Why don't you do it?" Felicity shouted angrily at Joel.

"No!" Marshall snapped. "He might lose the trail. Just keep going!"

Joel continued to guide Felicity. "Um, keep going up, up...oh, now to the right...no, no, just a slight angle upwards...oh! Go down—downward, no, not straight—angle to the right..."

Thirty, twenty-nine, twenty-eight...

"Now straight down. Okay, now keep going straight. Straight...oh! It's a—uh, it's one of these tower things—in the canyon—um, what are they called—"

Seven, six, five...

"Obelisk!" Marshall shouted. "It's in the shape of an obelisk!"

"CORRECT," the Heatwraith said in a neutral tone of voice.

Joel exhaled loudly. "Oh man, I don't know if I—"

"AND NOW, THE SECOND TEST."

Felicity screamed as their floating ledge lurched forward toward the spot where Joel had spotted the Heatwraith. Some of the murky darkness cleared away, and an amorphous cloud of Aura materialized directly in front of them. They watched as the cloud slowly took on the shape of an enormous flamefeeder that was perched on a web of thin red beams of light stretching from one canyon wall to the other.

"Okay, so now what?" Felicity asked.

"I don't know," Marshall said, "I suppose we wait for it to—"

"THREE CLOUDS OF AURA WILL APPROACH YOU. ONLY ONE WILL CARRY YOU SAFELY TO THE GROUND. YOU MUST CHOOSE THE CORRECT ONE."

"What?" Felicity said. "Wait, how do we know which is the correct—"

The ledge they stood on began to shake. Joel looked down and saw that tiny cracks in the rock had started to appear.

"Um, I think this thing is breaking apart!" he shouted.

"Great observation!" Felicity yelled back. Then she turned to Marshall. "Let's just levitate each other down!"

"No time," Marshall said. "Joel—can you see the clouds? Which is the right one?"

Joel anxiously looked in the direction of the Heat-wraith and saw a mass of crackling blue Aura energy quickly floating towards them. "I can't even tell them apart!" he yelled in frustration.

"Neither can we," Marshall said, working to keep his voice calm as the shaking of the ledge intensified. "But I think you have this thing, this Sight that it's talking about—you need to clear your mind. Just focus and concentrate."

Joel reached for something—anything—to distract him from the crumbling footing underneath them. Instinctively, his thoughts retreated to his own list of made-up band names that he thought he could use one day for a hypothetical group: Bluekick; Beat Up the Bad Guys; The Sinkstoppers; Kicking Ida...

As he did this, he noticed that the blue energy cloud did indeed have three separate parts to it, and that the part on the left was slightly darker in tone and appeared to be denser than the other two.

"Joel?" Marshall said as large chunks of the ledge began to fall away.

"Any day now!" Felicity yelled. The cloud was now just several feet in front of them.

"Um—the left—the left!"

"All right—jump!" Marshall shouted.

The three of them leaped off of the ledge just as its final pieces crumbled and plummeted to the ground below. During the split second that he was in the air, Joel fervently hoped that his guess was correct.

His hope was rewarded with the feeling of a soft yet solid landing as he tumbled onto the cloud's surface. The other sections of the cloud immediately dissolved.

"Okay, that was just a *little* scary," Felicity said as she sat up.

"Blimey, lad, you did it," Marshall said. "Very impressive."

Joel didn't reply as he tried to get his nerves under control. The cloud gradually descended straight down until it was just a foot above the ground. The three of them hopped off and were greeted by Greenseed and the slimebacks.

"Are all of you all right?" Greenseed asked.

"Uh, yeah, I—I think so," Joel replied.

"So, I believe it's obvious that our boy here has the Sight," Marshall called out to the Heatwraith, who still appeared as a giant flamefeeder. "Will you let us pass now?"

"THERE IS ONE FINAL TEST," the Heatwraith pronounced.

"Seriously?" Felicity grumbled under her breath.

"ON THE NORTH WALL, THERE ARE TWO PASSAGEWAYS OUT. ONE LEADS TO THE BRIDGE THAT WILL TAKE YOU TO THE CAVES. THE OTHER IS A SHEER DROP INTO NOTHINGNESS."

"Um, sounds easy enough," Joel said as they remounted their slimebacks.

"Wait for it." Felicity smirked.

131

"BOTH PASSAGES WILL BE OBSCURED. IF YOU TRULY HAVE THE SIGHT, YOU WILL BE ABLE TO IDENTIFY THE CORRECT ONE."

"So, uh, I'll just check one out, and if it's wrong, we'll go the other way," Joel said to the rest of them.

"TO ENSURE THAT YOU ONLY HAVE ONE CHANCE, MY CHILDREN AND I SHALL CHASE YOU TO THE EXIT," the Heatwraith intoned as it climbed down off of its web.

Felicity flashed Joel an ironic "I-told-you-so" smile.

"Let's go!" Marshall shouted as a thundering pack of flamefeeders began to bear down on them. The slime-backs took off at a faster pace than Joel had experienced up until this point; Felicity nearly fell off as Dreamer bolted ahead of the rest of their party.

"Let Joel take the lead!" Marshall yelled out to her.

"Fine!" Felicity yelled back. "This thing has a mind of its own, you know!"

Joel tried to clear his mind as they raced toward the north wall. As they drew closer, two arched openings came into view, each one of them covered by a hazy cloud of dark-violet Aura energy. He briefly looked over his shoulder to see if the others were following; they were, but right behind them were literally hundreds of flamefeeders, led by the Heatwraith. Joel knew that no shield would be able to hold them off. He had to get this one right.

"You can do it, Joel!" Marshall shouted. "Just like the first two tests!"

They were now just a hundred feet away from the openings. Joel could feel the white flames from the ground getting hotter—with actual heat. Destiny bellowed with discomfort.

He looked at the two passages. *Which one to choose?*

Fifty feet away...

His mind drifted. *What would be the best way to go—falling, burning, or being eaten? Burning would probably be slow and painful. So would being eaten. So yeah, falling would be the easiest. Except that I hate heights.*

Twenty feet...

"A sheer drop into nothingness"—I wonder how far down that is? If it's, like, super far, then that could be almost as slow and painful. You would know that you're gonna die, and you would see the ground approaching. Yikes. I don't even wanna think about that.

Six feet...

Okay, that looks like something there—

Joel and Destiny charged through the opening on the right and immediately found themselves without footing, hurtling through the air.

CHAPTER 11: CAVES OF WRATH

Unlike some phobias, which you can trace back to a certain traumatic event in your life, Joel wasn't quite sure where his fear of heights had come from. Nevertheless, it was quite intense—he even had to close his eyes while riding a Ferris wheel.

So it was probably an overload of terror that was giving him an oddly peaceful feeling as he plummeted toward, well, nothingness—there was nothing to be seen at all. Everything was just blank white, as if Spectraland really had been made up of watercolors or computer pixels and someone had just decided to wipe the easel clean, or perhaps press "delete."

It felt like he was falling in slow motion. He saw Destiny right below him. She was bellowing in a low, horrible tone, which Joel assumed was the sound that slimebacks made when they were plunging to their deaths.

Then he heard a piercing scream. He looked up over his shoulder and saw Felicity and Dreamer falling, followed closely by Marshall, Greenseed, and their respective mounts.

He felt terrible. He hated being wrong, and he hated when things were his fault. And now, after they had all trusted and believed in him, he had led them through the wrong passage, and they were going to die.

He shut his eyes. For a second, he didn't even realize that his fall had been arrested and that he was hanging suspended in midair. Even after the falling sensation was gone, it was hard to tell exactly what was happening without any visual points of reference, as they were all still surrounded by nothingness.

"YOU DO, INDEED, HAVE THE SIGHT," the voice of the Heatwraith boomed, with even more echo than before.

The nothingness suddenly turned into a thick, hazy mist that began to clear away. Joel noticed that his body was enveloped in a shimmering yellow net of Aura energy. Looking around, he saw that the others were similarly encased.

"WE HAVE BEEN WAITING FOR YOU. YOU POSSESS THE ABILITY TO SAVE THE LAND FROM ITS LATEST THREAT."

As the mist lifted, Joel looked up and saw the opening that they had charged through, some fifty feet above. It was located in the face of an enormous, sheer cliffside, and within it stood the figure of the Heatwraith.

"Um, but I—I picked the wrong passage," Joel said mostly to himself, only half expecting the Heatwraith to hear him from so far away.

"NO, YOU CHOSE CORRECTLY," the Heatwraith said.

The rest of the mist vanished, and Joel's eyes grew wide with astonishment. A tubular tunnel made up entirely of multi-colored light waves stretched for hundreds of yards over a seemingly bottomless chasm. The tunnel, which writhed and twisted as if it were a live snake, led toward another gigantic cliffside on the far end.

"THIS IS THE COLORBRIDGE," said the Heat-wraith. "IT WILL LEAD YOU TO THE CAVES OF WRATH, WHERE THE ARTIFACT YOU SEEK IS HID-DEN."

Joel noticed that they had fallen into the tunnel's mouth-like opening, which was pointed directly at the passageway he had chosen. The passageway next to it did, indeed, lead only to the endless abyss below. He exhaled in relief, partly because he was still alive, but also because he knew that he had not let the others down after all.

"Can—can you come too? And help us?" Joel felt bold enough to ask.

"I AM BOUND TO THE FIELDS OF FLAME. BEYOND IT, MY CONSCIOUSNESS CEASES TO EXIST."

"Oh," Joel said, disappointed. Even though the Heatwraith had basically tried to kill them, Joel felt that it had a valid reason for attempting to do so, and that its power would probably have come in handy down the road.

"THE SIGHT WILL GUIDE YOU. GOOD LUCK," the Heathwraith said, and with that, it disappeared.

Joel tried to stand up, but he found no solid footing. He waved his arms around. Moving through the waves of light that made up the Colorbridge felt like wading through very thick syrup.

"Good job, mate," Marshall said, his voice echoing within the confines of the tunnel. "Although you had me worried there for a second."

"Yeah, just a little," Felicity added.

They slowly made their way along the tunnel using a half-swimming, half-crawling motion. When the tunnel jerked or twisted, Joel felt as if they were going to be thrown out of it, but they always managed to remain safely within its borders.

After what felt like a very long time (but was, in reality, only nineteen minutes), they approached the end of the bridge. It ended about three feet away from the cliff, and what from a distance had originally looked like a large entrance in the cliff's wall was actually two separate lung-shaped openings adjacent to one another. Each opening was dark, so they were unable to tell what lay beyond.

"Looks like we'll have to jump for it," Marshall said. "But which one? Joel?"

Joel cleared his thoughts and stared at the openings. "Um—I dunno, can't tell. They both seem the same."

"You'd think the ancient shamans could have left us a map," Felicity muttered.

After staring a little more, Joel thought he saw a flicker of Aura within the right opening. "Oh—uh, there, I think I saw something. In the right side."

"Ah, brilliant," Marshall said. "Greenseed—you first, go ahead and jump over there. We'll follow right behind."

"Master?" Greenseed said, sounding a bit nervous.

"You heard me, go on," Marshall sighed.

"Um, it's okay, I—we can go," Joel offered. Destiny gave a little affirmative grunt.

"No, no, let her do it," Marshall countered. "She's supposed to be our guide here, remember?"

Greenseed urged her mount closer to the edge of the tunnel-bridge, where it sniffed at the air and croaked in a protesting fashion. "Master, there is something wrong—"

"Joel has the Sight, and he saw something in the right side, so it's perfectly fine. He hasn't failed us yet," Marshall snapped.

"Understood, but—"

At that moment, a creature that was mostly all jaws and teeth poked its head out of the right opening, hissing and gnashing violently. Greenseed gave a startled cry, and her mount reared its head defensively as it retreated a few steps.

"All right, then, I suppose there are some limitations as to what the Sight can do for us," Marshall said.

"Um, sorry," Joel mumbled. "I, uh, I did see something, though."

"Indeed you did. Anyway, I say we go in the *left* side," Marshall declared. "Agreed?"

Greenseed's slimeback made the leap into the opening on the left side without incident, and the rest of the group followed. They found themselves in a cramped, dark cave that forced them to travel single file. They lit up their wavebows as they made their way along its narrow, meandering path. The walls of the cave were brown, rocky and nondescript. Eventually, the ground began to slope downward, and Joel could detect the familiar smell of salty ocean air.

"So, um, is this the Caves—uh, I mean, Cave of Wrath?" he asked.

"Nothing bad's happened to us yet, so I really doubt it," Felicity replied.

"Greenseed," Marshall said, "I assume that this is not the place, correct?"

"I am not sure, Master," she answered. "No one has ever been this far."

Nine minutes later, after nearly sliding down a particularly steep section of the path, they saw light coming through an opening some twenty feet away. A warm, moist breeze wafted into the cave, along with the sound of crashing waves.

Upon exiting, they were greeted by the sight of a majestic, secluded cove that was bordered by incredibly high and steep mountain walls. Leafy red and purple bushes dotted the pale orange sand, and the ocean washed up additional vegetation onto the shoreline. In the face of the mountain opposite them was a large, circular cave entrance. It was adorned with a multitude of pointed stalactites, and faint wisps of multicolored Aura could be seen drifting out of it.

"Okay, so *that's* gotta be it," Felicity said.

"I believe you're right, my dear," Marshall said in an anticipatory tone of voice. "Here we go, then. Joel, keep an eye out for anything unusual along the way, would you?"

"Um, sure," Joel replied.

They cautiously entered the cave, which started out as a fairly large landing area with additional stalactites and lots of small rocks that covered the cave's surface. There was no obvious pathway to be followed, however.

"Okay, this can't be it," Felicity said, picking up one of the rocks by her feet. "'Cause that would just be way too easy."

"Oh—wait, look—over there," Joel said as he pointed to a dark spot at the edge of the cavern.

Upon closer inspection, the dark spot turned out to be a small tunnel that was large enough for perhaps only a single person to crawl through. Joel's eyes traced the wisps of Aura that they saw earlier back to the mouth of the tunnel.

"That looks like the way we have to go," Marshall declared. "The slimebacks will need to stay here. Greenseed, wait with them until we return."

"But, Master—" Greenseed started to protest.

"No buts!" Marshall barked. "You're starting to get a bit cheeky, I must say. *Wait here until we return.* Got that?"

"Yes, Master," Greenseed said with just the slightest hint of resentment in her voice.

"Joel, after you," Marshall said, gesturing toward the tunnel.

After witnessing Marshall's little outburst, Joel didn't feel in the mood to argue. "Um, okay."

He got down into a prone position and crawled into the tunnel. Marshall and Felicity followed. Ten minutes of uncomfortable wriggling later, relief arrived in the form of another large, open cavern area, this one a bit more circular than the first and illuminated by sporadic patches of glowmoss on the walls.

Joel stood up and looked around for any sign of an Aura-emitting shell. The only notable thing he saw, however, was a huge boulder, about twenty feet high, blocking what appeared to be another passageway on the far side of the cavern. Aura energy seeped out from the cracks between the boulder and the wall.

"Um, how are we going to get past that?" he asked.

"Uh, hello," Felicity said, raising her wavebow. "Remember these?"

"She's right," Marshall said. "But that thing is rather large, so we'll need to do it together."

They took aim, and on Marshall's signal, they each fired a levitation cast at the boulder. Waves of green light engulfed the giant rock, but it refused to budge.

"It's not working!" Joel shouted.

"Everyone move it to the right. To the right!" Marshall yelled.

Now that they were all on the same page, the boulder rose up off the ground and easily moved aside, revealing a large passageway that turned sharply to the left.

"Well done," Marshall exhaled. He lowered his wavebow and began briskly striding toward the passage.

"Um, I think I hear something coming—"

At that moment, a large, feathered head poked out from around the corner, followed by its equally large, feathered body. The creature, which resembled a cross between a tyrannosaurus rex and a chicken, filled up the passageway with its tremendous height and girth. It blinked a few times, shook its head, then let out a loud, screeching roar.

"I think maybe we woke somebody up," Felicity said as she backed up a few steps.

"Uh, maybe it's friendly?" Joel suggested, backing up as well. The rooster-saurus fixed its stare on them and started to approach.

"Not bloody likely," Marshall said, raising his wavebow. "Someone left it here as a guard."

The creature roared again and swiped at them with a large claw. They all managed to jump out of the way, just in time.

Joel aggressively strummed his wavebow, sending a stream of stunning light at the beast, but he only succeeded in gaining its attention. It turned toward him and swiped again. Joel ducked and fell to the ground, dropping his wavebow in the process. He frantically lunged for his instrument, but instead of recovering it, he ended up accidentally pushing it under the beast's legs, where it narrowly missed getting stepped on.

Joel saw Marshall and Felicity also firing at the creature and encountering the same lack of effect. His mind raced as he vainly waited for an opportunity to retrieve his instrument.

Woke somebody up...

Joel had an idea. "Hey!" he yelled. "Try—um, try a sleeping cast!"

"What?" Marshall shouted over the din.

"A sleeping cast! Maybe—maybe it wants to go back to sleep!"

Marshall shot Joel an "are-you-crazy?" expression. "I'll think it over," he said with a healthy dose of sarcasm as he continued to fend off the creature's blows. "Oh, bloody—all right! Felicity, hold this thing off for a bit!"

Marshall retreated to the back of the cavern while Felicity continued to fire various stunning and freezing casts at the giant reptile-bird. He started to play a gentle, ballad-like melody that Joel could barely hear among all of the other sounds that were going on.

A powder-blue wave of light drifted out and wrapped itself around the creature's head. The creature stopped slashing at Joel and Felicity, blinked a few times, and then slumped to the ground.

"It worked!" Joel exulted.

"Yes, yes, good idea," Marshall said dispassionately. "But you really need to take better care of your wavebow. Losing it in the heat of battle—not very good."

"Um, but I—"

"All right, come along now, we've got ourselves a Songshell to find," Marshall said as he walked around the sleeping rooster-saur and headed for the large passage.

Joel felt disappointed, and a little surprised at Marshall's unappreciative response to his idea. He grabbed his wavebow off the ground and glanced in Felicity's direction.

"Can't be the golden boy all the time, I guess." Felicity shrugged as she walked after Marshall. Joel had no idea what she meant by that.

After rounding the corner, they found themselves in a short, wide tunnel that ended in another cavern-like space. At the far end of the space was a tall, twisting stairway that was carved into the rock itself. Cautiously, they walked into the space and up the stairway with their wavebows at the ready.

They reached the top of the stairway and were faced with a stone door that had a triangle-shaped rune and native lettering etched into it. On each corner of the rune was a small, clear gemstone embedded in the rock. The door itself hummed with a vibrant Aura field.

"I'm guessing we can't just blast this thing open," Felicity said.

"Probably a bad idea to even try," Marshall said as he inspected the lettering. "Let's hope these are the instructions."

Aiming his wavebow at the door, Marshall played the same lick that he had used to translate the Songshell scroll back at the temple. A yellow wave covered the letters, and thirty-seven seconds later, their blurry English equivalents appeared. The three of them moved in for a closer look.

> When the time has arrived
> The three makers of the waves, and only the three
> Shall cast their primary lights at the corners
> Allowing them to pass
> And recover the power
> To be used only for good

"Not very poetic," Felicity said.

"I'm sure it rhymes in their language," Marshall said drily. "The main thing is that it tells us what we need to do."

"Uh—which is what, exactly?" Joel asked.

Marshall pointed at the rune on the door. "I believe that each of us needs to cast at one point on this triangle."

"Cast what, though?"

"Hmm, good question," Marshall mused. "'Primary lights,' it says."

"Maybe like primary colors?" Felicity suggested.

"Yes, of course," Marshall said. "That must be it. And the primary colors were, what again, red, blue—"

"Uh, yellow?" Joel offered.

"Yes, yes, that sounds correct. All right, let's try that. I'll take red on the top corner—Felicity, you do blue on the bottom left, and Joel, yellow on the bottom right. Got it?"

They each stood back and played a simple chord on their wavebows that issued forth the necessary streams of colored light. The streams hit their respective targets, but aside from the gemstones glowing faintly, nothing happened. They kept it up for a few additional minutes, trying all the different possible combinations, before Marshall spoke up.

"All right, all right, stop. We're wasting valuable energy. So that's obviously not the answer."

They stood there in uncomfortable silence for almost thirty seconds, each of them staring at the rune.

Then Felicity said, "Oh, wait—yellow is a primary color for art. *Green* is the other primary color for light."

Marshall aimed a skeptical eye at her. "Hmm, all right, let's try that. Joel—switch to green."

They tried again, this time with Joel generating a green wave. On the second combination (green—top, red—bottom left, blue—bottom right), the gemstones began to glow much more vividly, and the door started to shake. They continued until the door had slowly moved off to the side, revealing another tall stairway.

"You may prove to be useful after all." Marshall smirked at Felicity.

Felicity made a face at him as they started up the stairway.

I'd never talk to her like that, Joel thought with a mixture of irritation and perhaps—jealousy?

Pushing these thoughts aside, Joel found himself growing short of breath as they ascended the stairway, which, as it turned out, was much longer than the first one. The amount of Aura energy flowing down toward them steadily increased as they went, almost to the point where it felt like it had an actual physical presence—like a group of tiny crystalline particles being carried along by a gentle breeze.

Finally, they reached the top, which Joel was glad to see was absent of any stone barriers. Beyond the opening, however, was yet another incredible sight: a gigantic dome-shaped cavern, about as large as a football stadium, with a tempest of Aura energy swirling within it.

They stood on a ledge overlooking the scene at what would have been about the upper one-hundredth seating level of a stadium. However, instead of a turf field on the bottom—or any surface, for that matter—there was nothing but an endless hole where the energy seemed to be originating from.

"Seriously," Felicity said with a mixture of snark and awe. "How many bottomless pits can one tiny island have?"

"Look—up there," Marshall said.

The circular sloped "roof" of the cavern was covered in jagged stalactites. And there, suspended in midair a few feet below the formations, was what looked to be a small, brown, tear-shaped rock.

"Up where? What?" Felicity said, craning her neck.

"That must be it," Marshall whispered.

"Um—you mean, the Songshell?" Joel asked. He had been expecting something a bit grander, like perhaps a conch or nautilus-type of shell. "That's it? It looks kinda—uh, I dunno—"

"Plain? Ordinary?" Marshall said as he turned to face Joel with an excited, almost manic look in his eyes. "That's precisely it—one uses it to store energy, or to amplify it—so if it's not being used, it wouldn't have any energy of its own. We've found it!"

"Cool, so how do we get it down?" Felicity asked.

Before she had even finished her question, Marshall had taken aim with his wavebow. He fired a green stream of light that wrapped itself around the shell, but the little brown shape refused to move from its spot.

"You thought it was gonna be that easy," Felicity chuckled.

"Joel, take a look. Can you see anything unusual?" Marshall asked.

Joel cleared his mind and looked at and around the shell, but he could see nothing out of the ordinary. "Um, nope," he answered.

"Keep trying while I think," Marshall said.

Three and a half minutes passed by, but Joel still came up empty. He was starting to feel some frustration set in, which distracted him from his focus.

"All right, I've got an idea," Marshall declared. "We'll levitate up there and grab it by hand."

"What? That's crazy," Felicity said.

"Um, how are we gonna levitate ourselves?" Joel asked.

"Not ourselves," Marshall replied, "each other."

"Okay, you're nuts," Felicity said, looking up at the shell. "That's probably, what, hundreds of feet up?"

"Uh, just a little under one hundred, I think," Joel said.

Felicity shot Joel an angry look and then turned back to face Marshall. "Do *you* have enough power to lift someone up that far? 'Cause I'm pretty sure we don't."

"Hmm, I suspect not," Marshall mused. "Not safely, anyway. But I think that the three of us together might."

"What do you—oh. Oh, no," Felicity said.

Joel looked at them with a puzzled expression. "Um, what are you guys talking about?"

"We'll make a chain," Marshall announced. "I'll levitate you," he said, looking at Felicity, "while you levitate Joel. We should be able to get high enough that way."

"Yeah, okay, that doesn't sound dangerous at all," Felicity said, rolling her eyes.

Joel looked down into the pit below and shuddered. He also felt that it was a risky proposition, and of course, his acrophobia didn't help matters, but after everything they had been through so far, he couldn't see why this would be any different. He did have one request to make, however.

"Um, is it okay if someone tells me when I'm near the shell, just so—you know, I, uh, well—" he faltered, not wanting to directly admit that he was going to close his eyes.

"Yeah, yeah, I'll let you know," Felicity said. "Now let's just get this over with."

Raising her wavebow, she generated a green stream of light that wrapped itself around Joel's torso. He took a deep breath and shut his eyes as he felt the sensation of being lifted vertically up off the ground.

He tried to occupy his mind with random lists, to keep from thinking about the possibility of falling. *Let's see...World Series winners since 1976: Reds over Yankees. Yankees over Dodgers. Yankees over Dodgers, again. Pirates over Orioles. Phillies over Royals. Dodgers over Yankees. Cardinals over Brewers. Orioles over Phillies. Tigers over—*

His smooth ascent was interrupted by a sudden shaking, as if he were in a defective elevator. He made the mistake of looking down, and the sight made his stomach rise up into his throat. Before he shut his eyes again, he caught a fleeting glimpse of Felicity rising up into the air on Marshall's wave while simultaneously trying to keep her own instrument steady.

"Have I said that this is crazy?" she shouted rhetorically.

The rising feeling resumed.

Tigers over Padres. Royals over Cardinals. Mets over Red Sox. Twins over Cardinals. Dodgers over A's. A's over Giants. Reds over A's. Twins over Braves. Blue Jays over Braves. Blue Jays over Phillies. Strike year.

"Joel!" he heard Felicity scream. "Now!"

He opened his eyes. The shell was there, an arm's length away. It hung there ever so invitingly, like an apple waiting to be picked—a crusty, ugly, dirty brown apple.

Is this really it? He thought. *This is the powerful Songshell that will help us beat Fourfoot?*

"Hurry!" Felicity screamed.

Joel reached out and grabbed it. He expected something to happen at that moment—something majestic, like a flash of brilliant golden light, or even something a bit more undesirable, like a monster snapping at his outstretched hand—but nothing did. He plucked the shell out of the air and noticed that it really did feel like picking a fruit, as if it had been fastened there in midair by some invisible stem. The shell—which, upon closer inspection, resembled a solid brown cowry shell—was hard and cold in his grip.

"Got it!" he called out, keeping his vision focused upward.

"Bring us down!" he heard Felicity shouting at Marshall.

Joel felt his body start to descend, slowly and steadily. He closed his eyes again and clutched the shell tightly in his right hand, holding it to his chest. He exhaled deeply.

We did it, he thought.

Just then, however, he felt himself start to shake once again. He could feel a sudden warm draft start to rise up from below, but he dared not open his eyes.

"Um, everything okay?" he shouted.

"Hey, it's getting a little windy here!" Felicity yelled.

Joel heard Marshall yell back, but he couldn't make out exactly what Marshall was saying. Along with the gradually increasing updraft was an ominous rumbling noise that was not there before. He felt himself start to sway back and forth as the wind grew stronger. He began to feel nauseous.

"Uh—what are you doing?" he shouted.

When Felicity didn't reply, he decided to take a look. What he saw made him instantly regret his decision. The green light streams holding each of them in place were waving and wobbling as Felicity and Marshall struggled to keep them steady amidst a growing vortex of Aura energy rising up out of the pit. Joel wanted to scream, but managed to stifle the impulse, clenching his jaw instead and channeling the energy of his fear into an even tighter grip on the shell in his hands.

He vaguely heard Felicity and Marshall shouting things at each other, but they were completely unintelligible now as the rumbling began to resemble the sound of a jet engine warming up. The wind blew hot and fast, carrying small bits of assorted rocks, dust, and debris past Joel's face. Their levitation waves whipped wildly back and forth until the grip of Felicity's wave slipped, and Joel began to fall.

He closed his eyes again. Within his fear, he also felt regret, to have failed after having come so far. He thought of his mother and sister, and of the career that he would never have. Then, during the next fraction of a second, he found himself hoping that this was all, indeed, a strange dream that he would suddenly wake up from, safe in his own bed in that lousy apartment back home.

The jet engine sound reached a deafening climax, and a violent burst of wind and steam and Aura energy erupted from the pit. A huge hole broke open in the center of the top of the cavern, and the three otherworldly adventurers found themselves swept up and away into darkness.

CHAPTER 12: FOREST OF LIGHT

Joel had no previous life experience that even remotely compared to what was happening. Of course, he was still only sixteen years old, but even so, he suspected that most people even five times his age had never felt the sensation of being pushed upward by a hot blast of air through a narrow, winding cavern tube for hundreds of feet. The only similar image he could think of was perhaps a spider being shot through a furnace vent, or a piece of dust being expelled from a vacuum that was set to "reverse."

The cave tube was dark, so even when he opened his eyes, he could not see much. The only way he even knew that he was in a narrow passageway was because the air blast occasionally bounced him off of the rough, rocky sides like a pinball. Although these bounces definitely hurt, he focused on holding the Songshell as tightly as possible, not wanting it to become dislodged by any of the painful impacts.

Eventually, light came streaming into the tube. Joel looked and saw that a small hole had opened up some thirty-three feet away, and that the air blast was carrying him right toward it. The hole opened a little wider as he approached, little pieces of rock crumbling away from its borders and falling on his head. When he was only five feet away from the hole, he was shocked to see Greenseed's perplexed face peering back at him.

"Master? What is—"

He burst through the opening as the relentless pushing of the air blast carried him along with tremendous force. He briefly recognized that he was in the original cave where they had left Greenseed. The air and Aura currents swirled around in the cave, sweeping Greenseed and the slimebacks up like slips of paper before shooting all of them out of the cave's mouth into the cove outside.

The blast did not dissipate; rather, it gained strength as it mixed with the surrounding atmosphere. It quickly evolved into something resembling a massive tornado, and its swirling force filled up the entire space between the walls of the cliffs that surrounded the cove.

At this point Joel resigned himself to letting the wind take him wherever it would. He felt his body spinning in a clockwise direction and moving farther and farther upward, leaving the sandy ground farther and farther behind.

Then finally, the tornado ejected him. After flying in the air some twenty feet, he struck a solid but soft surface with surprisingly little impact and went rolling across the ground until he eventually came to a stop among a cluster of small plants. He heard approaching screams and thuds nearby and deduced that he had been joined by the others.

"Bloody hell!" Marshall yelled exuberantly as he stood up, roughly thirty-four feet away from Joel. "Now that was some ride! Joel? Joel? Ah, there you are. Do you have it? The shell?"

Joel looked at the crusty brown trophy, making sure it was still in his hands, before slumping back on the ground.

A few minutes later, they gathered together in the patchy field where the Aura tornado had deposited them. After Joel had given the shell to Marshall, they took stock of their physical condition. Amazingly, none of them had suffered any injuries beyond a few bad bumps and bruises.

"I have a feeling that being Wavemakers ourselves may have had something to do with that," Marshall said, attempting an explanation of their well-being. "It was probably designed to expunge intruders who weren't meant to recover the shell. Our unique Aura patterns probably saved us."

"Um, but what about Greenseed? And the slime-backs?" Joel asked.

"Lucky to be with us, I suppose." Marshall shrugged.

"Well, anyway," Felicity said, "we have the shell now, right? So can we beat that Fourfoot guy and go home?"

"Yes, yes, of course," Marshall said, thoughtfully turning the shell over in his hands. "Odd, though, it seems rather...cold. Let me try something. All of you, stand back."

Marshall placed the shell on the ground. He aimed his wavebow and fired a red stream of light at it. The shell rolled over as the light struck it, but other than that, nothing noteworthy happened.

"Hmm," Marshall said. He played a different chord, this time sending out a slower, steadier yellow wave. The light surrounded the shell for a few seconds, then faded away.

Marshall picked up the shell and inspected it. "Nothing," he muttered. Then, kicking at the ground, he yelled: "Nothing! Blast it! What a bunch of—"

"Wait, wait," Felicity interrupted, "what do you mean, 'nothing'? What was supposed to happen?"

"It should've either stored or magnified the Aura energy that I cast at it," Marshall griped.

"Uh—maybe we got the wrong shell?" Joel suggested.

"Not bloody likely," Marshall grumbled, pulling the scroll from his vest and looking it over. "There wasn't anywhere else for us to go. This has to be it."

"Master, if I may," Greenseed said meekly. Everyone turned and looked at her.

"I now seem to recall," she continued, "some of the Wavemakers spoke of the shell needing to be reforged, so to speak, in the White Fire of the Dragoneye. A result of the attempts to destroy it."

"What?" Marshall snapped as he shot Greenseed a suspicious look. "How do you know this? Why didn't you tell us this before?"

"I apologize, Master. I had...forgotten," Greenseed said, looking at the ground. "My memories of those times are painful, as you know."

Marshall made a noise that was a cross between a growl and a sigh. "Very well. Dragoneye it is."

"Why do I get the feeling that we're not going home any time soon?" Felicity said.

"Dragoneye is a volcano quite far from here," Marshall explained. "But we have no choice. We'll need to hurry, though, otherwise—"

"Um—I have a problem," Joel blurted out, suddenly realizing that he was missing something.

"What?" Marshall snapped.

"I—uh, I lost—I lost my wavebow."

"You lost—are you sure?" Marshall said with narrowed eyes, looking Joel over from head to toe as if that would reveal something.

"Uh, yeah," Joel said sheepishly. "Do any of you guys have it?"

Marshall turned and looked at Felicity, and then at Greenseed; both of them shook their heads no.

"How in blazes did that happen? I mean, I know there was that wind and all, but what about your strap?"

"I—I dunno." Joel shrugged. "I was so focused on holding onto the shell, it must've just fallen off, or something."

Marshall looked like he was on the brink of exploding. "I can't believe it! You know, there aren't any more of those—Fourfoot destroyed the rest. We need three fully functioning Wavemakers *with* instruments in order to complete this quest and save this bloody island *and* ourselves! Not to mention, we're going to need all the help we can get, going to Dragoneye. Who knows what manner of vile creatures lurk between here and there!"

"Um, sorry," Joel murmured. He felt like crawling into a hole and never coming back out.

"I'm really not sure what we're going to do now," Marshall continued with a heavy sigh. "At least your 'Sight,' or whatever, can make you somewhat useful, hopefully, and maybe we can—"

"Master?" Greenseed said.

"Yes?" Marshall said through clenched teeth.

"There is a place where we can get Master Joel a new instrument—and it happens to be on the way to Mount Dragoneye."

Marshall looked at Greenseed with a curious expression. "Oh, really? Funny, I never heard of that before."

"I—er, believe that perhaps the other shamans simply forgot to tell you," Greenseed said, her voice faltering, "seeing as how there was so much else to be concerned with at the time."

Marshall regarded her for a few seconds before he replied. "Yes, I suppose you're right," he said. "So, tell me, where is this place?"

"At the end of the Forest of Light," she said. "There is a sacred tree there. Within it dwells the Luthier."

Marshall furrowed his brow. "Interesting...go on."

"The Luthier is another wraith," Greenseed explained, still seemingly a bit nervous. "She is the only being in Spectraland with the ability to craft new wavebows. It is usually done only at the time a Wavemaker's power is first identified, shortly after birth. Perhaps she might make an exception now, however, given the present circumstances."

"All right," Marshall said, fingering the scar on his cheek. "Our path has been laid out before us, it seems. Well, let's not waste any more time."

Joel quickly moved over to Destiny, happy that Greenseed had managed to stop Marshall's ranting at him.

"Oh, and by the way," Marshall said to Greenseed as he prepared to mount his slimeback.

"Yes, Master?"

"If you have any more useful information, feel free to let us know any time."

Greenseed looked away and said nothing as she hurried over to her mount.

Eighteen days until the Nadir

Joel dodged the red bolts of light just in time. He turned and saw that the bolts had struck a large stalagmite behind him, shattering it into hundreds of tiny pieces. The shadowy figure firing at him continued to approach, yelling something in a language that Joel couldn't understand.

Scrambling to get away, Joel narrowly avoided falling into a pool of bubbling silvery-white lava that had suddenly opened up in his path. He looked up and saw the night sky through the opening of an enormous caldera and realized that he was standing in the middle of an active volcano.

He ran as fast as he could as another round of red bolts came streaking toward him. More pools began to open up in the surface of the caldera, and a thick, hot steam started to pour out of them. Joel was frantically searching for a means of escape when suddenly he heard Felicity's voice.

"Joel!" she cried.

Joel looked around, but she was nowhere to be seen. Her voice seemed to come from everywhere at once.

"Joel!" she called again.

He took off running once more, not knowing exactly where he was headed. There was no sign of Felicity wherever he looked—only red streaks of light, steam, and white lava.

"Joel!"

Abruptly, there she was, hovering over him—and the entire caldera was gone, replaced by the shimmering Aura of a shield-tent, through which the first rays of morning sunlight shone.

"About time you woke up," she said. "Marshall wants to get moving again."

Joel rubbed the sleep out of his eyes, still slightly disoriented by the extremely vivid images of his caldera nightmare. "Sorry—was, uh, having a dream."

"Don't apologize," she said. "What were you dreaming about?"

"Um, I—nothing, really," he said. "Just, like, volcanoes and stuff."

Joel was undecided about whether to mention his dream to anyone. This was actually the fourth time he had had visions of the caldera with the pools of white lava, but up until now, he had attributed the recurrence of the similar scenes to coincidence. Now that he knew that such a place potentially existed—and that they were going to travel there—he felt a bit unsettled.

Walking out toward where the slimebacks were gathered, Joel took a swig from his water flask and looked around at his surroundings. They had arrived at the edge of a thick and lush forest, where all of the trees were hundreds of feet tall. Long, willowy leaves that faintly glowed in various shades of green and yellow adorned the many branches.

Felicity turned and headed for a particularly dense grouping of trees.

"Uh, where are you going?" Joel asked.

"Ladies' room," she said casually. Feeling himself blush, Joel did an about-face and made a beeline toward Marshall, who was feeding a handful of leaves to his slimeback.

"Where's Greenseed?" Joel asked.

"Fetching some more edibles," Marshall replied. "How was your nap?"

Joel looked down at the ground. The grass there was thin and curly, like tiny green pigtails. He cleared his throat. "Well, um, remember what you said earlier, about how the Aura can warp time within our subconscious?"

"Yes," Marshall said. "Why, are you having strange dreams?"

"Um, yeah," Joel said, unsure of how much he wanted to say. "Kinda, anyway."

"About what?"

"That place that we're supposed to go to, I think. The volcano."

"Dragoneye?"

"I guess."

"What did you see?"

Joel started to feel uncomfortable, although he was not quite sure why. "Uh, like, pools of white lava, lots of steam, and, um...someone casting red waves at me."

"Hmm, interesting," Marshall said. "Well, we can't be totally sure that what you're seeing is actually a vision of the future—only very experienced Wavemakers can do that. It could merely be that you're having some anxieties about what we're about to face. I wouldn't blame you, given all that we've been through so far."

"Um, but...these have been going on for a while now. Like, ever since I first got here, almost."

Marshall raised his right eyebrow. "Is that so? Why haven't you told me about this before?"

Joel suddenly felt quite nervous. "I, uh, didn't—didn't think that it was important, until I found out where we were going."

"You could be seeing a vision of Fourfoot," Marshall mused ominously, looking at the ground in front of Joel. Then, as if snapping out of a trance, his demeanor suddenly brightened, and he raised his head and put a reassuring hand on Joel's shoulder. "What am I saying?" he chuckled. "Really, mate, I honestly don't think there's anything to it. Remember, only master Wavemakers can see the future. Are you telling me that you're a master?"

Joel shook his head no.

"Well, then. Listen, I'm glad you told me about this now, but try to put it out of your mind, all right? In fact, I wouldn't mention it again—especially to the ladies. We wouldn't want to worry them unnecessarily now, would we?"

As if on cue, Felicity came sauntering over to them at the same time Greenseed emerged from behind a tall cluster of bushes with a half dozen lifepods in her arms.

"Ah, perfect timing," Marshall said. "Shall we?"

They rode for three days with very little rest, and it seemed to Joel as if the forest would never end. Greenseed assured them that she did, indeed, know where they were going, and that they were not simply riding around in circles.

Fourteen days until the Nadir

On the fourth day, it started to rain heavily. Even though they were sheltered somewhat by the trees, enough water managed to find its way through the canopy that within a few hours, they were all totally soaked. By nightfall the rain had intensified into a full-blown storm, so they decided to set up camp early.

As it was their turn to keep watch, Joel and Felicity sat under an extension of the shield-tent that functioned as a sort of awning while Marshall slept inside. Greenseed and the slimebacks slept huddled together under a large tree that provided sufficient cover from the rain.

"Um, pretty crazy storm, huh?" Joel said.

"Yeah," Felicity agreed. "I like this kind of weather, actually."

Her statement reminded Joel of something that Marshall had mentioned one night back at Headsmouth, before their ill-fated concert. "Oh—hey, uh, remember that time when Marshall said we were from the same area? And you got all mad after that? Does—does that mean you're from Seattle?"

"Yeah," Felicity chuckled. "Well, Bellevue, actually. And I wasn't mad. Not more than usual, anyway."

"Oh, uh, cool," Joel said, grateful that he had found something else they had in common and relieved that she was, in fact, not upset about that.

"This rain is kinda different, though," Felicity said, sticking her hand out and letting the drops fall through her fingers. "It's warm. And the air is still warm. Not like all those forty-degree days back home."

"Yeah, I know," Joel said. "It's kind of like Hawai'i, actually."

"Oh yeah? You've been there?"

"I, uh, was born and raised there. We moved to the mainland when I was ten and a half. Well, ten and seven months."

"Oh, cool," Felicity said, wiping her hand on her already-wet tunic. "I've always wanted to go there."

"It's, um, it's pretty nice, I guess. Are—were you born in Bellevue?"

"No, Vancouver."

"Oh—British Columbia?"

"Washington."

"Oh, okay—um, by Portland, Oregon. Across the Columbia River."

"Wow, you're one of the few people who actually seem to know that," Felicity said without her usual sarcastic tone.

"I—uh, I memorized a map of the U.S. when I was eight," Joel admitted.

"Of course you did," Felicity chuckled.

"Um, do your parents still live in Vancouver?" Joel asked, feeling braver by the minute.

"No, they died in a car accident a few years ago," Felicity said in an oddly impassionate tone.

"Oh—um, I'm sorry," Joel said, his courage wiped away by embarrassment and chagrin.

"It's okay," Felicity sighed. "Stuff happens, I guess."

Joel didn't quite know how to respond to that.

"So my sister and I lived with our grandparents until I graduated, then the two of us moved up to Seattle," Felicity continued. "I know I don't sound like it hurts, but it still does. Just because I can't express emotions well doesn't mean I don't have them, you know?"

Joel just nodded.

"What about your parents?" Felicity asked.

"Um, they got divorced. That was kinda why we moved," Joel replied softly.

Felicity twirled a lock of her hair around her finger. "Sucks, huh."

"Yeah."

Two minutes and twenty seconds passed by with nothing but the sound of the pouring rain. Joel found himself counting the trees surrounding them when suddenly, Felicity spoke up again.

"You know that's why we're here, right?" she said as more of a statement than a question. "Why we can do the things we do, with the wavebows and casting and stuff?"

"Uh, because we're musicians?" Joel replied, puzzled.

"Well, yeah, but also because of our 'spectrum disorders,'" Felicity said, making the air quotes motion with her fingers, "or whatever they want to call it. Like it's some kind of disease that can be cured, or whatever."

"Um, wait—what? You have—"

"Yeah, of course. What did you think? I told you I was in those 'special' classes, remember?"

"Oh—um, but I didn't think that—I thought maybe you were—you don't seem like you have—"

"Well, we're all different, you know," Felicity said, again reaching out for the rain. "That's why they call it a spectrum. Some are on one end, some are on the other. Some are in between. And it can show up in different ways. Haven't you read up on your own condition?"

Connections were starting to form in Joel's head. "Um, wait—so that means that Marshall—he's—"

"He's like us," Felicity finished his sentence. "I thought you knew that?"

Joel couldn't believe that there was some detail about his idol that he wasn't aware of. "Wow—um, no, I didn't."

"That's mainly why I was such a huge fan," Felicity explained. "I mean, his songs are great and all, but I felt like if he could make it, then so could I, you know? And then all my problems—"

"Would be solved," Joel said, making the briefest of direct eye contact with Felicity for the first time.

"Yeah," she said, quickly looking away. "Anyway, he explained it to me when I first got here. Something about the frequency of our brain waves being different. I guess we—"

"Whoa, um—what's that?" Joel said, noticing a flash of movement out of the corner of his eye.

"What's what?" Felicity said, sounding a bit annoyed that Joel had interrupted her story.

"I, uh, saw something—over there," he said, gesturing to their left.

Felicity craned her neck. "Over where? I don't see—"

"There! Right there!"

A few feet away stood a small animal that looked like a cross between a squirrel and a monkey. About a foot tall, it was covered in light gray fur, and its wide, dark eyes stared at Joel and Felicity with a proverbial deer-in-the-headlights expression. Attached to the end of its tail was a tiny glowing sphere, and in its hands was what looked like a small, crusty brown rock.

"It has the Songshell!" Felicity exclaimed as she reached for her wavebow.

"Shh," Joel said, keeping his gaze firmly fixed on the tiny creature, which continued to stand in its spot as if it were frozen. "Don't scare it."

"What? I need to stun it," Felicity hissed. "It's stealing the shell."

"Um, no, it's just hungry," Joel whispered, cautiously inching closer to the animal. "Just—just give me a chance to—"

Then, with a sudden burst, the creature dashed away.

"No!" Joel cried as he charged into the rain after it. He heard Felicity and Marshall shouting at each other behind him, but he did not look back—he was determined not to lose sight of the little beast that was making off with their only hope of saving themselves.

The creature skittered past the trees, leading Joel deeper and deeper into the forest. Fortunately, it was not quite as fast or agile as a normal squirrel, otherwise Joel would not have been able to keep up with it like he was. The glowing bulb end of its tail also helped Joel follow its path. Still, he had to keep a very close eye on it as it darted across the ground.

"Joel? Where are you?" Marshall called out.

"Um, over here!" Joel replied as rainwater dripped down his face. "I'm following it!"

Finally, after a nine-minute chase, Joel saw the creature scamper up a tree that was unlike the others surrounding it; its trunk was not straight and thick, but sloped, like a ramp, and only a foot wide. At about fifteen feet in height, it was also much smaller than the other trees. At its top it split off into dozens of thin, crooked branches that were intertwined with each other and were covered with circular leaves that glowed a faint orange. The creature settled on one of the branches that provided the best protection from the rain and began gnawing on the Songshell.

"No—no, um, don't do that," Joel said to it. "That's not food."

The creature's head jerked, squirrel-like, as it looked down at Joel, and then back at the shell in its hands.

"Uh—that's right, not—not food," Joel repeated. "We—we need that. Very important. Please, give it to me."

The creature regarded Joel intently, its dark eyes reflecting the orange light of the leaves. It took a tentative step forward.

"Good, yes," Joel said encouragingly. "Um—we have—we have food, we can trade. Food for the shell. Okay?"

The creature took another step, but then its head jerked up and it scurried backward, obviously startled. Joel whipped his head around and saw that Marshall and Felicity had caught up to him.

"Where is that bloody thing?" Marshall sputtered, his wavebow at the ready.

"No, no—um, don't hurt it," Joel protested. "I think—I think it was listening to me. It was gonna give the shell back."

"What, now you can talk to animals as well?" Marshall said, wiping rain out of his eyes. "Joel, listen to me. We need that shell. I don't know how that thing managed to steal it from my vest while I was asleep. It would have taken a very stealthy effort to pry it from my grasp. That animal could be Fourfoot, for all we know."

"It's not—it's not—"

"Ah, there it is," Marshall said, looking up at the tree. He quickly raised his wavebow and plucked a string with the efficiency of a trained marksman. A single laser-like bolt of red light shot out toward the tree's upper branches.

Joel whirled around, just in time to see the shell falling out of the tree toward the ground below, followed closely by the creature.

"No!" Joel cried.

CHAPTER 13: THE LUTHIER

Joel dove for the squirrel-like creature without a second thought. He had always had an affinity for animals. They usually listened patiently to all of his ideas and observations and never seemed judgmental in any way. His old dog, Sammy, would pay rapt attention whenever Joel recited his favorite lists of minutiae or explained the various nuances of license plate numbering systems. And animals never got mad, unless you did something really bad to them—which Joel never did.

Despite his lack of athletic prowess, Joel surprised himself and somehow managed to catch the creature just before it struck the ground. Its eyes were closed, and the light in its tail-bulb had gone out. Joel cradled the animal in his arms and stroked its soaking wet fur, unsure of what else to do.

"Did—did you kill it?" Joel asked, trying to hold back an oncoming feeling of hysteria.

"Thank goodness, it's safe," Marshall said, ignoring Joel as he inspected the Songshell, having already picked it up off the ground.

Joel started to feel the familiar angry fog sensation creep into his head. "You didn't have to kill it!" he shouted.

Marshall looked up at Joel with an irritated expression on his face. Just as he was about to say something, the end of the animal's tail started to glow once again. It opened its eyes and shook its head, spraying Joel with rainwater.

The angry fog in Joel's mind abruptly dissipated as he smiled and breathed a sigh of relief. "Oh, wow, it's okay."

At that moment, Greenseed appeared, having finally caught up with them. "Master, is everything all right? I heard yelling and followed—oh. Oh my," she said, stopping and staring at Joel.

"Um, what?" Joel said, puzzled at Greenseed's expression. The animal shook itself off again, ran up Joel's arm, and then perched on his shoulder.

"A silvertail," Greenseed said softly, taking a few slow steps in Joel's direction. The slightest hint of a smile crossed her face, the first Joel had ever seen. "The rarest of creatures on Spectraland—no one alive today has actually seen one before. They were thought to be extinct. Where did you find it?"

"It—uh— it—" Joel began.

"The filthy bugger was trying to steal the Songshell," Marshall interrupted, obviously annoyed. "Fortunately, we were able to catch up to it."

"Master," Greenseed said, turning to Marshall, "according to legend, these creatures are harbingers of good fortune. A good sign, I think, for our quest. Also, they are supposed to be extremely intelligent."

"It's a bloody squirrel, for Pete's sake," Marshall said.

"Well, it seems to have taken a liking to Joel, here," Felicity noted as the silvertail ran in circles around Joel's neck.

"Intelligent—um, does that mean it can understand us?" Joel asked.

"I am sure it can," Greenseed said, still sporting a look of fascination as she stared at the animal. "It is supposed to have many other unique abilities as well—its claws supposedly can dig through stone, and it can track things from hundreds of miles away."

"Oh, cool," Joel exclaimed, excited that someone else seemed to share his passion for details and facts. "I've, uh, heard of cats and dogs being able to do that—find their owners after they were lost or abandoned."

"What kinds of creatures are those?" Greenseed asked.

"Great, just what we needed," Marshall grumbled, turning away from the burgeoning conversation between Joel and Greenseed. "A bloody mascot."

Twelve days until the Nadir

The silvertail gave no indication that it wanted to leave, nor did Joel make any attempt to force it to do so, so it just became an unspoken understanding that their traveling party had gained a new companion. Their arrangement became even more firm with Joel's bestowal of a name upon the animal: Sammy.

The rain finally stopped on their sixth day in the forest, which made Joel a little happier, although this happiness was offset by an increased level of tension in the air. Marshall had become increasingly agitated since Sammy had joined their little crew, and he complained loudly about a great number of things, including the amount of lifepod meat that Sammy consumed (which was not much), the weather, and the length of their journey through the glowing woods. Greenseed assured him that they would reach the Luthier soon, and that this was the path they needed to follow to get to Mount Dragoneye anyway.

I hope he calms down soon, Joel thought as they made their way through a cluster of trees. *I really hate it when people are like this.*

Ten days until the Nadir

On their eighth day, Joel noticed that the tenor of the forest began to change. The trees were sparser but bigger, and the glow of their foliage had increased in intensity. Dense waves of Aura energy filled the spaces in between the trees, and Joel could almost make out a faint humming in the air. Sammy began to chitter excitedly.

"We are very close now," Greenseed said. "Just be careful. The Luthier—she can be, well, somewhat unpredictable at times."

The humming sound continued to grow stronger until finally, after dismounting and slipping between a pair of particularly thick trees, they emerged in the middle of a circular clearing, at one end of which stood a majestic, shimmering tree that towered over all of the others. Joel craned his neck, but still, he could not even begin to see the top of it. Dozens of Aura streams circled around the tree, producing a dizzying visual effect. The tree itself throbbed with a pulsating golden light that seemed to be timed to a heartbeat, and its massive trunk appeared to be made of the same mother-of-pearl-like material as the wavebows. Instead of branches and leaves, tentacles of glittering light fanned out from the tree's immense base and eerily swayed about, as if alive.

They all stood staring at it for a few moments, until Felicity broke the awed silence.

"So why didn't we see this from, like, miles away?" she asked.

"The Aura warps the visual space around this area," Greenseed said in a reverential tone, "so that no one but those who know can find it."

"Um—the Luthier lives in this tree?" Joel asked.

"She *is* the tree," Greenseed replied.

As if on cue, the tree's luminous tentacles twitched. Everyone jumped back a step.

"So, how does Joel get a new wavebow?" Marshall asked.

Greenseed paused before replying. "Truthfully, I do not know. Normally a formal ceremony is involved, and only newborn Wavemakers receive instruments. To approach it in the manner we are now has never been attempted before, to my knowledge."

"Great," Felicity muttered, rolling her eyes. "Always breaking more ground, aren't we?"

The humming abruptly grew much louder. So much so, that even Marshall—his hearing dulled from years of playing high-decibel rock shows—was forced to cover his ears. The golden glow stopped pulsing and expanded into a constant floodlight that bathed the entire clearing in blinding illumination.

"Another newborn in need of an instrument already? That was fast," a pleasant yet powerful female voice rang out, cutting through the din like an aural knife.

Squinting and shielding his eyes, Joel looked toward the spot where Greenseed had stood, expecting her to answer, but she was no longer there.

Bewildered, Joel looked around some more, and saw Marshall wearing a similarly confused expression. Joel shrugged to indicate that he did not know where Greenseed had vanished to.

"We—are here because of dire circumstances," Marshall improvised loudly in response to the voice as he quickly regained his composure. "We are on a quest to save the people of this island from a great evil."

"*Are you now?*" the voice said, almost cheerfully. "*That is wonderful. But I see no newborns here. What do you wish from me?*"

"We merely require a new wavebow for my companion here," Marshall said, gesturing in Joel's direction, "and then we shall be on our way."

Joel could have sworn he heard the voice chuckle.

"*You are not of this world, are you?*" the voice said after a pause.

"No," Marshall replied, "no, we are not. However, we too can wield the energy, as you say. I can demonstrate, if you like."

"*No need,*" the voice said liltingly. "*What makes you think you deserve a new wavebow? The ones you have are not even yours.*"

Joel was not sure what she meant by this. Felicity's wavebow, perhaps, could be considered a hand-me-down from a previous shaman, but hadn't Marshall received his own instrument when he was first brought over?

"Perhaps you are not concerned about the people of this island," Marshall said in an increasingly defiant tone, "but surely you must have some regard for your own fate. If we do not stop the evil force at hand, I am certain that he will eventually attempt to usurp your power."

This time, Joel was sure that he heard a sound that resembled laughter.

"*That is unlikely,*" the voice said. "*My energy has dwelt within this forest for ages, surviving much.*"

Joel grew worried. Perhaps he would have to carry on without a new wavebow after all. He looked at Marshall, who seemed uncharacteristically stumped and unsure of what to say next.

"Show her the shell, moron," Felicity hissed at Marshall.

"Oh—of course," Marshall said before flashing Felicity a wry smile. "I was just about to do that."

Felicity made a face at Marshall as he dug through his vest. He pulled out the Songshell and held it aloft like a trophy.

"We have the Songshell," he declared. "We are the three Wavemakers mentioned in the secret prophecy."

There was a long pause, during which the humming sound seemed to vacillate a bit. Then there was a noise that sounded like a sigh.

"*Very well,*" the voice continued, "*perhaps the time has indeed arrived, at last. There does seem to be something unusual—and perhaps worthy—about the young one. But he is no newborn, and thus, he must be tested. Please, approach.*"

Joel glanced at Marshall, who gave Joel an affirmative nod and then motioned his head in the direction of the giant tree.

More curious than frightened, Joel began to take a cautious step forward. But before his foot even reached the ground, he found himself swept up into the air by the tree's Aura-tentacles. Whipping his head around just in time to see Sammy falling off of his shoulder, Joel tried to call out to his animal friend but found that his voice had been silenced.

Then, over the next few seconds, Joel began to experience a very peculiar feeling. It was as if the tree's Aura energy was seeping into his skin and filling up his body, like water flowing into a sponge. It was warm and unnerving, but not altogether unpleasant. This feeling was followed by a series of tingling sensations that coursed through his body, as if he were receiving hundreds of tiny, mild electrical shocks.

Suddenly, he became aware that he was not only receiving sensory input from his own limbs and organs but from the extremities of the tree itself. He closed his eyes, but even still, he felt as though he could "see" Marshall and Felicity standing on the ground below with confused looks on their faces and Sammy darting around their feet. He attempted to "look" for Greenseed, but he saw no sign of her.

A voice that sounded like the Luthier's soothing female tone, but with Joel's own voice as an echo, spoke in his head: "*A newborn Wavemaker is focused only on the moment. Not on the past, of which they have none, nor on the future, of which they have no concept. They have needs and know of unhappiness, as such is the way of life, but they are not dependent upon vague, distant dreams to cure what ails them, nor do they have any regret about prior actions or mistakes.*"

The part of Joel's consciousness that was merged with the Luthier's heard and understood these words, but the part of him that was his own had difficulty grasping and comprehending the ideas that it was trying to communicate.

"Newborn Wavemakers are taken from their parents to train at the Wavemaker Temple. They must overcome the fear and pain that is associated with this traumatic event and learn to stand on their own while forging their own individual identity. They must embrace change, or else be carried away by the ever-shifting winds. They quickly realize that the only thing they truly have control over is themselves."

Joel still struggled to understand. What kind of a test was this?

"Perhaps this will help."

The electrical shocks returned, stronger this time. Joel started to feel a kind of pressure in his head, as if each side of his brain were pushing against each other.

Then, all at once, a flood of painful memories rushed into his mind, memories that he thought were buried forever. His thoughts whipped back to the events of six years ago, when seemingly overnight, his entire world had been turned upside down. He again felt trapped in a nightmare that he could not wake up from. His consciousness was locked in a roller coaster of emotions that zoomed through a dark tunnel with no end in sight.

In an instant everything that he knew had changed. All of his comfortable routines, all the security and predictability of everyday life, all of the familiar surroundings and traditions and memories—all of it, gone, in the blink of an eye. And there was absolutely nothing that he could do about it.

One day he lived in a house in Hawai'i with his entire family. The next day he lived in an apartment in Seattle without his father.

It was like he was a...*newborn*, ejected from the warmth of the womb into a cold, scary, unfamiliar new world.

Joel wanted to scream, but no sound came out. He wanted to cry, but he found that he could not. There was no alternative but to steel his will against the pain and simply push through—just as he had done six years ago. He remembered how he had to contain his fear of the unknown and simply live life one day at a time. He forced himself to recall how, even though the scar was still there, the wound eventually did heal.

What did Art say that one time? "This, too, shall pass." Okay, now that makes sense...

The memories began to subside.

"*Very good,*" the soothing female voice said. "*Finally, newborn Wavemakers are innocent and good of heart, without any of the bias or hatred that is acquired throughout a life of suffering. You have suffered, young one, but you retain your purity of intent. I can see now that you are, indeed, worthy of what you seek. You have passed my test. Our island is in your hands.*"

A second later, Joel could sense the tentacles of the tree becoming extensions of his own body, as if he had gained several additional arms. Some impulse in his mind prompted him to move them, so he did. With the tentacles, he stripped away pieces of himself and fashioned the parts into something odd, yet familiar. Everything that was happening felt predestined, as if he were in control of his own actions yet following a path that had already been laid out for him, like a river flowing out to sea.

For a moment, he thought he sensed another Aura— a third presence, almost—but the feeling quickly passed.

And then it was over. The tree's energy rushed out of him, and he found himself lying face down on the ground, gasping for breath. He felt Sammy jump onto his back. He heard Marshall and Felicity saying things that he could not make out, as the humming noise was still too loud. He used what little strength he had left to raise his head slightly, and the last thing he saw before everything went dark was a beautiful new wavebow, lying on the ground a few inches from his face.

CHAPTER 14: THE LANDVEIN

Nine days until the Nadir

Joel awoke with a start. For a moment, he thought that the whole experience with the Luthier had been another dream, like the ones he had been having about the caldera.

"Oh, good, you're up," Marshall said as he turned a wavebow over in his hands. It was similar to the one that Joel had lost, except that its finish was much brighter, and the glow of the strings was stronger.

Wow, I guess it wasn't a dream after all, Joel thought as he pulled himself into a sitting position, rubbing his eyes to get the blurriness out. Sammy quickly hopped up onto his lap.

Marshall walked over to Joel and handed him the instrument. "Here you go. Seems like it put you through quite a lot. It was worth it, though, I suppose."

"Yeah, except now we have some other problems," Felicity said. "But what did you expect, right?"

Joel felt the neck and body of the new wavebow and was amazed at its smoothness. He glanced around and saw that they were still in the Forest of Light, surrounded by the now all-too-familiar trees.

"Um, where are the slimebacks? And what happened to Greenseed?" he asked.

"Good questions, both," Marshall sighed. "After the Luthier released you, she literally flushed us out of her presence with some big blast of energy. We were pushed out somewhere into the forest, and now we can't find either Greenseed or the slimebacks."

"Tell him the best part," Felicity chuckled.

Marshall gave her an annoyed look. "Think this is funny, do you? When Fourfoot shows up, I'll just tell him that you volunteered to be skewered first. Then we'll see who's laughing."

"Hey, don't snap at me," she retorted. "I'm just getting a little tired of all this crazy running around, almost-getting-killed business. I didn't sign up for this."

"Sometimes," Marshall said, seething, "things happen that are beyond our control. Ever noticed that? Or have you been too busy living a carefully choreographed little princess lifestyle, hmm?"

"You have no idea what kind of life I've had," Felicity growled, her eyes narrowing. "You think that just because—"

"Okay, okay," Joel said with a raised voice. "Um, can you guys please—please, just stop. I hate arguments. It stresses me out. Just tell me, what—what's the other problem?"

"We're lost," Felicity said. "We've been wandering through the forest for hours now, and we have no idea where we are. Rock-star-man here was carrying you the whole time you were unconscious. We had stopped for another break when you finally woke up."

"I told you," Marshall said, "we're not lost."

"Riiight," Felicity said, full of sarcasm. "Face it, we're trapped in here, unless we can find Greenseed, or some other miracle happens."

Sammy made a little squeaking sound. Joel looked at his face, which was a curious blend of rodent and simian features. Shiny, almond-shaped eyes; slightly turned-up nose; tiny, round ears...Joel recalled reading something in a textbook about squirrel monkeys (genus: *Saimiri*, subfamily: *Saimirinae*) that lived in Central and South America, and wondered if they were similar at all to the creature that was sitting in his lap. He made a mental note to look into it some more when—if—he ever got home.

Suddenly, he had an idea.

"Um, why don't we just ask Sammy to guide us?"

Marshall and Felicity looked at him like he was crazy.

"I mean, he lives here, right? And remember what Greenseed said about his tracking abilities? Maybe he, uh, maybe he knows a fast way out of here."

"That's a brilliant idea," Marshall said, "except that in case you haven't noticed, *he's an animal*. He can't talk, otherwise the translation cast would have let us know what all his infernal chittering and squeaking has been about."

"Well, yeah," Joel said, "but that doesn't mean he doesn't understand what we're saying. Animals back home can do that. And Greenseed said that silvertails are extremely intelligent."

Marshall rubbed the scar on his face as if he were expecting a genie to pop out of his mouth. "This is all just getting a bit out of control," he grumbled to himself. Then, to Joel, he said, "So, what, I suppose you're just going to ask it to lead us out of here, then?"

"Um, sure, why not?" Joel replied. Before he actually had a chance to do so, however, Sammy hopped out of his lap and scampered off over a large tree root to their left. Moving quite a bit slower than when he had taken the Songshell, the little animal stopped just beyond the root and looked back at the three humans, apparently waiting for them to follow.

Joel looked at Marshall and Felicity as he stood up. "Um, shall we?"

"Make sure he knows we're trying to get to Mount Dragoneye," Marshall huffed.

They followed Sammy through the forest for a couple of hours. Joel didn't recognize any of the trees or areas that they passed through, and although most of the forest looked pretty much the same, he was sure that he would know when they were someplace he had been before.

"I don't know if either of you had thought of this," Felicity said, trying to catch her breath, "but this is gonna take us forever on foot."

"We're, uh, we're not going back the way we came," Joel told her as he jumped over a large rock. "I think we're headed away from there."

"That's good, because we can't afford any more delays if we're to stop Fourfoot," Marshall reminded them, beginning to sound like a nagging mother.

"Um, I actually think we're almost at the edge of the forest," Joel said, without really understanding how he knew that.

Sure enough, after twenty-six more minutes of following Sammy, the trees thinned out quickly and they emerged on the bank of a large river. Sammy ran over to a nearby cluster of purple bushes and began chittering wildly.

"What now?" Marshall sighed.

Joel rushed over to investigate. He pushed aside the prickly leaves and branches, and his eyes widened at what he saw.

"It's—it's Greenseed!" he called out to the others.

The tiny native was lying on her side, apparently asleep or unconscious, with her supply pack next to her. She did not show any external signs of injury as far as Joel could tell.

Marshall walked over and brusquely dragged Greenseed's limp form out of the vegetation.

"Greenseed," he said, shaking her shoulders. "Wake up."

Joel picked up her supply pack and noticed that it seemed rather bulky. For a brief moment, he considered opening it to check what might be inside besides lifepods, but he decided against it, figuring that to do so would be quite rude. A quick glance told him that it appeared to be tightly sealed, anyhow. He found this to be somewhat curious, but he decided to set his suspicions aside—for now.

"Unhh...Master?" Greenseed said as her eyes fluttered open. "Where—where are we?"

"At the edge of the forest," Marshall replied. "What happened to you? Why did you disappear? How long have you been here?"

"I'm fine," she said, apparently ignoring Marshall's line of questioning. "The last thing I remember is seeing the Luthier appear—then everything went dark, and now I am here. Were you—were we successful?"

"We were. Joel has his new wavebow. But we've lost much time in the process. We simply must get to Mount Dragoneye as quickly as possible."

"Yes, of course," she said, getting to her feet. "Where—where are the slimebacks?"

"Don't know," Marshall said. "We were hoping they were with you."

"That is unfortunate," Greenseed said as she received her supply pack from Joel and glanced around at the surrounding area. "This river, though...if I am correct, it could help us expedite our journey."

"What are we gonna do, build a boat out of these trees?" Felicity asked skeptically.

"The trees here are sacred—cutting them down is forbidden," Greenseed explained as she walked closer to the edge of the rushing river. "However, we seem to have been fortunate enough to have found the Landvein."

"The what now?" Felicity said.

"The Landvein," Marshall answered. "I read about it in the archives—it's the largest river on the north side of the island. The water in it is heavily charged with Aura energy—and infested with all manner of wild creatures, as well."

"Yes, but its energy would help support an Aura shield generated by your instruments," Greenseed said. "And if memory serves, its currents should lead us in the direction of Mount Dragoneye. The only risk—and it is a big one, to be sure—is that taking the wrong path could lead us to the Prism Valley."

"I swear, all these names are driving me crazy," Felicity grumbled.

"Prism Valley—it's real?" Marshall asked.

"Um, what is—" Joel tried to interject.

"It is," Greenseed replied. And then, turning to Joel, she explained, "The Prism Valley is a place inhabited by a dangerous race of creatures called the Lightsnakes. They prey on our people, but they cannot venture far from their lair. So we normally avoid any contact with this river or the surrounding area. Given the circumstances, however, it would seem that we have no choice."

"Well, I've always been a gambling man," Marshall said. "And you're right, we have no choice. We only have nine days left."

"But how are we gonna know which is the correct way?" Felicity protested.

Greenseed pondered for a moment before replying. "Dragoneye's silver magma contains very powerful Aura properties. There should be residuals of it flowing through the river's tributaries. Master Joel's Sight power could—"

"He could use it to see the correct path toward the mountain. That's brilliant," Marshall said.

"No pressure there," Felicity chuckled.

Joel was having trouble keeping up with the rapid-fire conversation that was taking place. "Wait, um—what are we doing again?"

"We're going surfing, with you as our tour guide," Felicity told him. "Since you're from Hawai'i, it should be pretty easy for you, right?"

"Um, yeah...sure," Joel said hesitantly.

Marshall was already forming a saucer of yellow light and testing it for buoyancy. "This is perfect," he said, "the Aura helps keep it afloat and watertight, and we don't have to expend as much energy as with a normal shelter-strength shield."

Joel looked at the shimmering, rough waters with more than a fair amount of trepidation. "Are you sure this is, you know, safe?"

"I can't believe you're asking that, after everything we've been through." Felicity laughed. "C'mon, this might actually be fun."

Joel played a chord and conjured up his own approximation of a large yellow saucer. Despite the fact that his shield looked neither as circular nor as solid as the ones that Marshall and Felicity had managed to produce, the new wavebow felt good in his hands, and the casting process had been much smoother and quicker than with his previous instrument.

He placed a tentative foot on the saucer and looked back at the others. "So, um, just like this, right?" he asked, trying to hide his nervousness.

"Perfect," Marshall said as Greenseed moved to join him on his Aura-board. "Now, on the count of three, everyone push off into the water. Joel, you take the lead. One—"

"Wait! Um—I don't even know what—"

"Two—"

"I'm supposed to be looking—"

"Three!"

"For!"

Not wanting to be left behind, Joel pushed off, with Sammy perched on his shoulder. At first he was sure that he was going to slip and fall off into the raging water, but to his pleasant surprise, he found that the shield was remarkably balanced. After several minutes, his fear subsided, and he actually began to enjoy himself.

Carried by the current, they raced along the waterway at a great speed, leaving a foamy, sparkling trail of water and Aura energy in their wake. Marshall whooped and hollered as they went, the wind whipping through his hair, his shield occasionally bouncing on the river's surface like a skipping stone.

Riding alongside Marshall and Greenseed, Joel managed to gain enough confidence to speak while he surfed. "So, how do I know which way we're supposed to go?" he shouted, rephrasing his earlier question.

"Look for silvery trails in the water," Greenseed yelled back, "and follow them. It is very important that you not go the wrong way!"

Joel nodded. He tried his best to relax while he recited random fact lists in his head. A number of different colors became evident within the river, but it was difficult for him to really make any clear distinction between them, due to the speed at which he was traveling. As the river was not splitting off into multiple directions just yet, he figured that he had at least a few minutes to get it sorted out.

"See anything?" Marshall called out.

"Um, not yet," Joel responded, trying not to lose his focus. At that moment, he saw clusters of concentrated red Aura suddenly appear in the water about a hundred feet ahead.

"Wait, uh, there's something, but I don't know what it—"

By then, however, it was too late. Before anyone knew what was happening, dozens of large, eel-like creatures with glowing red scales and alligator heads were leaping out of the water all around them.

"No! They are not supposed to be this far upstream! We must—" Greenseed yelled.

"Bail out!" Marshall shouted.

Joel steered toward the riverbank, but the grotesque eels blocked his path, forcing him to spin several times. He barely kept his balance while the river gushed fast under his shield. Sammy's claws dug into the skin of Joel's shoulders as the little animal tried to keep from flying off.

Greenseed screamed as one of the eels knocked her from Marshall's shield and into the waterway. Marshall tumbled onto dry land next to where Felicity had already landed.

In a single acrobatic move that was reminiscent of his days on stage, Marshall rolled, turned, got up into a half-kneeling position, and fired several bolts of red light in the general direction of the eels. Since Joel had not yet managed to make it to the riverbank, one of the bolts whizzed by him, alarmingly close to his legs.

"They've got Greenseed!" Joel shouted as the eels took off in the direction of the current.

"Go! We'll catch up!" Marshall yelled, barely audible to Joel as he was already zooming away.

Joel followed the red trail in the water. He also noticed what he thought was Greenseed's Aura mixed up among the red streaks.

I hope natives like her can hold their breath, or have gills, or something.

Sooner than he expected, he saw a fork in the river up ahead. He caught a glimpse of a bright silver streak within the water that appeared to lead off to the left. Unfortunately, the red mass seemed to be headed down the right side. Joel briefly looked over his shoulder and saw Marshall and Felicity following behind. He heard Marshall yelling something, but he could not make out what it was.

For a split second, Joel wondered which way he should go—left, which most likely led to Mount Dragoneye and the end of their quest, or right, to save an alien creature that he barely even knew and still had his suspicions about.

There really was no debate, however. He was going right.

After several hundred more yards, the river's path took a sharp turn around a tree-covered bank. Then Joel saw something that his mind had difficulty processing: another fifty yards out or so, the river became a very long waterfall that flowed up into the air, without anything else surrounding it. It was hard to tell what lay beyond the waterfall, as it seemed to lead straight into a huge misty cloud.

He had heard of the Upside Down Falls back in Hawai'i, but they were nowhere near as big, and their name came simply by virtue of the winds blowing a normal waterfall back upward. This was an actual inverted cascade, as if someone had taken a photo and rotated it a hundred and eighty degrees.

Joel snapped out of his shock and looked back down to make sure he was still following the gator-eels, which he was. From behind, he heard Marshall and Felicity shouting things at each other as they rounded the corner.

It appeared that the gator-eels were taking Greenseed with them into the falls, so Joel resolved to continue his pursuit. Sammy dropped to a hanging position from Joel's neck, his tiny arms squeezing so hard that Joel struggled to breathe.

Joel did not close his eyes this time. In fact, they were glued wide open as he and Sammy rode their Aurashield-board over the "edge." Somehow, incredibly, they remained on the water's surface during the initial steep incline of the falls, and Joel felt a rush of excitement flow through him.

Must be getting used to this sort of thing, he thought as the wind whipped through his bangs and sprays of water splashed his face.

The water leveled out as they approached the mist cloud. Joel suddenly developed a splitting headache, and he could feel the energy of his shield start to waver. He replayed the appropriate chord on his wavebow to recast the shield, but instead of the desired effect, dozens of tiny green bubbles floated out from his fingertips.

"Um—" Joel said, as he and Sammy were swallowed up by the cloud with a large *whoosh*.

CHAPTER 15: PRISM VALLEY

Joel was pretty certain that what he had landed on was soft, marshy ground. It was hard to know for sure, however, as the surrounding scenery was in a constant state of flux, in contrast to what he had now become used to, where the landscape only shifted with each Aura manipulation. One minute, the surface he was lying on looked like grass, mud and weeds; the next, it resembled a pattern of leaves and bird feathers before it mutated again into something else altogether. Tall spiderlike trees and large gray boulders that changed into random stripes and circles dotted the area around him. Joel felt as if he had entered a giant kaleidoscope that someone kept on turning.

He stood up and took inventory: wavebow still in hand, Sammy still hanging around his neck, and a throbbing pain still in his head. There was no sign of the gator-eels, or of Greenseed.

He was startled by two thumping sounds next to him. He whipped his head around (which made his headache worse) and raised his wavebow, only to see Marshall and Felicity lying on the ground, deposited there as if out of nowhere.

"Ugh—seems like we're always falling in, on, or out of stuff," Felicity groaned as she rubbed her head.

"Are you sure we went the right way?" Marshall asked Joel as he stood up and brushed himself off.

"Um—what do you mean?" Joel asked, still a bit rattled.

"There was a fork in the river. Did you see any silver Aura in the water?" Marshall said, his volume rising.

"Uh, well, I guess, but—"

"You guess? You followed it, I hope?"

Joel felt a lump develop in his throat. "Well, um, not—uh, not really—I, uh—"

"Blimey, mate, don't tell me you went the opposite way!" Marshall yelled, his face turning red. Joel wanted to disappear into the ever-morphing background.

"Oh, c'mon, give him a break," Felicity snapped as she got to her feet. Joel's spirits lifted a little.

"A break?" Marshall sputtered. "My dear, we could've been well on our way to completing our task and *getting you home.* Instead, now we're probably trapped in—in—"

"Prism Valley?" Felicity said wearily.

"Yes, bloody Prism Valley," Marshall barked. "And I have no idea how we're going to get out. What were you thinking, Joel?"

"I—uh, I—"

"You were trying to save Greenseed, right?" Felicity asked, turning toward Joel.

"Um, yeah," Joel gulped.

Marshall grimaced before letting out a huge sigh. "Admittedly, we still may need her services to find our way into the mountain," he said, as if trying to rationalize their situation to himself, "but I think we could've figured it out for ourselves, since we were so close."

"Well, not to mention it was just the right thing to do," Felicity offered. Joel's spirits lifted even further.

"Sometimes, sacrifices need to be made for the bigger picture, my dear," Marshall said in an unusually menacing tone. "I figured you, of all people, would understand that."

"What's that supposed to mean?" Felicity said, hostility creeping into her voice.

"I mean, you don't seem like the type who cares—"

"Um, okay, okay, please," Joel interrupted. "Please, just—just stop. Look, I—I'm sorry I went the wrong way. I, uh, I just figured that we still needed Greenseed and that we wanted to rescue her, that's all."

Marshall paused and appeared to be collecting himself. "Fine," he sighed. "You're right. We should rescue her. It is the *right thing to do*. Let's just get a move on, all right? Joel, see if you can find her Aura trail."

"Okay, um—let me see what I can do," Joel said, noticing that Felicity was fuming, her lips tightly pursed.

His head was still pounding painfully, making it difficult for him to even think, much less focus and concentrate. He scanned the ground in front of him and could see nothing but an undulating blur of colors and shapes.

"I—I can't see anything," he admitted after several minutes of trying. "This place is, um, weird, to say the least."

"Well, let's just start moving, then," Marshall said. "Keep looking. Hopefully something will become evident soon."

They walked for twenty minutes into the psychedelic wetland before Felicity finally spoke up again, having calmed down somewhat.

"Is it just me, or does this seem pointless?" she complained. "I mean, we have no idea where we're going, or where to even start looking."

This made Joel feel guilty for losing the trail and did nothing to help his headache. "Sorry," he said ruefully.

"Don't apologize," she sighed. "It's not your fault. But, like, now what? We can't tell how big this place is, or where it ends. And how do we even know if Greenseed is still alive?"

Joel glanced at Marshall, who remained oddly silent. Apparently, no one had any answers for Felicity's questions.

They trudged along for what felt like hours. The ever-changing colors, while beautiful to look at, were becoming quite disorienting, and Joel started to feel light-headed and dizzy, on top of the pain in his skull.

"Um, I have to sit down for a minute," he said, looking around for a suitable place to rest.

"We can't afford to lose any more time," Marshall grunted. "Why do you need to sit down?"

At that moment, as Joel's eyes scanned the horizon, his head cleared for a second, and he saw what looked like the outline of a large cat-like creature with four long tails seamlessly camouflaged amongst the shifting scenery.

"Uh, there's something—" he started to say.

You can see me. Very interesting, a calm, silky voice echoed in Joel's head.

"What is it?" Marshall said, raising his wavebow.

"Like, um, an invisible tiger, or something—"

"What? Where?"

Joel pointed in the general direction of the outline. "Um, over there," he said.

Marshall quickly aimed his wavebow and played a short, aggressive riff. The red wave that emanated from his instrument instantly turned white and drifted off like smoke.

"What the—"

Why are you here? the voice said, unfazed by Marshall's unsuccessful attack. The soothing voice was neither male nor female, or perhaps it was both simultaneously; Joel found it hard to tell.

Joel glanced at Marshall, expecting his idol to provide the voice with an answer, but Marshall simply gave Joel a befuddled look.

I believe only you can hear me, the voice said. *Your mind is open to communication via the Aura. Your brain wave frequencies are rather—unique.*

"Who—me?" Joel asked.

"Who are you talking to?" Felicity asked.

Yes, young one, you, the voice said without a trace of impatience. *I ask again, why are you here?*

"Um—we're, uh, we're looking for our friend," Joel replied as he saw the four tails flick back and forth. "We need to save her."

Interesting. You must be referring to the latest villager to be taken by the Lightsnakes.

"Yes! Do you know where she is?" Joel asked, excited.

"Who are you—" Felicity started to ask again before Marshall shushed her.

Our meeting was not a coincidence, the voice said, seemingly to itself. *This is the moment that I have been waiting for.*

"Um, okay, but can you—"

Yes. I can help you.

The outline stepped toward Joel. In doing so, it emerged out of its chameleonlike camouflage and became fully visible to all. It had the general shape of a large tiger, but its coat resembled sheep's wool, and where a tiger's ears would normally be was a pair of ram's horns instead. Each one of its four tails was tipped by a bulbous, unblinking eyeball.

"Whoa—cool," Joel whispered as Sammy cautiously moved from one shoulder to the other.

My name is Nineteen, the voice said. *I will take you to the Lightsnakes' Lair.*

"Oh, your name is a number," Joel observed. "That's, um, different—but still cool! I—um, I'm Joel."

I know, Nineteen replied. *I can see into your thoughts and emotions.*

"Uh," Joel said, unsure how he felt about that.

Do not worry, Nineteen said. *My intentions are pure, as are yours.*

Joel suddenly felt himself flooded with feelings of reassurance, and somehow he knew that Nineteen was telling the truth.

"So, what's going on? You're talking to this thing, I assume? Is it going to help us?" Marshall asked.

"Hey, I thought you wanted us to be quiet," Felicity grumbled.

"Um, it is—I mean, yeah, its name is Nineteen, and it said it'll take us to the Lightsnakes' Lair, where Greenseed is."

"Nineteen? Can we trust it?" Felicity said.

"Um, yeah, we can," Joel replied.

"How do you know?"

"I just know," Joel said with uncharacteristic confidence.

"I don't think we have a choice, anyway," Marshall added. "It'll be able to get us out of here, though, right?"

"I didn't ask that yet. I, uh, thought that we wanted to save Greenseed first?"

"Yes, yes, but—"

At that moment, Nineteen's form became blurry. Within seconds, it transformed into a large, transparent sphere, rather like a giant soap bubble.

Please, enter.

Joel took a cautious step toward the bubble. Before he had a chance to think it over, he found himself encased in the bubble's thin membrane, looking at Marshall and Felicity with a sheepish expression that said *I guess you should come along?*

"Are you serious?" Felicity exclaimed. "This place gets more and more like a video game all the time."

"Just get in," Marshall snapped.

Nineteen floated up into the air and began to drift along on a gust of Aura that seemed to come out of nowhere. Joel looked around in amazement. He knew exactly what Felicity was talking about, as he had played a number of different video games where you rode in a bubble, guiding it along while trying to avoid bumping into sharp objects. He never imagined that one day he would be doing it for real.

Prism Valley is a place where the Aura does not behave as expected, Nineteen's smooth voice explained in Joel's head as they started to pick up speed. *That is why your companion's wavebow did not function, and why you feel the painful sensation in your head.*

"Oh," Joel replied, surprised that his question had been answered just as he was about to ask it. "So, um, what—"

You are very inquisitive. It will be easier to answer all of your questions if you look into my thoughts.

"Um, how do I do—"

Relax.

Joel took a deep breath and closed his eyes. Images began to flow into his mind, and his headache subsided a bit. It felt as if he were having a dream while still awake.

In his mind, he saw fuzzy visions of multiple Nineteens, or other similar tiger-sheep beings, engaged in some sort of melee with the gator-snakes from the river. The snakes sported arms and legs, three of each, and were standing upright.

Our races were the original inhabitants of the island now known as Spectraland, Nineteen narrated. *We were all powerful users of the Aura. A great war broke out between us, and the Lightsnakes were victorious—I am the only survivor of my kind.*

Joel then saw a vision of a huge explosion, drenched in multiple colored streams of Aura, as if someone had blown up a paint factory.

Their victory came at a price, however, Nineteen continued. *They accidentally created an unstable parallel plane of existence in which they found themselves trapped—the same place that you find yourself in now.*

Joel felt another question coming on, but decided to remain silent while he let the visions play out.

The Lightsnakes were eventually able to create a portal between here and their former home, but they found themselves unable to remain on the island for any significant period of time, due to their now-permanently unstable Aura presences. A new race of beings—the ancestors of your villager friend—came to populate the island.

Joel then saw horrific images of the gator-snakes attacking and abducting terrified Spectraland natives. Instinctively, he closed his eyes, but the images carried on.

The Lightsnakes were miserable, and jealous of the new race, who they viewed as usurpers of their land. They began to prey on the new race, killing them out of anger and vengeance, and kidnapping them in hopes that they could assimilate enough of their Aura energies to someday make a successful, permanent return. They believed that once they could accomplish this goal, they would be happy.

Joel furrowed his brow. That last sentence resonated with him for some reason.

Nineteen paused for two full seconds before continuing. *In the meantime, I hid in exile, also bound to Prism Valley forever. During my time alone, I gained much wisdom and knowledge about myself and the nature of existence. Although I spent the early years in sorrow and misery, missing my former home and companions, I eventually learned the value of appreciation.*

Joel saw an image of Nineteen slowly walking through rapidly changing surroundings that looked like they were filmed with time-lapse photography.

One night, I had a vision that a strange being with a noble mission would appear in Prism Valley. Unlike the Lightsnakes, this being would be able to see through my perfect disguise, and it would then become my life's purpose to aid him. I believe that this vision has now become a reality.

"So, I assume that this thing has been telling you its life story, correct?" Marshall asked impatiently. "Did you check if it can get us out of here?"

"Um, I haven't had a chance to—"

I am aware of your larger goal, beyond saving your villager friend. I do believe that if we are able to defeat the Lightsnakes, everything else should fall into place. That is my hope, at any rate.

"Uh, yeah, everything's cool, don't worry," Joel announced to the others after clearing his throat.

"Hey, so I assume that your new friend here can help us beat these snake things, right? Since our wavebows apparently don't work here?" Felicity said.

Joel's stomach tightened as he realized that Felicity had just asked a very good question. How in the world were they supposed to defeat a group of beasts that had wiped out an entire race of powerful creatures like Nineteen's? And without their wavebows to boot?

"Yeah, um, well, you see—"

We shall figure that out once we arrive, Nineteen's voice echoed impassively in Joel's head. *Stay in the moment. Have faith.*

Joel gulped. "Um, it'll be fine, you'll see. Just, uh, have faith."

Although he focused his eyes squarely on the surreal scenery whizzing past him, Joel still felt like he could see the suspect glares that Marshall and Felicity were probably sending his way.

"Why do I not feel good about this?" Felicity muttered.

They continued to float along at an ever-increasing speed. Joel was glad that Nineteen could steer himself, as they swooped around and between various obstacles shaped like trees and other miscellaneous objects. The distortions in the Aura and the scenery were getting more severe the farther they traveled, until eventually their surroundings looked like one big Roberto Matta painting.

One feature in the landscape was stable, however: a large, light-green lake that sat in the middle of a shifting palette of colors and textures. Nineteen came to a stop on the ground just on the edge of the lake.

This is the way to the lair, he said.

"Um, okay," Joel said. "Then why are we stopping?"

I cannot travel through this lake in my current form, Nineteen replied as his bubble shape began to shrink. *There is no propelling force to move us. Hence, we must swim.*

Joel's heart sank. "Uh...there's a problem with that."

There was no reply. The three of them were ejected from the bubble, which then changed back into Nineteen's original tigerlike form. Marshall and Felicity looked at Joel inquisitively.

"I, uh, I can't swim."

"Are you serious?" Felicity said, laughing. "I thought you grew up in Hawai'i!"

"Um, yeah...I just never learned how. I tried. Couldn't get the hang of it, for some reason."

"Wow." Felicity shook her head in disbelief. "Just—wow."

"Well, mate, looks like you're gonna have to fake it," Marshall said. "You're the only one who can talk to tiger-boy here, and we need him to tell us where we're going."

Joel gulped. Memories of his youth came rushing back in an instant: of long afternoons spent at the beach with his dad, carefully wading out into the warm, shallow water before flailing in panic once he realized that his feet no longer touched sand; of after-school lessons at the neighborhood pool, where everything was fine until he had to put his head under the water, at which point he ran crying into the locker room, to the laughter of the other kids. He eventually came up with the theory that if past lives did indeed exist, one of his had drowned after falling out of a plane into the ocean (thus, his accompanying fear of heights).

I may have a solution, Nineteen said.

Moments later, Joel found himself plunging into the lake as he held on to Nineteen's back, while Sammy, Marshall, and Felicity all swam alongside. With Nineteen as sort of a self-propelled flotation device, Joel mostly kept his eyes shut and let his new friend do the work until they slowed up halfway across the lake's surface.

Here, we must dive, Nineteen said. *Inform the others.*

"Um, we must what?" Joel said, before he decided that protesting would do no good. He sighed, passed the message on, and then took a deep breath.

CHAPTER 16: LIGHTSNAKES' LAIR

Joel never really understood how people could keep their eyes open underwater. It just didn't seem natural to him. For some reason, however, this time he decided to part his eyelids just ever so slightly as Nineteen pulled him down deeper into the water, as if perhaps he would be missing out on something special if he didn't at least take one small peek.

What he saw did not disappoint him.

Streaks of colored light danced and intertwined in elaborate patterns, flowing in and around each other like massive schools of tiny fish. Small sparkling bubbles rose up in billowing columns around them. There were circular objects floating everywhere that at one moment resembled dinner plates with tentacles and the next, glowing underwater UFOs. Every so often the objects would float through a streak of light, and little crackling electrical bursts would result.

They dove right through all of the objects and into a dark hole at the bottom of the lake. The hole led to a tunnel that took a number of twists and turns before finally leading upward in a straight path. Joel began to feel an increasingly urgent need for air; he fervently hoped that they would be out of the water soon.

His prayers were answered when the tunnel opened up into a shallow pool. Joel gasped as his head broke the surface of the water. He looked around and saw that they were in a relatively normal-looking cavern that was lit by sporadic patches of glowmoss on its walls.

Do not be fooled by the appearance, Nineteen said as he shook water off of himself. *The Aura is just as unstable down here as it is up on the valley's surface.*

Joel relayed the message as they clambered out of the pool onto rocky ground. Marshall cursed as he tried a test cast with his wavebow that produced nothing but tiny sparks.

The air was cooler here, and Joel shivered a little as he wiped water from his eyes. At the far end of the cavern was a half-circular opening that was covered by what looked like a film of soap bubble liquid.

We are here, Nineteen said.

"Wait, um, what? Already?" Joel said, slightly taken aback. He started to feel a mild sense of panic, not knowing what to expect or what their plan of action was, but he didn't want to alarm Marshall and Felicity by saying too much.

It was too late for that, however. "Already what?" Felicity asked. "We're here? At their lair? So we can lean on your friend, right?"

"Relax," Marshall admonished her. "I'm sure Joel knows what he's doing. Right, Joel?"

"Um, yeah, sure," Joel mumbled.

Without further word, Nineteen moved quickly toward the opening, and the others followed. As they passed through, Joel noticed that the soapy film felt thicker than he had expected, as if they were walking through a wall of gelatin. He looked down at his feet as he pushed his legs through the goopy substance.

Then he was free of it, and he looked up.

"Whoa," he whispered.

"Oh, gross," Felicity said.

They were in a large domed cavern about fifty feet high. Hundreds of the eerily glowing red snakes completely covered the ceiling and walls, crawling and swarming all over each other. Drops of the gelatin substance fell from the snakes' jaws onto the ground like a thick, sticky rain.

Hanging in the air in the middle of the cavern, surrounded by a spherical cloud of misty green Aura, was a pale-white gator-snake that was slightly larger than the red ones. It sported a pair of curved horns on its head and six long, insectlike limbs, four of which ended in pincers, the bottom two of which ended in birdlike claws. And below it was Greenseed, lying unconscious on a writhing pile of the red drone serpents.

The large white Lightsnake shrieked something in an unrecognizable tongue that did not translate. Joel was quite sure that whatever it was saying contained a fair amount of surprise and anger at seeing a surviving member of an enemy race long believed extinct.

"You're sure this is gonna be cool, right?" Felicity asked Joel out of the side of her mouth.

"Um—yeah, totally," Joel replied, trying to muster up as much reassurance in his voice as he could.

The white Lightsnake jerked its head around and waved its pincers menacingly. Every member of Joel's party jumped back a step except for Nineteen, who calmly spoke out loud in a similarly untranslated language. A conversation between the two ancient foes ensued,

SECRET OF THE SONGSHELL

lasting for several minutes before Nineteen's voice sounded once more in Joel's head.

This is the Queen of the Lightsnakes. I have negotiated a deal with her.

"All right, mate, so what are they saying?" Marshall asked. "Are they going to release Greenseed and let us get on with our business?"

"Um, what kind of deal?" Joel said, ignoring Marshall for the moment.

The queen knows that if she truly wanted to, she could command all of her drones to attack us, and we would not stand a chance.

Joel did not like the sound of that. "Uh—"

However, having been trapped in Prism Valley for all this time, she is...in a word, bored. She has agreed to play with us before she destroys us.

Nineteen paused. After three long seconds, Joel asked, "Um, what? Play with us? Okay—so, uh, what's the rest of the deal?"

That is it.

"That's it?" Joel blurted out.

Have faith, young one, Nineteen said in his smooth, relaxed tone. *Events will unfold in the manner in which they were meant to happen.*

Joel gulped. This certainly brought new meaning to his personal philosophy of "just go with it."

"So, what's this about a deal? What do we have to do?" Felicity asked.

"Um, we have to—play, uh, some kind of game, I guess." Joel improvised.

"Ah, I get it," Marshall said with a smile. "Some kind of challenge, correct? And if we win, we get Greenseed and go free?"

Joel hesitated, unsure of how to respond. He was let off the hook when Queen Lightsnake let out a loud, horrific scream that rattled the walls of the cavern.

She wants to begin with a riddle, Nineteen said.

Joel exhaled. A riddle, he figured they could handle. "Uh, the first game—it's—it's a riddle."

"Classic," Felicity snickered.

Joel sneezed. The temperature felt at least twenty degrees cooler here than on the island's normal surface. He caught himself wondering *why would snakes live here when reptiles usually like warmer climates?* before refocusing his attention on Nineteen's words, as the latter translated what the queen was saying.

"Okay, um, here we go," Joel told the others. "We are the same, yet different. We are united, then divided."

He sneezed again.

"Are you getting sick?" Felicity asked.

"Shh," Marshall hissed at her.

"We, uh, we are the living vision at the still river's edge," Joel continued, wiping his nose. "What are we?"

Marshall asked Joel to repeat the riddle, so he did. He also noticed that Greenseed seemed to have lost a lot of her color.

"The same, yet different," Marshall repeated again to himself as he rubbed his scar. "What the devil...Joel, does your cat-ram-whatever friend there know the answer? I can't think right now with all of this goop dripping on my head."

Before Joel had a chance to ask Nineteen, however, Felicity raised her hand as if she were in a classroom.

"Oh, wait, I got it: twins," she said. "That's the answer. Twins."

"Are you sure?" Marshall asked her, raising an eyebrow.

"No, I'm making stuff up so we can get killed," Felicity said with a tilt of her head. "Of course I'm sure."

"You'd better be right," Marshall scowled at her. "Okay, Joel—relay the answer."

Joel was already in the process of doing so as he glanced admiringly in Felicity's direction.

Your companion is rather wise, Nineteen said to him.

The pale snake raised her head and bared her fangs in what possibly could have been a smile. She said a few more things in her strange language.

"That's correct!" Joel raved before he sneezed again, twice.

"Not bad, huh?" Felicity said with a smug smile on her face.

"So, is that it?" Marshall muttered.

Joel felt his excitement vanish as Nineteen communicated the details of the subsequent challenge.

"Well, what now?" Marshall demanded, apparently noticing the sudden change in Joel's demeanor.

"Um, it's—it's a duel," Joel replied. "She, uh, she's challenging Felicity to a duel of some sort."

"A duel? With what? Wavebows at forty paces?" Felicity scoffed.

A humming, buzzing noise began to fill the air. The pale queen snake swelled to almost twice her original size, and then with a sickening, ripping sound, she split herself into two fully formed versions of herself, each with its own set of horns and elongated limbs.

"Hey, twins," Felicity said drily, with the comic timing of a cartoon coyote about to get blown up by a thousand tons of dynamite. "I get it."

The cocoon of green Aura surrounding the two queens melted away, and both creatures descended to the ground, using the pile of drone snakes below them as a stepping stool. The humming noise grew louder.

"What do I have to do?" Felicity yelled at Joel.

"I—um, I'm not—I'm not sure!" Joel stammered. "I can't really understand—"

"Well, forget this already," Marshall said, raising his wavebow. Before he was able to play anything on it, however, one of the queens dismissively waved a pincer, and his instrument went flying into a nearby pile of red drone snakes.

Joel's and Felicity's wavebows met the same fate a split second thereafter. Then, with another, slightly more complex pincer motion, all the travelers save for Felicity were flung through the air against the cavern walls, where they landed amongst swarms of the drone snakes, who immediately moved to restrain them. Joel nearly gagged as they slithered over his face and around his neck. He tried to pull them off but found his arms and legs bound by clusters of the snakes wrapping themselves around each other.

"At least they don't smell too badly," Marshall managed to say before he, too, was covered in the red reptiles.

The queens slowly advanced on Felicity, who took a few cautious steps backward while keeping her eyes firmly fixated on the twin snakes. With another wave of their pincers, the queens cleared the floor of drones, sending them—including the pile that Greenseed was on—all sliding into bunches up against the bottom of the cavern's perimeter.

They will engage her in hand-to-hand combat, Nineteen's voice said in a tone reminiscent of a golf announcer. *This is how all of our leaders perished. I hope your friend is as skilled with her limbs as she is with her mind.*

Joel tried to quell the rising sense of panic that he was starting to feel. He was not only worried for Felicity but also realized that he did not know what happened to Sammy after they were thrown against the wall. He struggled against the bonds that the drones formed around him, but to no avail.

Halting their approach, the queens raised their pincers, each of them striking something that resembled a mantis pose. Felicity apparently recognized what they were about to do and assumed her own defensive position.

Then, without warning, they struck. Felicity managed to deflect the first couple of blows, but the third one landed on her left arm and knocked her to the ground. She quickly rolled over and stood back up, but Joel could tell that she was hurt by the way she was grabbing her shoulder.

One of the queens took a huge swing that Felicity was able to duck under. Seizing the opportunity, Felicity connected with a kick to the queen's abdomen, which pushed it back a few steps but did not seem to do much harm otherwise. The other queen then attempted a kick of her own that Felicity dodged just in time.

Joel tried to ask Nineteen what Felicity should do, but he was unable to make a sound with a drone snake covering his mouth, and the telepathic communication channel apparently only worked one way. Since Nineteen did not proactively offer any suggestions on his own, Joel assumed that he had none.

Felicity baited each queen into approaching her from either side. Just as they were closing in, she executed a perfect backflip to move out of the way while the twins just managed to avoid crashing into each other. Their horns did get locked together for a few seconds, however, an interval that Felicity used to deliver a ferocious kick that sent both of them tumbling to the ground.

Joel was impressed. Felicity had shown him some basics when they were back at Spearwind, but he hadn't guessed that she was capable of moves like these.

As the fight wore on, though, it was becoming more and more obvious that Felicity's shoulder injury was beginning to wear on her. The queens pressed their advantage at every opportunity, and they did not seem to be getting tired at all.

They appear to be enjoying the contest, Nineteen said. *They have not had a challenge like this in some time. It is highly impressive that your friend has lasted this long—although it seems that she is slowly growing weaker.*

Joel tried again to free himself, but his movements just made the snakes squeeze him harder.

Felicity cried out in pain as she was hit again on the arm. A follow-up slash with a claw-foot struck her in the lower back, tearing through her tunic and opening up a long, shallow wound.

Joel's eyes went wide as Felicity crumpled to the ground. He doubled his efforts, straining mightily to move his arms and legs, but the result was something akin to a Chinese finger trap; the more he tried to get away, the tighter his bonds got.

Well, my friend, it was a good effort, Nineteen said with just the faintest hint of sadness.

Good effort? Joel thought furiously in his mind, even though he knew that Nineteen could not hear him. *What happened to "faith"?*

A memory came rushing into Joel's mind. Two years ago, a hamster named Nibbles that his science class kept as an unofficial pet became very ill. Everyone, including his teacher, was resigned to letting it quietly pass away. Joel, however, simply refused to accept this fate, having been conditioned into delusional stubbornness by the previous traumas in his life that he could not control or reverse. And so, Joel temporarily overcame his own social awkwardness and managed to raise enough money from his classmates and teacher to pay for an overnight vet visit for Nibbles, which ended up saving the little creature's life.

Never give up—how could I have forgotten?

Felicity scrambled to get up on one knee as the queens closed in. They could have finished her off right then and there, but instead, they circled around, regarding her like cats inspecting a dying mouse. They seemed almost disappointed that their little game was about to come to an end.

Joel figured that there was one last thing he could try. He let his body go completely limp as he stared off into space. Releasing his anxiety, he let his mind drift aimlessly for two full seconds before he started counting the red drone snakes covering the walls.

He barely got to one hundred (in another two seconds) when his senses were overwhelmed with an explosion of color and sound. His headache, which had subsided without him noticing, was suddenly back, stronger than before.

Just when he felt as if his skull was about to split open, he noticed something interesting: an elliptical spot on each of the queen's chests, right about where the heart would be on a human being, that seemed to pulse with a volatile, even combustible concentration of Aura energy. Something—an instinct, perhaps, or maybe wild conjecture—told him that a well-placed impact right on that spot could possibly...

His train of thought was interrupted by an uncontrollable urge to sneeze once again. He did so, almost violently. Whether his captor snakes were caught off guard by the lack of tension in his body, or by this strange, involuntary human action of nasal expulsion, he was not sure. But either way, he suddenly had a brief window of opportunity where his mouth had been freed up, and he went charging through.

"Felicity! The chest—hit them in the chest!" he yelled, his thoughts clearly and cleanly articulated.

The drone snakes, quickly realizing their mistake, slithered swiftly to cover Joel's face. He could feel them also tightening their grip around his torso, this time with the intent not to restrain but to crush the very life out of him.

In the brief instant before his line of sight was obscured by the red reptiles, Joel saw Felicity lash out with a vicious punch that landed squarely on the first queen's breastplate with a satisfying *crunch*. Then, a fraction of a second later, her foot whipped around in a furious arc that struck the other queen in the same exact location.

The queen serpents fell back, clutching at their chests with their pincers. The entire cavern began to shake with earthquake-like force. Joel gasped for air and slid to the ground as the drones released their grip on him.

Well done, Nineteen said, in a tone so casual that Joel wasn't sure if he was being sarcastic or not. Did strange tiger-ram creatures from an alien world (within another alien world) understand sarcasm?

Their lair is breaking apart. Its existence is dependent upon their personal Aura energies. They did not expect to lose.

The queen snakes fell to the ground. All of the red drone snakes began to wither and dry up like burning leaves. Joel saw Greenseed sit up and look around, obviously disoriented and startled by what she was seeing.

"Ha-*ha*!" Marshall exulted as he ran around, gathering up their wavebows. "Bloody things thought they could mess with us! Now, how do we get out of here?"

Joel ran over to Felicity, who had slumped back onto the ground, clutching her shoulder. Blood from her lower back was running down her legs.

"Are—are you all right?" he asked her as the cavern's shaking intensified.

She gave him a perturbed look that said *are you seriously asking me that?* before she broke into a smirk. "I'll live," she said.

"That was awesome!" Joel exclaimed. "You're great, seriously—"

"Yeah, yeah," Felicity said with a grimace as she tried to move her arm. "See, I told you I'm not the damsel-in-distress type."

Joel still wasn't quite sure what she meant by that, but he smiled anyway.

Greenseed came over to them, her supply pack still miraculously strapped around her waist.

"What happened? What is going on?" she asked.

You must leave immediately, Nineteen's voice echoed in Joel's head with absolutely no urgency whatsoever. *If you are still here when the Aura disintegrates, you will not survive.*

"Um, wait, where's Sammy?" Joel shouted. "We can't leave yet, we need to find him!"

I will attempt to rescue the silvertail, Nineteen said. *After I transport you and your friends out.*

"Wait—what? You can do that? What about you?" Joel asked. The cavern began to disintegrate into blurry fields of light and color.

Thanks to your valiant efforts, I can now access enough Aura energy from the Lightsnakes to perform such a feat. I will be fine. Where do you want to go?

"Joel! Can we get out of here or what?" Marshall yelled.

"Uh—Nineteen—he said he can transport us out now! Can we go back to Headsmouth? Felicity is hurt!"

"No, Fourfoot will kill us all! She'll just have to hold on!"

"But—"

"What good will healing her do if we're all dead?"

"I'm fine," Felicity said sternly as she tried to get to her feet. "Let's just go."

Marshall looked Joel directly in the eyes with such a frightening determination that Joel had to immediately turn away.

"Dragoneye," Marshall said. "Tell him we want to go to Dragoneye."

CHAPTER 17: DRAGONEYE

It dawned on Joel that he had now been transported three times: from Earth to Spectraland, from Spectraland to Prism Valley, and then back again. He started to wonder why *those* journeys were possible, and yet teleporting within Spectraland was not, as Marshall had assured him back when they were outside of the Wavemaker Temple. Wouldn't it basically be the same principle—just the shifting of matter from one area to another? In fact, wouldn't it be even easier, given that the state of the Aura seemed more or less the same all around the island? The no-flying explanation he could sort of understand, but there just didn't seem to be any logical consistency to the whole no-teleporting thing. He made a mental note to ask Marshall about it later, when he did not seem to be so upset.

"Why did that blasted creature have to send us down here, to the base?" Marshall ranted, his face red. "When I said Dragoneye, I meant *directly into the caldera*, not all the way down here. Now we have to navigate our bloody way in!"

Joel felt fortunate that Nineteen had at least saved them from the collapsing Lightsnakes' Lair, but Marshall did have a point. Although she put on a brave face, Felicity did look to be in some nonmarginal amount of pain. Joel wanted to get their mission completed as quickly as possible, so that she could get some medical attention.

"Um, how...how much more time do we have?" he asked cautiously.

"Looks like about two days," Marshall growled as he inspected the positions of the moons in the night sky. "Apparently, we lost almost a week in Prism Valley, even though it didn't feel that long. Must've been a time warp of some sort."

"Good thing we're here, then," Felicity said, grimacing.

"Yes...good thing..." Marshall said absently.

They entered a large lava tube that was fifteen feet high and just as wide. Its rocky, corrugated walls gave off a soft white glow without any apparent source of illumination. The air was warm and thick, like soup, and Joel could feel streams of sweat running down his forehead. Eventually, the tube split off into several different directions, and it soon became evident that they were in a maze.

"Are you sure you know where we're going?" Marshall snapped at Greenseed. He had not yet inquired as to her well-being, acting as if she had never been taken by the Lightsnakes.

"Yes, Master," Greenseed replied. "We will get there."

"We need to hurry," Marshall barked.

"Yeah, yeah, we know already," Felicity said, annoyed. "I thought we had a couple of days? What do you want us to do, start running? I think you're the only one who didn't get hurt by those stupid snakes."

Joel gingerly rubbed his ribs. Now that she had said that, he did notice that his breathing had been somewhat labored since he was released from the crushing grip of the drone serpents, and that the pain around his chest area had not yet dissipated.

"Just no more delays," Marshall said in a menacing tone that Joel had not heard before.

As they continued on in purposeful silence, Joel became aware of an uneasy feeling in the pit of his stomach. It was similar to when he was about to receive the results of a school test he knew he had failed, or when the other team's all-star came to bat with the bases loaded, down three in the bottom of the ninth—that foreboding feeling of inevitable, unavoidable disaster.

He wanted desperately to ask Marshall again about his volcano dream, but he recalled that Marshall asked him not to mention it again—especially in front of Felicity and Greenseed. In retrospect, he wasn't quite sure what the reasoning behind that request was, but he knew this was not the time to be broaching the subject.

Joel glanced over at Marshall. There was definitely something different about him—where before he had always seemed carefree and casual, even in the most precarious of situations, he now gave off a vibe of agitated, uptight intensity, like a starving dog eyeing up a steak that was just beyond its reach. Joel chalked it up to anxiety over being so close to their final goal; probably the same reason that he, himself, was not feeling quite right.

They rounded a corner. A large pile of rocks and silvery straw-like reeds assembled together in a bowl-shaped formation blocked their way. Joel heard tiny squeaking and chattering noises coming from the bowl and was suddenly reminded of Sammy. He hoped that his little friend was safe, and that Nineteen would be sending him back to them soon.

"What—is—this?" Marshall bellowed. "I thought you knew where we were going?"

"Master, please," Greenseed said in a hushed tone. "This is a sunlion nest. They live here in the volcano."

"They're gonna die here in the volcano if they don't get out of my way," Marshall growled.

"Master, they are normally good-natured, but they can be very territorial if provoked. We need to proceed carefully—"

But Marshall was not listening to her at this point. He had already drawn his wavebow, and with a quick, aggressive riff, a red wave burst forth and blew open a large hole in the middle of the nest. Tiny bits of rock flew everywhere, and Joel raised his hands in front of his face to deflect them.

When he lowered his hands a couple of seconds later, Joel saw a veritable river of small, lizard-like creatures pouring out of the remains of their nest.

"We need to go!" Greenseed shouted. She and Marshall led the way as they jumped over the swarming creatures, who were now squealing like an army of frightened pigs.

Joel and Felicity followed. Several sunlions had latched on to his legs as he tried to leap over them, and one of them sank its tiny, pointed teeth into his ankle. Joel howled in pain. He swatted at the creature and managed to dislodge it. As he glanced back, he saw that the rapidly growing pile of sunlions had quadrupled in size, nearly filling up the entire bottom half of the lava tube.

Marshall stopped, turned, and fired a quick succession of red bolts into the pile, momentarily stemming their tide. Felicity was about to do the same when Greenseed grabbed her by the arm.

"No! Stop!" the tiny native cried. "It is futile—there may be millions of them—your energy will run out. We just need to keep going!"

Forcing himself to ignore the burning sensation in his leg, Joel turned and broke into a run, as did the rest of them. The flood of sunlions now filled up the tube from top to bottom, and their cacophonous squealing was nearly drowned out by the thunderous rumbling caused by their cascade.

"So now we're running. Happy?" Felicity yelled at Marshall.

They continued to run even as the tube started to take on a noticeable incline, which did nothing to slow down the onrushing flood of lizards. The pain in Joel's leg was getting worse, and he was not sure how much longer he could keep up. At one point, he stumbled and had to be quickly propped up by Felicity, who winced as she used her bad arm to grab him.

The tube twisted and turned, and the incline got steeper and steeper. In addition to everything else, Joel's side was now aching, and every breath he drew was a chore. He and Felicity were lagging behind Greenseed and Marshall, who both momentarily disappeared from sight as they rounded a corner.

"I—I can't make it," Joel panted. His leg was throbbing. His chest was burning. The lizards were almost upon them.

"C'mon! You have to! Don't give up now!" Felicity shouted at him.

She's right—don't give up.

Fueled by Felicity's words, Joel clenched his jaw and pushed forward. They rounded the corner, just in time to witness a series of events that seemed to occur in slow motion.

The tube ended in an opening, beyond which Joel could see nothing but billowing columns of white smoke. Greenseed and Marshall came to an abrupt stop. Greenseed turned her head, as if she were about to say something. Marshall bumped into her. She fell forward, disappearing from Joel's view. He heard a scream that got progressively softer until it could be heard no more.

Felicity and Joel scrambled up to where Marshall stood, on a ledge overlooking an enormous caldera, about three hundred feet above the crater's surface. Joel looked out and saw a pile of large rocks but no sign of Greenseed. Marshall turned, raised his wavebow, and began firing at the oncoming lizards.

"What happened?" Joel yelled, still frantically searching for any sign of their native companion.

"No time!" Marshall yelled back. "We'll need to levitate each other down to the base! Quickly!"

Joel and Felicity glanced at each other. Without a word, Felicity wrapped Joel in a sheath of green light and lowered him to the crater's surface next to the pile of rocks. For a second, Joel noticed a strange blurriness in the Aura around the rock pile, but he chalked it up to heat shimmer and fired a levitation cast up to the ledge. A few seconds later, Felicity touched down next to him.

"You bring Marshall down, I'll look for Greenseed!" he yelled, with a sureness and authority that surprised even himself. Felicity nodded.

He searched around the pile of rocks, climbing over some and lifting some of the others, but there was no trace of Greenseed—no body, no supply sack. Joel began to have a sinking suspicion that both her fall and her disappearance were not accidental.

There was no more time to contemplate any conspiracy theories, however, as Felicity had swiftly floated Marshall off of the ledge and down to where she stood. On his way down, Marshall played an unusually loud chord that caved in the opening of the tube in front of the lizards, blocking most of them. The few that trickled out ended up plummeting to the surface, where they landed with a *plop* and did not move thereafter.

"Over there!" Marshall shouted, pointing his finger toward the middle of the caldera, where the largest column of smoke was originating from. "The White Fire Pool!"

For the first time since he was bitten by the sunlion, Joel looked down at his ankle. It was bright red and horribly swollen, and the bite mark itself was foaming. Suppressing an urge to gag, he looked away from the wound and moved as quickly as he could to follow Marshall, who was now positively sprinting toward the center of the crater.

As Joel trailed after Marshall with Felicity beside him, he noticed that their surroundings looked almost exactly like those in his dreams: the trails of white and silver lava, the columns of smoke, the thick waves of red and orange Aura in the air. Rocks and stalagmites were scattered about the otherwise barren surface, and the night sky shone with the light from the twin moons. He looked around for a mysterious, malicious figure, but there was no one there besides the three of them.

The heat became more and more unbearable the closer they got to the fire pool, which was circular, fifty feet in diameter, and filled with a bubbling platinum liquid. They stopped thirty feet away from the pool's edge, unable to get any closer without baking themselves. Smoke was everywhere, making Joel's eyes water and his chest sting with every effort-filled breath. He slumped over and rested his hands on his thighs.

"We're here!" Marshall said giddily with a manic smile on his face. "We made it!"

"Yeah, but now what?" Felicity said, dropping to one knee. Joel looked at her, and it was obvious that she was in just as much physical pain as he was at that moment.

"We need to get closer," Marshall said as he pulled the crusty brown Songshell from his vest. He seemed very distracted and lost in his own thoughts. "But how?"

"I dunno—shield cast? Freezing cast?" Joel suggested, wanting more than ever to get this ordeal over with.

"Good idea," Marshall said with such an intense gaze that Joel had to instantly look away.

Marshall slowly walked toward the pool as he attempted a variety of shield and freezing casts to ward off the heat, but none were effective enough.

"Ah, I know," he said. He placed the Songshell on the ground and played his wavebow, wrapping the shell in a cocoon of green light. As he levitated the shell toward the pool, he turned to face Joel and Felicity.

"You two, help me do this," he commanded.

"What? Why?" Felicity asked.

"Just do it!" Marshall barked in a voice that Joel recognized from the harshest, heaviest Biledriver songs.

Joel and Felicity stood up without moving any closer to Marshall, who now looked completely maniacal with his hair in his face and his teeth bared like a wolf about to devour its prey. They shakily cast their own green waves onto the shell, and the three of them slowly moved it over the smoking pool.

"Now," Marshall growled, "lower it—slowly!—into the magma."

Joel felt a mixture of fear and confusion as he did what he was told. They were finally about to accomplish their goal (for real this time, he hoped)—so why did something feel so strange, so...not right?

He glanced at Felicity, whose expression mirrored his misgivings. He recited a few lists in his head, to see if the Sight would show him anything that would confirm his concerns, but there was nothing significant there as far as he could tell.

Then he realized why Marshall wanted all of them to levitate the shell together; the second it touched the pale magma, it started to sink, quickly and heavily, as if it were being pulled down by a magnetic force at the bottom of the fire pool. Plumes of colored smoke hissed out at the shell's point of contact. The three of them yanked up on their wavebows like they were fishermen reeling in a gigantic shark, barely managing to maintain their holds on the shell—if only one of them were levitating it, it surely would have been lost.

For a moment, they all stared at the Songshell. Or, more precisely, the bottom half of it, which began to gleam with a bright, majestic silver light as the magma dripped off.

"Again! Carefully this time," Marshall ordered. Slowly and deliberately, they once again lowered the shell into the pool. Joel braced himself against the magma's pull as a searing pain shot up and down his leg. He fought to maintain a solid hold on the shell as they fully submerged it beneath the surface and clouds of colored smoke blew past his face. After a few seconds, Joel felt a sensation of the shell "locking" itself into place.

"Now, play the same routine that I taught you for your concert back at Headsmouth," Marshall snapped.

"Are you kidding?" Felicity shouted.

"Do it!" Marshall yelled so loudly that Joel winced.

Somehow summoning up a third wind, Joel numbly went through the various notes and chords that he had memorized for the performance that seemed to take place so long ago. This time, there were no obvious pyrotechnics or effects; each of the different colors and waves simply jetted out in a straight line directly into the magma pool. More plumes of smoke poured out, making Joel's eyes water as they wafted over him.

Marshall grinned widely after their routine was complete. "All right, now levitate it back up!"

Joel fired out a green stream of light. Weakened by his injuries and exhausted from performing the routine, however, Joel felt his Aura energy rapidly slipping away, and with it, his tenuous grip on the Songshell. His arms began to shake, and he started to lose his footing.

"Up! Bring it up!" Marshall yelled.

Joel dug deep. With one last burst of energy, he pulled up on his wavebow. A blinding light came shooting out of the fire pool amidst a mushroom cloud of smoke.

With the pain too much to bear, Joel's leg finally gave out, and he collapsed to the ground, dropping his instrument. When he looked up a few seconds later, he had to squint to shield his eyes from the brilliant glow emanating from Marshall's left hand. All seemed strangely silent, except for a faint humming sound in the air that was not there before.

Marshall brought the new Songshell up to his eye level, seemingly unaffected by its blazing radiance. With a triumphant expression on his face, he turned the shell around in his palm, inspecting it as one would a cherished childhood toy.

Joel would have exhaled a huge sigh of relief, except that he felt like he was going to pass out from the pain.

"Thank you very, very much—both of you," Marshall said softly. "You've been great."

An alarm went off in Joel's head.

Marshall pocketed the shell—an act that, for a moment, seemed to extinguish all the light in the caldera, even that of the twin moons above. He raised his wavebow. "But, well, it's time for me to go solo."

It is amazing what can happen in a single second. You can say the word "one," followed by the entire four-syllable, eleven-letter name of the twentieth state of the United States of America. Members of a basketball team can throw an inbounds pass, catch it, turn, then shoot the ball twenty-five feet through the air into the hoop and win the game. A neuron in the human brain can fire a thousand times.

Likewise, the next few events happened within the span of a second: Joel's eyes grew wide. A bright red wave shot out of Marshall's instrument and streaked directly at Joel's face. From off to Joel's right, a yellow burst of light flew in and formed a shield in front of him that absorbed Marshall's blast. Joel turned his head and saw Felicity, who had just saved his life.

Marshall turned and redirected his assault at her. She played a loud chord that expanded the golden shield into an umbrella-like semicircle that covered her and Joel at the same time. Fueled by adrenalin and anger at Marshall's betrayal, Joel worked up the strength to pick up his wavebow and fire off a stunning cast at the man who had been his idol. Taken by surprise, Marshall dodged but could not get completely out of the way in time. The cast grazed his arm, and he dropped his wavebow, which landed with a clatter at his feet.

"Stop!" Joel yelled as Marshall bent over, reaching for his instrument. Joel's lower lip was trembling as he felt an angry fog drifting into his head. He fought back the impulse to blast Marshall straight out of the crater. "Why are you doing this?"

Felicity halted her shield cast and took a cautious step forward, keeping her wavebow trained on Marshall. "You used us," she said to him in a steely voice that was full of hurt and resentment. "There is no Fourfoot, is there? You just made all of this up so that we would help you get this stupid shell!"

"No, really?" Marshall sneered mockingly, holding his palms forward and out in a defensive, semisurrender gesture. "I'm glad you figured it out on your own, my dear. For a second there, I was afraid I would have to do one of those movie-style bad guy monologues."

"Well, this isn't a movie, but it's gonna have a happy ending," she said, raising her wavebow.

"Perhaps," Marshall said, "for one of us."

In an instant, Joel noticed a flicker of movement—Marshall was about to reach into his vest. Joel strummed a chord and let fly a wide red wave at Marshall, who simultaneously drew out the gleaming Songshell and held it out in front of him. Felicity followed with a red wave of her own.

The Songshell immediately swallowed up both casts like a vacuum. Its pure silver-white sheen turned blood-red, and the humming in the air grew louder. The shell shook violently in Marshall's hand, and, for a moment, he seemed unsure of what was going to happen next.

But then he regained his composure and gripped the shell tightly with both hands. He aimed it at Joel and Felicity, who glanced at each other.

"Run!" Joel cried.

They turned and managed to run eleven whole yards before a huge red light wave came pouring out of the shell, which, because it was still vibrating wildly, spoiled Marshall's aim. The light wave crashed into the ground, setting off a large explosion that sent all three of them hurtling through the air.

Joel landed on his back, missing a trail of white magma by inches. He groaned and forced himself into a sitting position. Smoke was everywhere, and now the surface of the crater itself was beginning to tremble. He looked for Felicity but could not see her.

"Felicity!" he called out. It hurt so much to speak that he collapsed back onto the ground.

Then, a few seconds later, he saw a red bolt of light flash through the air. Then another, and another, all heading in the same direction—his.

"Heeere's Johnny!" Marshall's voice rang out from somewhere behind the smoke. The agitated Aura carried his words through the air and made him sound like he was speaking through a fuzz box. "C'mon, kids, come out to play! Let's jam, shall we? Rock 'n' roll! Free Bird! Wooo!"

Joel scrambled to his feet and ran. His injured leg had gone numb, so he didn't notice that he had stepped into a spot of magma until his leggings had caught on fire. The trembling grew stronger, and through the smoke, he saw other fountains of white fire begin to erupt out of the ground. Red bolts of light continued to streak by, one of them narrowly missing his head.

"The place is gonna blow! Good night, everybody!" Marshall's voice yelled from a distance. The red bolts stopped.

Marshall has left the building, Joel grimly thought to himself in a moment of dark humor.

Joel dropped to the ground and rolled, but the fire stubbornly refused to go out. Joel closed his eyes and wondered which would finish him off first. The fire? His injured and probably infected leg? His broken ribs? Smoke inhalation? Third-degree burns? The entire caldera erupting?

Then, through the smoke and his own blurry vision, he thought he saw an unfamiliar Aura outline of a small figure rushing toward him.

"Felicity?" he said weakly, even though he knew it was not her.

Dizziness set in, followed by a major feeling of *deja vu,* which he barely managed to recognize before he blissfully escaped into unconsciousness.

CHAPTER 18: FIREFLOWER'S TALE

Within the darkness there floated an amoeba-shaped spot of bright light, like what you see with your eyes closed after looking too closely at the sun. The spot shifted its form several times as it swam around aimlessly. Joel sensed warmth coming from the spot, although it was not a physical warmth, or anything that he could detect with his normal five senses; instead, it was just something that he knew was there, an awareness independent of regular human perception.

He tried to move toward the spot, but movement, as he was familiar with it, was irrelevant. It was as if he were already there, encased in the light's warm glow, able to stretch out his thoughts and feelings within its infinite borders. In fact, he *was* the light, and the light was him.

Could this be what death is like? he wondered. *And if so, why can I still think these thoughts to myself? Does that mean there is consciousness after death?*

He recalled reading somewhere the idea that the supply of energy in the universe was finite. Whether that was a religious belief or a scientific hypothesis was a detail that oddly escaped him at the moment, but either way, if it was true, could it be that all of the Aura energy that was visible here on Spectraland was interconnected somehow, and that death was merely a release of one's energy into the greater whole?

This train of thought started to make Joel somewhat excited, as he felt that he was stumbling onto a major discovery. He was actually somewhat disappointed, then, when the light suddenly vanished and his physical eyes fluttered open. He felt himself lying on a hard surface that was shaking like a vibrating bed.

Hovering above him was the light-green face of an unfamiliar native. Her features were stern and handsome, and she projected a reassuring air of confidence and knowledge unlike any of the other natives that Joel had met so far.

"You are fine now," she said in a voice that sounded remarkably like Greenseed's. "We need to find Felicity and get out of here as quickly as possible."

Joel sat up and saw that he was still in the caldera. His clothes were no longer on fire, and all of the pain in his body was gone. The native helped him stand, and as he did so, he saw that his sunlion-bitten leg looked completely normal.

"Um, who—what—" he stammered.

"I will explain later," she said, handing him his wavebow with one hand. In her other hand she carried another wavebow that looked similar to his, except that its body had a shiny jet-black finish with faint streaks of various colors running up and down its surface. She plucked a two-note chord on it, generating a loud, piercing tone, and a spot of bright green light appeared about thirty yards away, clearly visible through a wall of smoke.

"Over there," the native said before she dashed off. Joel scrambled to keep up.

They reached the source of the light, which turned out to be Felicity, lying on the ground in a crumpled heap. The native with Greenseed's voice knelt beside her and played a short progression of lush, complex chords. The green light disappeared and was replaced with a pulsating golden Aura.

After five seconds, give or take, Felicity opened her eyes and raised her head. The golden glow quickly dissipated.

"Your injuries are healed," the native said to her. "We must leave this place immediately. The volcano is going to erupt."

"Who are you?" Felicity asked as she stood up, looking back and forth between the native and Joel with a confused expression on her face.

"I am Fireflower," the native replied. "Follow me—this way."

Fireflower took off running. Joel shrugged in response to Felicity's questioning glance before he turned and followed the mysterious native through the smoke.

"Wait—my wavebow! I lost it!" Felicity yelled as she trailed behind. Joel heard a ringing note originating from Fireflower's direction, and a second later, a wavebow came flying through the air. Joel turned his head just in time to see Felicity catch it in midstride.

"Whoa—nice!" he said.

"Hurry!" Fireflower yelled without looking back.

Joel sped up and almost lost his balance as the shaking of the ground intensified even more. Fountains of silver magma started to spring up around them, and the smoke was so thick that he had to fixate on Fireflower's Aura glow in order not to lose her.

He thought about how much easier it was to run with no pain in his leg, and with the ability to breathe free and easy. Then he remembered Marshall's betrayal, and he suddenly felt very angry. How could his idol, his hero, take advantage of him like that? For years Joel had looked up to and tried to emulate this person, studying everything he wrote, said, wore, and thought. Joel truly felt as if he knew Marshall, inside and out, before he even met him. As it turned out, Joel realized that he had never really known him at all.

Momentarily lost in thought, Joel almost crashed into Fireflower as she came to an abrupt stop. She played a couple of chords, and Joel heard the sound of rocks crumbling as the smoke around them cleared away. He saw that they had arrived at the edge of the caldera, and that she had opened up a passageway in the rock wall. She turned her head to make sure Joel and Felicity saw her, and then she ducked into the hole she had created.

Joel followed. It was pitch black for a second, but then Fireflower lit up her wavebow so brightly that Joel didn't feel the need to do the same. They were in a narrow tunnel that looked like a miniature version of the lava tube they used when they first entered the mountain. They ran through its twisting, downward-sloping path for several minutes while the rumbling of the volcano continued.

Then the rumbling stopped.

Fireflower turned around, her eyes wide. "Get down!" she cried.

Joel heard an enormous explosion coming from nearby. He instinctively covered his ears with his hands and dropped to the ground. The tunnel shook with tremendous force, and bits of rock fell from its roof.

Moments later, the shaking subsided. An acrid smell, similar to the scent of the smoke in the caldera, wafted through the tunnel. Joel felt like the temperature had suddenly gone up twenty degrees.

"She has erupted—the lava is coming down the tunnel," Fireflower declared.

The three of them immediately stood up and continued running. Joel could hear what sounded like the rush of an oncoming river.

Lizards going up, lava coming down. Why are we always being chased by something? And why do those things have to move so dang fast? And why am I asking myself questions like these? Felicity must be rubbing off on me.

The tunnel straightened out. About a football-field length ahead, it seemed to go no further.

"Um—is this a dead end?" Joel asked as he skidded to a stop.

"Just keep going," Fireflower replied.

Joel looked back and saw a smoking flood of silver lava bearing down on them at a much greater speed than any lava flow he'd ever seen before (on video—he'd actually never seen a lava flow in person). He turned and continued running.

As he got closer to the end of the tunnel, he saw that it did not terminate in a solid wall, but rather, in an opening that led to (yet another) sheer drop.

"Do not worry!" Fireflower yelled as they approached the opening. "Just jump!"

In a fraction of a second, Joel concluded that this unfamiliar native would probably not be tricking them into leaping to their deaths, given the fact that she could have easily killed them or left them to die back in the caldera. The lava was almost upon them when he closed his eyes and launched himself off of the edge.

He expected the sensation of falling to end quickly, but it did not. He opened his eyes and saw that they were still hundreds of feet above the ground, where a jungle of yellow palm trees awaited. Oddly, he did not feel the urge to scream. He looked over at his companions and saw that they were similarly calm.

We really must be getting used to this, he thought.

He looked up and saw the lava pouring out of the side of the volcano like a waterfall of the regular downward variety. Fortunately, the act of jumping out of the opening put them on a different trajectory than the lava, thus ensuring that they wouldn't get burned to a crisp once they hit the ground—which, because of Joel's trust in Fireflower, was something that he assumed they would survive.

Sure enough, once they were about fifty feet from the surface, Fireflower played a few chords on her wavebow. Suddenly, Joel felt the air below them growing thicker, as if they were falling through syrup. Moments later, they floated safely to the ground amidst a cluster of yellow palms. The lava-fall landed a relatively safe distance away, setting a different group of trees on fire.

"Well, that was fun," Felicity said, dusting herself off.

"Thanks for saving us, uh—Fireflower?" Joel said.

"After you risked your lives rescuing me from the Lightsnakes, I was convinced that your hearts were in the right place," she responded.

Joel gave her a funny look. "Uh—wait, what?"

"Ohh—you're Greenseed!" Felicity said with a faint hint of a smile. "I thought your voice sounded familiar."

"Um, but how did you—why didn't—"

Fireflower turned and started to head off. "We need to catch up with him. I will tell you everything along the way."

"Him?" Joel asked. His head was spinning.

"Marshall," Felicity answered for Fireflower. Then, calling after the native, she said, "Do we have to worry about the fire?"

"The trees will eventually recover. They have been through worse before," Fireflower said, ducking under a cluster of large, low-hanging fronds. "Right now, we have a much bigger problem."

Joel ran to catch up with her. "How—how are we going to catch him?"

Fireflower emerged from behind the fronds. Right behind her, a pale, yellow amphibian head poked out and croaked a warm greeting.

Joel broke into a wide grin. "Destiny!"

♪♪♪

Reunited with their slimebacks, Joel, Felicity, and Fireflower (née Greenseed) charged through the island terrain as quickly as their mounts' legs would allow. Prior to their departure, Fireflower had performed a complex incantation allowing her to communicate telepathically with Joel and Felicity, alleviating the need for her to shout her story at them as they traveled.

Twenty minutes into their journey, this is what Joel had learned:

There really is—or was—a native leader named Fourfoot. Three years ago, Spectraland time, he was the new young Chief of the village of Nightshore. For reasons unknown to Fireflower, he became inspired to unite the four main villages under his leadership. A civil war broke out on the historically peaceful island.

A handful of Wavemakers lived in each village, serving as general peacekeepers and healers. The Wavemaker Elders back at the temple issued a directive for them to remain neutral in the conflict. This proved to be rather difficult, however. Not only did they have friends and families who lived in their villages, but they had also developed loyalties to their chiefs, who had been granted measures of authority over their village's shamans by the Elder Council.

Eventually, the Wavemakers of Nightshore decided to ignore the Elders' directive. They began to assist with the war effort, using their abilities to gain an advantage for their village. This drew the shamans of the other villages into the conflict.

The other three villages—Headsmouth, Spearwave, and Bluecrest—joined forces to put an end to Fourfoot's campaign. With their combined strength, they quickly achieved the upper hand in the war and were moving to finish it off. Desperate, one of the Nightshore shamans uncovered an old and forbidden incantation which allowed him to scan the universe for others with similar— or stronger—powers, and to open a portal by which he could bring them over.

And thus, Marshall Byle came to Spectraland.

Normally, Fireflower explained, *Wavemakers are identified and trained from the time they are infants. Marshall received some very quick, basic training— similar to what the two of you received—and then it was off to fight.*

But how could someone who had so little experience defeat others who had a lifetime of it? Joel asked.

He had one ability that the rest of us did not: the ability to kill.

Oh, Joel thought.

Fireflower paused before explaining. *The Aura is highly resistant to wavecasts that purposely release additional energy—the energy of life—into its folds. That fact, along with the moral concepts that all Wavemakers learned and lived by, had always served to prevent us from destroying other living creatures.*

Marshall, however, was bound by neither restriction. With his help, Nightshore turned the tide. In the final battle, I was gravely wounded, and my body lay comatose at the bottom of a ditch.

After I awoke, possibly months later, I returned to find that Marshall had killed Fourfoot and taken over as High Chief of the Four Villages. The other Wavemakers had also been killed off, and our temple was ravaged, as you saw.

To protect myself, I—

Fireflower paused again. Joel looked at her and saw an expression on her face that seemed to communicate great sorrow. He had an urge to stop and comfort her, but as she continued to press on, urging her slimeback to maintain their rapid pace, he did so as well.

I—assumed the form of my younger sister, Greenseed. She was not a Wavemaker, but a servant to our chief, and both of them were killed in that final battle.

I also suppressed my Aura presence so that Marshall would not be able to detect me. I knew that he would destroy any surviving shamans that he discovered.

Everyone seemed so accepting of him, though—why is that? Felicity asked.

He had learned of an incantation that clouded the memories of everyone on the island. It was a grand deception, although it had no effect on me, because of my training.

And so, I assumed my sister's former position as a servant, figuring that I could stay close to him until an opportunity to vanquish him arose—but such a chance never quite arrived. He was very careful to protect himself, and I could not risk using my powers, even in the smallest fashion, lest he discover my identity.

They had exited the yellow palm jungle and were now riding through a vast swath of open field. The alien sun blazed as it rose over the horizon. Joel wondered for a moment why he did not feel tired, as he hadn't slept in days.

When I healed you in the caldera, I also eliminated your fatigue, Fireflower explained.

Ah, gotcha, Joel thought in response.

One day, Fireflower continued, *purely by chance, I happened to stumble upon Marshall as he was formulating a plan. He had learned of the Secret of the Songshell. He wanted to gain its power.*

For what? Felicity asked. *Seems like he already had all the power he needed here.*

Precisely. He grew bored...discontent. With the Songshell, he would be able to store enough Aura energy to maintain his powers back in his homeworld—your homeworld.

Wow, okay, Joel thought, *that's not good.*

No, you think? Felicity thought back. *Just imagine if he—hey, wait, Joel. You talk a lot clearer when you're thinking.*

Yeah, 'cause I know what I want to say in my head—I just have trouble getting that to my mouth. He turned to face Fireflower. *So Marshall already has the shell. Does that mean we're too late?*

Not yet, Fireflower replied. *But we must catch him before the Nadir arrives. He is taking the shell to*

Crownrock, a tiny offshore islet where the Aura concentration is very high. Once there, he will attempt to absorb all of Spectraland's energies—an act that will surely spell the end of life on the island.

Suddenly Joel felt very guilty. *This is my fault*, he thought. *Marshall wouldn't have recovered the shell without my help. I was caught up in chasing my stupid dream, believing in him, thinking that I could—*

"Stop that!" Felicity audibly shouted at him. "You need to stop blaming yourself. You need to stop being sorry all the time. What happened, happened! And I was just as involved too. He tricked us. Now let's go fix this thing!"

Joel looked at her, this time maintaining eye contact for two full seconds. He set his jaw and nodded.

You're right, he thought.

Of course I am, she replied, her mouth upturned ever so slightly at one corner.

As they continued to ride, Fireflower answered as many of their questions as she could.

She admitted that she did not trust them at first, believing that they were Marshall's otherworldly friends, there to not only help him recover the Songshell but to share in its power as well.

She admitted that she knew most of what Marshall was telling them was a lie—which was a bit confusing to her, seeing as how she originally thought that they were friends with him—but she did not say anything, as she wanted to see the quest through to its completion, then possibly wrest the Songshell away from Marshall.

She admitted that she caused Joel's wavebow to become lost back at the Caves of Wrath, necessitating a journey to the tree of the Luthier. She had disappeared at that time in order to gain a new wavebow of her own, which she kept hidden in her pack.

She admitted that she sent the slimebacks away, asking them to wait near the base of Dragoneye in the expectation that they would be needed—and she was right.

She did not expect to be kidnapped by the Lightsnakes.

She did not expect that Marshall would try to kill her by pushing her off of the ledge at the caldera. Fortunately, he was too occupied with thoughts of reforging the shell to notice her use of a wavecast to save herself. She had, however, been knocked unconscious, which prevented her from coming to their aid sooner.

After this last bit of information, the telepathy cast wore off, and Fireflower decided to spend some time recharging her energy. At any rate, Joel and Felicity felt satisfied with their new level of knowledge, so they rode along in relative silence as the day passed by.

One day until the Nadir

The shock and disbelief at everything that Marshall had done really began to sink in now. Joel choked a little when he recalled what had happened to Suntooth. The helpful native had been possessed all right—not by Fourfoot, but by Marshall himself! And then, after Marshall had used him as his talking puppet, he simply disposed of him with no remorse whatsoever.

Joel felt his anger rising again. His hands started to shake. He couldn't wait to confront his "hero" and take out all of his hurt and frustration on him.

"Um, how much longer to Crownrock?" he asked, a bit testily, when they had slowed to a trot.

"A few hours," Fireflower replied. "Fortunately, we are not very far behind. Based on the tracks I have seen, he is riding on a scaletop, which are much slower creatures."

"Our creatures seem to be getting a little tired," Felicity said, patting Dreamer on the neck. Dreamer turned her head and nibbled at Felicity's hand. "And hungry, I think."

"We will be passing close to Nightshore soon," Fireflower said. "We can make a very quick stop for supplies. We can still reach Crownrock by dawn."

"Nightshore? Um, isn't that the village that started the whole war?"

"They will not be hostile now. Marshall placed the entire island under his memory cloud."

As they entered an area populated by a variety of trees and other assorted flora, Joel recalled something that his Uncle Dave (who was not really his uncle, but his dad's friend) always used to say: "And now that you've said that..." This statement was Uncle Dave's way of expressing his superstitious belief that a confident declaration of an optimistic outlook is almost always followed by an event that proves the declaration wrong; for example, saying "it won't rain—it hasn't rained in weeks" will invite six inches of torrential downpour the very next day. Or saying "our team's quarterback is so durable" will guarantee said player's ticket to the injured reserve list.

So it was with this thought in mind that Joel began to have an uneasy feeling. And whether it was due to instinct, superstition, the Aura, or whatever, Uncle Dave was soon proven right once again.

CHAPTER 19: NIGHTSHORE

They appeared, seemingly out of nowhere, from all directions. First, Joel felt his wavebow get snatched away. Then, with a few swift, efficient motions by their attackers, he was pulled off of Destiny and hogtied with lengths of thin, wiry rope that chafed his skin when he struggled against them. His head was wrapped in a smelly mesh cloth that clung to his face, allowing him to breathe and hear but not to see or speak. Right before that, he had managed to catch a glimpse of their assailants: short, muscular natives wearing only leggings and abstract war paint designs on their faces and chests. He heard one of them speak.

"Well done," it said in a voice that sounded like it had been gargling gravel and glass shards. "Take them back."

Joel felt himself being lifted and carried. He felt leaves and branches brushing his sides as he was carted off to some unknown destination. He heard no further voices until thirteen minutes later, when he was unceremoniously dumped onto warm, hard ground.

"Remove their—*hic*—masks," a familiar voice said in a soft, serpentine tone.

A gruff pair of hands grabbed the edges of the mesh cloth by Joel's jawline and peeled it off like an old bandage. Another pair of hands raised him up into a kneeling position. Joel's eyesight took a second to adjust, and when it did, he furrowed his brow in anger at what he saw.

Standing a few feet in front of them was a wrinkled and scarred native with an empty eye socket that resembled an endless cavern.

"Hello, offworlders," Darkeye purred. "And Fireflower! What a nice—*hic*—surprise. I thought you were killed at the Battle of Red—*hic*—Gulch."

"Release us, Darkeye," Fireflower growled. "We have urgent business that is bigger than any of us."

Darkeye smiled broadly, revealing a mouth that was absent all of its teeth. "You refer to Chief Byle and the—*hic*—Songshell, I believe?"

Joel's muscles tensed. Fireflower did not respond.

"Oh, I know all about your—*hic*—'urgent business,' as you say."

"Then you know that we're trying to save your island, you idiot!" Felicity snapped. "So let us go!"

Darkeye recoiled mockingly. "Such a feisty—*hic*—child, when not rendered inert by the bloomfish poison!"

"You'll find out just how feisty if you don't let us go right now," Felicity snarled.

"Remember, my dear, I—*hic*—saved your life with my antidote. You should be bowing to me in—*hic*—gratitude."

"Um, she doesn't have to thank you," Joel said. "We paid your price."

"A price that was—*hic*—duly refunded," Darkeye said as he gestured toward the slimebacks, who were being held a few feet away by several of the war-painted natives.

"If you know what Byle is planning to do," Fireflower said, "then you know that you are wasting valuable time. We need to stop him before he steals all of Spectraland's Aura."

"Ah, but that is precisely the—*hic*—point. You see, Chief Byle negotiated a new deal with me to get your—*hic*—trusty mounts back."

As Darkeye spoke, Joel looked around at his surroundings. He saw the familiar trappings of a village—tree houses, huts, and so forth—but they all looked a bit more damaged and ill-maintained than the ones in Headsmouth and Spearwave. Standing near Joel and his friends were fifteen of the burly natives who had kidnapped them, eight of whom carried elaborately carved wooden spears that were pointed toward their heads.

There has to be a way to escape, he figured. *This whole thing so far has been like a movie, so don't the good guys always manage to escape situations like this and win in the end?*

"Chief Byle believed that he would—*hic*—kill all of you once he recovered the Songshell," Darkeye continued. "But being the wise man that he is, he—*hic*—needed a contingency plan in case his efforts to eliminate you were—*hic*—less than successful."

"Will you get to the point, already?" Felicity snapped.

"The point"—Darkeye grinned—"is that he had me—*hic*—come here, to Nightshore, to intercept and kill you, if you—*hic*—made it this far."

That's why Marshall never told us how he got the slimebacks back, Joel realized.

"Wow, what a great deal," Felicity said, her voice reeking with sarcasm. "Return our rides *and* do his dirty work? You really got the best of him there."

Darkeye started to walk around them in a circle. "Ah, but here is the rest of my—*hic*—story. In return for those favors, Chief Byle has promised to take me with him, back to your world, where I understand there exists many opportunities for a master alchemist—*hic*—such as myself."

"What?" Felicity nearly laughed. "You'd be a freak— an alien. The military would lock you up and do all kinds of experiments on you."

"And, um, besides," Joel added, "I don't think you can trust Marshall to keep his word. He's probably just gonna let you die here with us."

Darkeye made a noise that sounded like a snicker. "Believe me, children, I—*hic*—thought about all of that. Surely you do not think I am that naive, do you? No, shrewd as I am, I—*hic*—made Chief Byle drink a bit of my truth potion, to confirm that he meant everything he said. And with his power, no one will be able to touch me there. We will make—*hic*—an omnipotent team."

"Do you not see now?" Fireflower said to the war-painted guards. "Why are you helping this animal? He is going to leave our world to die, and all of you along with it! Release us, and stop him, your true enemy!"

"Save the effort," Darkeye scoffed. "These fools are all under—*hic*—mind control. They will do whatever I ask of them."

Joel cleared his mind and tried to inspect Darkeye for some kind of weakness that he could exploit. As he saw back in Spearwave, Darkeye lacked a true Aura presence, with only scattered blotches of dark purple orbiting the native like spilled ink. Joel wasn't sure what this meant, or if there were any advantages to be gained by it.

"So why haven't you killed us yet?" Felicity asked with a great deal of contempt. "That's what your orders are, right? You know the longer you let us hang around, the more chances we have to escape."

Joel looked at her with an expression that screamed *why are you telling him that?*

"Funny," Darkeye said as he twirled a lock of Felicity's hair around his long, crooked finger, "Chief Byle—*hic*—said nearly the same thing. 'If they show up, kill them—*hic*—immediately.' Miraculous feats of escape must be—*hic*—commonplace in your realm. Well, I intend to do just that—"

"Oh—I know," Felicity said in an understanding yet acidic tone, "I get it, you scumbag. You're going to experiment on us first, aren't you? Like how I said you would be, in our world? Since you're such a 'master alchemist,' or whatever?"

Darkeye appeared to pause in his tracks. Joel glanced at Felicity, who was scowling, but turned her head ever so slightly to give Joel a knowing wink.

"Well, we're not gonna let you do that, right, guys?" Felicity continued. "We're not gonna give you the satisfaction of—"

"Silence," Darkeye growled. "Of course that is what I—*hic*—intended. A great mind such as myself would not—*hic*—pass up an opportunity to test out my various potions on you, before dissecting your bodies to see—*hic*—what makes you tick."

"Ugh, gross," Felicity muttered.

"So you see, you will—*hic*—be dead in time," Darkeye said, as if justifying his chosen course of action to himself. "But I have a while before Chief Byle returns, so I will—*hic*—take advantage of that. You are helpless without your—*hic*—precious instruments anyway."

Darkeye produced three tiny vials from the folds of his silky gray robe. "I shall begin to—*hic*—prepare my various experiments. These should ensure that you are unable to—*hic*—escape in the meantime."

Darkeye opened the first vial and poured the contents on Joel's head. Shutting his eyes and mouth tightly, Joel could smell the potion's pungent, sickly sweet odor as it trickled down his face.

"This better just be shampoo," Felicity said as Darkeye repeated the procedure on her.

After a minute Joel felt every muscle in his body suddenly seize and stiffen up. He tried to resist the impulse, but within seconds, he realized that he had become completely paralyzed from the neck down. From his kneeling position, he toppled to the ground like a fallen tree. Out of the corner of his eye, he saw that his friends had suffered a similar fate.

"Take them to the—*hic*—holding cell," Darkeye ordered, making a dismissive gesture with his thin, bony fingers.

Joel, Felicity, and Fireflower were picked up by the war-painted natives and carried through the dilapidated village, which Joel noticed was uninhabited, save for the occasional small spinedog scurrying about. Eventually, they arrived at a small, windowless hut near the village outskirts. The hut's exterior had been painted with thick, vertical black lines, making it look almost humorously like a jail. Joel waited for a remark from Felicity about the hut's appearance, but none came as the natives opened the door, tossed them inside, and then shut the door, leaving them in total darkness.

After several minutes, Joel opened his mouth to say something, but found that his larynx had been paralyzed as well.

No wonder Felicity's been so quiet, he thought.

Joel lost track of time as they lay on the ground, although he estimated that at least several hours had passed. Even within the confines of the hut, he could feel a noticeable change in the air—literally, as if the heat and humidity were slowly being sucked out of the atmosphere. He wanted to wrap his arms around himself for warmth, but the paralysis potion—not to mention the wiry rope tied around his wrists—made that impossible.

"Why is it getting so cold?" a raspy, nasal voice sounded from outside the hut. "And why do we have to stay here? The prisoners are not going anywhere."

"Who knows. Stop complaining," a deeper voice said.

Great, guards. Guess Darkeye thought of everything.

After about another hour, Joel thought he heard a tiny croaking noise coming from within the hut. His heart raced for a second. Could Destiny somehow have escaped her own captivity and managed to break into their cell to set them free?

His hopes were dashed, however, when it became apparent that the croaking noise was actually Fireflower trying to speak.

"Aura...draining," she struggled to say. "The Nadir...has arrived. He is there. At Crownrock. Only hours left."

What? Oh no! How do you know that? is what Joel wanted to say, but the words only sounded in his head. Apparently, Fireflower was better at overcoming Darkeye's potion than the two Earthlings were.

SECRET OF THE SONGSHELL

"Did you hear something?" the deep-voiced guard said.

"No, but it is getting too cold for me," the other one replied.

Joel thought feverishly about what else he could do. He had tried using the Sight at least twenty-five times over the past several hours, but it had yielded nothing. He was still unable to move at all, and if Fireflower wasn't able to rescue them, who could?

"This is crazy," exclaimed the raspy voice. "We are going to freeze out here."

"I am beginning to agree," the deep voice said.

Joel tried very hard to remain optimistic. He reminded himself that over the length of this wildly improbable journey, he had been certain that they were going to die several times, and each time, something had happened to pull them out of it.

"I am going to see Master Darkeye," the raspy voice grunted. "Maybe someone else can take over for me."

"For you? For me as well," the deep voice said. "I will join you."

Joel took a deep breath. He was determined to hold on, to not give up. Something would happen, he was sure of it. He just had to relax and let fate take over.

"What about the prisoners?" the raspy voice asked.

"You said it yourself," the deep voice responded. "They are not going anywhere."

Joel let his mind drift freely on an undercurrent of faith that everything was not as bad as it seemed, that everything was going to be okay. A feeling of calmness and tranquility came over him. Is this what Art meant by "Zen"?

And then his peaceful bliss was interrupted by an annoying scratching sound. At first he tried to ignore it,

BRIAN TASHIMA

but it kept getting louder and louder, like a dog wanting to be let in from the rain.

A dog...I had a dog once, Joel thought. *That's why that sound is familiar. And that dog's name was—*

Joel's eyes grew wide in the dark. He could feel his insides practically bursting with excitement as the scratching noise continued.

"Something...trying...to get in..."

Joel was sure that if Felicity could speak, she would have chided Fireflower for stating the obvious.

Finally, the scratching stopped. Cool air and a little moonlight seeped through a newly clawed-out hole in the back of the hut. A tiny glowing ball slipped in, lighting up the darkness like a reading lamp. Attached to the ball was a small, gray creature that was a cross between a squirrel and a monkey.

Sammy! Joel thought.

"Wavebows...hurry," Fireflower said.

Joel thought he saw Sammy nod before the tiny animal scurried back out through the hole.

Twelve minutes later, the scratching resumed, as did the voices of the guards.

"I told you he would not be pleased," the deep voice grumbled.

"You said no such thing," the raspy voice retorted.

With a few more insistent scratches, Sammy enlarged the hole just enough for him to squeeze Fireflower's wavebow through it, bowl end first. The instrument fell on the ground with a hollow-sounding *thunk*, and Sammy crawled in after it.

"What was that?" the deep voice said.

"Over...here," Fireflower instructed. Sammy pushed the wavebow in front of her face, and then stood there expectantly.

250

A very faint polychromatic glimmer of light, accompanied by a barely audible series of notes, began to rise up from Fireflower's instrument.

The door of the hut flung open.

"What is going on in here?" the deep-voiced native yelled as he waved a glowmoss-covered stone around like a flashlight.

A few more notes sounded. Joel felt his calf twitch. And then, all at once, feeling and mobility returned to his entire body. The ropes around his wrists and ankles loosened and fell off on their own.

"Get help! They are—" was all that the deep-voiced native managed to say before he and his raspy-voiced companion were both felled by quick bursts of red light.

"Um, how—how did you do that?" Joel asked Fireflower as he jumped to his feet.

"Yeah, Marshall told us you can't do a cast without touching your instrument," Felicity said, tossing her ropes aside.

"A lifetime of training," Fireflower said, exhaling sharply. "Sometimes experience trumps talent."

Sammy leaped up into Joel's arms. It was all Joel could do not to smother the tiny creature with the intensity of his hug.

"You saved us!" Joel exclaimed before Felicity shushed him. Then he continued in a whisper, "Thanks, buddy. We owe you one."

"Yeah, we do, but can we save the mush for later?" Felicity said. "I thought we only had a few more hours before this place goes poof."

"That is correct—if I understand 'poof' correctly," Fireflower said as she peered through the hole that Sammy had made. "Marshall is absorbing the remainder of Spectraland's Aura as we speak. We have lost precious time."

"Um, okay, so now what?" Joel asked as Sammy climbed up onto his shoulder.

"First, we have to recover your wavebows," Fireflower replied. "We will need them if we are to successfully confront Marshall. We also have to locate our mounts."

"Uh, Sammy found your wavebow. Should we just follow him?"

"We could," Fireflower said as she picked up her instrument. "Or we could use a more direct approach."

"What about Darkeye and his goons?" Felicity asked.

"They will be good practice," Fireflower said with just a hint of a smirk before she strode out of the hut.

"Now you're talking," Felicity said, following closely after her.

Upon exiting the hut, Joel was immediately struck by how different the landscape looked and felt. The formerly vibrant colors in the air were of a duller contrast, as if someone had turned down that particular setting on their television, and patches of the sky were visibly gray. The temperature was at least thirty-five degrees cooler, if not more. The twin moons, although both full and bright, seemed more like desolate pools, in stark contrast to their previous roles as central chandeliers in a festival of lights.

Fireflower played two ringing notes. After a short delay, a pair of wavebows came shooting out of the air from somewhere within the village. Joel put his hands up in an automatic defensive gesture and was surprised to find that the instrument had settled neatly into his grip.

"Let's go," Fireflower said.

The three of them moved quickly but cautiously into the village, wavebows at the ready. Everything seemed eerily quiet and still.

"Um, where are we going?" Joel whispered.

"Stables," Fireflower answered. "I am quite sure that is where they are keeping the slimebacks. Those animals are too valuable to destroy."

"Think they know we're free, and armed?" Felicity asked as she looked around.

"Probably," Fireflower replied. "If not, they will soon."

They slipped between two rows of heavily damaged huts, some of which had been knocked completely off of their wooden foundations. Joel started to feel some of the bruises he had incurred while he was paralyzed and thrown around, but the pain was nothing compared to what he had felt when they were back in Mount Dragon-eye, so he was able to shrug it off for now.

They rounded a corner and crossed into an open courtyard area. A larger-than-life-size stone statue of a skinny native lay on its side on the ground. Although he had nothing to base it on, Joel had a feeling that the statue was of the actual Fourfoot, who—judging from the statue's less-than-imposing physique—appeared to be not quite as menacing as the antler-horned image that Marshall had conjured up.

"Over there," Fireflower said, pointing to an open structure at the far end of the courtyard.

Just then, Joel's ears picked up the sound of many approaching footsteps.

"They're coming!" he blurted out.

Fireflower's head whipped around. "Duck!" she yelled.

Joel hit the ground as a volley of spears whizzed by. Both Fireflower and Felicity tumbled, rolled, and came up firing red bursts of light from their wavebows. Joel quickly stood up and followed suit.

From behind an approaching mass of hostile natives, Darkeye's voice rose up out of the din. "Get them!" he cried unnecessarily.

Joel stopped casting for a moment to see if he could locate Darkeye, but the shriveled old potion master appeared to be hiding himself well behind his wall of followers.

"I will hold them off—see if you can get to the slimebacks!" Fireflower yelled as she struck several of Darkeye's forces with stunning casts.

Joel and Felicity both turned toward the stable, but another group of natives emerged from that area, all brandishing some sort of weapon or weaponized accessory (pots, torches, and so on). In fact, as Joel looked around, he saw that they were being surrounded, as natives of all types—including women and children—came at them from every direction, like in some sort of bad zombie movie.

"Um, where are they all coming from?" he shouted.

"Never mind," Felicity said, "just shoot!"

"Some of them are kids!"

"We're just stunning them, remember? Darkeye probably has them under mind control!"

Joel swallowed hard and began casting waves of light that knocked down the oncoming hordes like bowling pins. His mind wandered to the question of why Darkeye didn't put the three of them under mind control as well. He considered filing that question away to ask Fireflower later, but as he continued to fend off the hapless villagers and the occasional household projectile, the answer made itself evident: it was their so-called spectrum disorders—the way that their brains were wired. The reason that they were able to perform these feats of musical magic was the same reason that Darkeye, or Marshall Byle, for that matter, was unable to force them to do their bidding.

So that was why he had to make up all those lies about the concert, and Fourfoot, and everything else, Joel realized as he followed his own train of thought. *He couldn't just force us into it. And if he threatened us, there was a chance we could stop him along the way. So he had to get us to buy in, to make the whole thing seem like it was in our best interests as well.*

Thinking about Marshall's deception flustered Joel and threw off his concentration, so he stopped thinking and refocused on the task at hand. But he suddenly felt a bit fatigued. Breathing heavily, he stepped around the fallen villagers and headed toward the stable.

He caught a glimpse of Destiny, Dreamer, and Fireflower's mount, all standing next to each other and tied securely to wooden posts. Destiny saw him and let out an excited croak, while Dreamer grunted in the manner of one saying "well, it's about time."

Then there was the sound of an explosion. A relatively small one, but an explosion nonetheless. Joel and Felicity turned and dashed back into the center of the courtyard, where Fireflower was standing in the middle of a ring of stunned natives, their bodies all lying motionless on the ground. A cloud of green smoke drifted out of a broken jar that was near her feet. Her wavebow was trained on Darkeye, who stood twenty feet away near the edge of the courtyard with his arms in the air.

"Um, what happened?" Joel asked. "We heard an explosion."

255

"He," Fireflower said, pausing for breath, "threw a combusting potion at us. I was able to blunt most of its effect, just in time."

"So what are you gonna do, just stun him?" Felicity asked.

"He is too dangerous," Fireflower responded. "I cannot kill him, but I can render him unable to—"

"Please—*hic*—let me help you," Darkeye called out to them. "I see the error of my—*hic*—ways now. I can help you stop—*hic*—Byle."

"Pfft, we're not gonna trust you," Felicity scoffed.

"Oh, but you will need—*hic*—my help."

Fireflower's eyes narrowed. "How so?" she asked skeptically.

"Surely, young shaman, you can—*hic*—feel the Aura slowly draining away. By the time you get to—*hic*—Crownrock, you will not have the necessary power to defeat Byle and—*hic*—save our worlds."

"That is a risk we have to take, Darkeye," Fireflower said, raising her wavebow. "And that is why we need to leave, right now."

"Wait! Allow me to— *hic*—finish. I have potions that will help you maintain—*hic*—your strength, at least until we get there. Without them, you—*hic*—will have no chance, and all your valiant efforts will be—*hic*—in vain."

"I don't like this," Felicity muttered.

Fireflower kept her wavebow aimed squarely at Darkeye's head. "Just give us the potions, then, and we will be on our way."

"They must be—*hic*—freshly prepared right before consumption, meaning that you will—*hic*—need to bring me along...conscious and unharmed, of course," Darkeye said with a toothless grin.

Joel, Felicity, and Fireflower all glanced at each other without making direct eye contact.

CHAPTER 20: JUNGLE OF DARKNESS

So as you can see, it was—*hic*—fortunate that I did not destroy your instruments, my natural scientific curiosity—*hic*—leading me to keep and inspect them so that I could figure out how they work. I have a—*hic*—theory that some kind of force generated by your bodies interacts somehow with the—*hic*—sonic wavelengths produced by the instrument, thusly allowing you to manipulate the Aura. Anyway, now that we are—*hic*—working together, it seems almost serendipitous that I did not follow through with my—*hic*—original intent, as you still retain the means with which to—*hic*—accomplish your lofty and noble goals. I am not sure if this—*hic*—Spectraland saying translates into your language, but 'everything happens for a—*hic*—reason.' And I think that, perhaps, we should—"

"Oh man, can we *please* put a gag on him?" Felicity groaned.

For a very brief moment, Joel actually felt a little pang of sympathy for Darkeye. He recalled the countless times that he himself would recite his many thoughts and insights—which were all very important and interesting, mind you—to his classmates, only to be ignored at best, or at worst, told to shut up, that he was boring, or when Mitch was involved, thrown against a locker or subjected to some other form of physical bullying. So Felicity's request kind of hit him in a sensitive area, even if Darkeye *was* their enemy who had tried to kill them just a short time ago.

"Um, kinda hard to do that unless we stop," Joel said to her. Reunited once again with their slimebacks, they rode along through a barren stretch of land that seemed strangely familiar to Joel. He had drawn the assignment of riding tandem with Darkeye, whom they had bound with rope and vine rather than with a binding cast, in order to conserve as much Aura energy as possible.

"No stopping," Fireflower said. "Not until we get to Stonelight Tunnel."

"Stone-what?" Felicity asked.

"Stonelight Tunnel," Fireflower repeated. "An underground passage that allows us to avoid the Jungle of Darkness."

"I can't stand all these lame names," Felicity muttered under her breath.

"The Jungle of Darkness is extremely dangerous," Fireflower continued. "It is inhabited by all manner of deadly creatures. Even the Elder Wavemakers feared that place. That is why they built the tunnel."

"Fireflower," Darkeye said, "I did not realize you had—*hic*—achieved Elder status. Where is your symbol?"

Fireflower went silent. Joel looked at her expectantly, awaiting her response, but none came.

"Oh no, do not—*hic*—tell me," Darkeye said mockingly, "you are not an Elder? How do you—*hic*—expect to open the tunnel's portal?"

"I thought you were on our side now, *potion-man*," Fireflower growled without looking back.

Although Darkeye was seated behind him, Joel felt like he could see the cunning native's toothless grin as he spoke. "Oh, of course I am—despite the fact that—*hic*—you still keep me tied up, indicating your continued—*hic*—mistrust. I am merely asking an honest and important question. If we—*hic*—cannot enter the tunnel, we will—*hic*—be forced to traverse the Jun—"

"I realize that!" Fireflower snapped as she urged her slimeback into a faster gait.

As Destiny sped up to keep pace, Joel thought about asking Darkeye what he meant by symbols and such, but thankfully, pieces of memory happened to come together at that moment, making additional questions unnecessary.

Joel recalled the unfamiliar tattoo that he had seen on Marshall's left forearm back when he first arrived in Spectraland. He remembered that Marshall had pressed that tattoo against a boulder at the end of a long tunnel, causing the boulder to roll aside. The rest then fell into place: Crownrock must have been the site of the Rift where Marshall brought him over. Then Marshall used an Elder Symbol—probably ill-gotten, Joel figured—to take them through Stonelight Tunnel and out toward Headsmouth.

"She seems very—*hic*—temperamental," Darkeye said. "As does your offworld companion. Why do you choose to—*hic*—ally yourself with them? You seem to have the potential for great power, you know. Why, after we—*hic*—vanquish Chief Byle, the two of us could band together, minus those—*hic*—unstable female—"

"Shut up," Joel said.

"I am merely suggesting—"

"I said, shut up," Joel barked.

Darkeye complied as they rode on. Joel shuddered, partly out of anger and partly because the temperature felt like it had plunged into the low forties, making the island more reminiscent of Seattle in December than of midsummer Hawai'i. He was still in his sleeveless vest, as the idea of jacket-like clothing was a foreign notion in a place that was used to year-round tropical conditions. Neither Felicity nor Fireflower had said anything about the chill yet, so Joel was determined not to either.

The landscape was now downright dreary, having completely shifted from watercolor pixels to a sort of blurry charcoal-and-pencil look. Off in the distance, Joel spotted a thin, swirling ribbon of light that was funneling down to a point on the horizon, and he knew that it was there that they would find Marshall.

After riding through a swath of seaweed palms, they arrived at what looked like a dome-shaped adobe hut with a boulder for a door. Joel recognized the area, although he had been too busy marveling at his surroundings his first time here to really remember all of the details. It felt almost like returning to a childhood home, where reality did not exactly match up with one's memories of the place.

Fireflower drew her mount to a halt, and the others followed suit. She hopped off and ran up to inspect the carving on the boulder.

"This is where we will need your potion, Darkeye," she said with a steely look in her eye. "I will need the strength if I am to break this enchantment."

"Indeed," Darkeye said. "I—*hic*—must be untied, of course."

"I'll keep an eye on him," Felicity volunteered as she slid off of Dreamer and pulled out her wavebow in one smooth motion.

"Um, me too," Joel said, dismounting as well. He had planned on helping Darkeye down, but Destiny quickly lowered her backside, causing Darkeye to tumble ungracefully onto the ground.

"Insolent little—" Darkeye muttered before abruptly changing his tone, "Yes, I—*hic*—suppose I deserved that."

Joel undid the vine-ropes tied around Darkeye's wrists then took a few steps back while readying his wavebow. Felicity and Fireflower stood right in front of them, eyes fully locked on the wizened native as he rose to his feet and reached into his robe.

"No funny stuff," Felicity warned.

"Of course—*hic*—not." Darkeye smiled as he pulled from his robe a tiny aqua-blue jar. He peeled a thin membrane off the top of the jar, then proceeded to repeat the same nauseating ritual that Joel had witnessed back at Spearwave. After he finished regurgitating into the jar, he handed it to Fireflower.

"*So* gross." Felicity grimaced.

Fireflower did not seem fazed as she sniffed the smoking contents of the jar.

"Uh, how do you know he isn't poisoning you?" Joel asked.

"We have a highly developed sense of smell that can detect most dangerous substances," Fireflower explained as she held out the jar. "But just to be sure, I would like to ask if you could inspect it as well."

Joel nodded as he took the jar from her. A few seconds of examining the potion with the Sight revealed nothing that he found unusual.

"Seems—seems okay to me," he said, handing it back to her.

Fireflower glanced once more at Darkeye, who word-lessly gave her a Spectraland shrug, before she drained the contents of the jar in a single gulp. After a period of five seconds, during which nothing strange or bad hap-pened, Fireflower ran back over to the boulder and be-gan to play a particularly aggressive-sounding series of notes. Joel kept one eye on Darkeye while observing her efforts, which, after a full minute and a half, did not seem to be producing any discernible results.

She tried for a bit longer before she trudged back to them with a disgusted look on her face. "No use," she gasped. "The seal is simply too strong."

"So this freak tricked us?" Felicity asked angrily, waving her instrument in a threatening manner at Dark-eye's head.

"No, the potion did restore some of my strength. The Elders just did not want anyone going to Crownrock without very good reason. It is a special, powerful place. Unfortunate that Marshall was able to secure a symbol for himself."

"Um, so now what?" Joel asked, even though he al-ready knew the answer.

♪♪♪

The Jungle of Darkness was nothing at all like what Joel had expected. In his mind, he had envisioned an eerie, dim, misty swampland not unlike Dagobah, or perhaps a tropical version of the Forbidden Forest.

But in reality, the jungle didn't appear to be much different from any of the other tree-filled regions he had been to so far. All of the vegetation seemed like standard Spectraland fare, and any gloominess was probably more attributable to the rapidly dissipating Aura than to any aspect of their immediate surroundings. Bright moonlight filtered through the overhanging fronds, providing more than adequate illumination.

"This, um, this place seems pretty normal," he said to no one in particular, even as Sammy skittered nervously about his neck and shoulders.

"Do not be fooled," Fireflower whispered. "This place is feared for good reason."

"What reason is that?" Felicity asked.

Fireflower paused before answering. "To be honest, I do not know. No one has ever entered the jungle and returned to tell about it."

"Great," Felicity muttered.

They continued to ride along at a steady but cautious pace, desperate to catch up with Marshall but taking pains to not attract any unwanted attention. Darkeye, who had not been retied, remained uncharacteristically quiet until after they had been in the jungle for about an hour, at which point he spoke up in a rather loud voice: "Perhaps—*hic*—the jungle is not as dangerous as everyone has claimed."

Joel suddenly had a very bad feeling. "Um, and now that you've said that—"

There was a flash, like that of a large camera, and then everything went dark.

It was an absolute kind of darkness, as if something had sucked out all of the light in the surrounding area, leaving nothing for the eye to latch on to. Not even Sammy's tail-orb was visible. Joel grabbed his wavebow and tried to initiate a light cast, but the note that sounded from his instrument was not the one that he had expected. An errant blue wave shot out and was quickly swallowed up by the dark. He heard two other incorrect notes being played at roughly the same time as his, and he knew that Fireflower and Felicity had met with the same lack of success.

"What's going on?" he shouted. His voice sounded tinny and distant to his own ears.

A voice that sounded vaguely like Fireflower's shouted a reply, but it was garbled to the point of sounding like a different language.

He tried the light cast again. Another unintended note sounded, and a purple wave came out that briefly lit up a figure in a silky gray robe, running away in the direction that they had come from.

"Darkeye!" Joel felt himself yell, although the sound that came out was more like a whisper in an empty soup can.

Then he heard a distorted growling noise that seemed to be coming from everywhere at once. This was followed by Felicity shouting, as if from miles away, "Use your Sight!"

Joel went through his now-familiar routine of setting his panic aside and pushing his mind towards a comforting list of miscellaneous details. Instantly, three outlines became visible within the darkness: Felicity on her slimeback, Fireflower on hers, and something very large looming right in front of them.

"Whoa—" he managed to say, right before he felt Destiny collapse, as if something had swept her legs out from under her. He hit the ground on his arm with a hard thud. Felicity cursed as she fell on top of him.

Joel quickly scrambled to his feet and backed away from the large shape. It had numerous long thorns extending from the top of its egg-shaped outline, and it was supported by thick cylinders, like a Medusa's head on tree trunks. He heard the growling sound again and saw one of the legs lifting up, as if preparing to strike.

"Get back!" he yelled as loud as he possibly could, but it came out in a mere whisper.

Felicity and Fireflower leaped backward, just in time to avoid a swift swipe by the leg, which also fortunately missed the slimebacks, who were still lying on their sides on the ground.

Joel attempted a stunning cast, but even though he was sure his fingers were in the right positions and his visualization was correct, he ended up with a very sour, dissonant chord that produced nothing more than a handful of green sparks. But it produced just enough light for him to catch a fleeting glimpse of their adversary: a frighteningly grotesque, rhino-sized angler fish with no arms and four furry, mammoth-like legs. Its primary filament was topped by a microphone-shaped blob that seemed to be pulsing with dark Aura energy.

An idea struck him. He ran over to the outline of Fireflower, leaned over, and awkwardly grabbed at her ankles. Letting out a startled, garbled yell, she kicked at him as one might kick at an annoying little dog, and landed a painful blow on his knee. Wincing but undeterred, he continued reaching until he felt the handle of the knife that she kept in a sheath around her leg.

He grabbed the handle and pulled the blade out as another growl sounded. Recognizing this as the signal that the fish-beast was about to strike again, Joel geared himself up to jump. Sure enough, another swipe came, directly at him this time. He launched himself as high and as far forward as he could, barely clearing the creature's leg and landing up against its face. Feeling its salivating fangs, he was glad at that moment that he could not see what he imagined to be its horrifying visage.

He slashed the knife at the outline of the fish's primary filament. Expecting to lop it off like a tall weed, he was instead surprised when it nimbly danced out of the way as if it had a mind of its own. Two more flailing attempts also struck nothing but air.

Joel felt the creature opening its gigantic, toothy maw, presumably to swallow him. He took another lunge at the filament, which again easily dodged his attack.

Out of the corner of his eye, he saw the outline of the creature raising its leg with a bit of an inward twist. Realizing that it probably intended to stuff him into its mouth, he frantically tried to clamber up its face. His fingers dug into something soft and gooey, and the creature howled. That bought him the split second he needed to boost himself up, just as the creature hit itself in the mouth with its own leg. This time, he slashed at the base of the filament, severing it in a single stroke.

Another bright flash followed, along with an even louder howl from the fish-beast. The filament tumbled to the ground as light poured out of its microphone-like appendage, returning visibility to the area.

Joel felt two jolts strike the fish's head as he held on to it, and suddenly the creature became limp. He turned his own head and saw Felicity and Fireflower with their wavebows aimed at him.

"That's a pretty ugly fish you're hugging," Felicity said with a smirk.

"What? Oh," Joel said, quickly jumping off of the creature. Seeing that he had bits of the fish's eye on his hand, he wiped it off on his vest while trying not to gag. He handed Fireflower's knife back to her as Sammy jumped off of his shoulder and dashed over to where the slimebacks still lay on the ground.

"Oh no," Joel said, following the silvertail.

Fireflower wore a grim expression as she inspected the animals, all of whom were clearly in pain. "Their legs are broken," she announced. "We will have to continue on foot."

"Um, can't you heal them?" Joel pleaded.

"Healing casts require a great deal of Aura energy, of which there is precious little left," she said, shaking her head. "And since Darkeye has escaped, we have lost our only way of augmenting my strength."

"I knew we couldn't trust him," Felicity grumbled. "He was just waiting for a chance to escape. Probably knew all about that Aura-sucking fish thing."

"I can ease their pain and give them a protective shield that will hopefully keep them safe until we return," Fireflower said. "But that is all."

She played a brief melody, and a thin, pale layer of yellow light settled over the slimebacks like a blanket.

"We'll be back," Joel said to Destiny, leaning over her head. "I promise."

"What about fish-face?" Felicity asked.

"It should be stunned until long after we get back," Fireflower replied. "If we take too much time, then it will not matter anyway."

Leaving the slimebacks behind, they dashed off through the jungle as quickly as they could, following the spiraling ribbon of Aura energy in the sky. They often heard the rustling and stirring of nearby creatures, but they did not slow down, choosing to risk the incitement of a chase from deadly jungle denizens over the loss of any more time and Aura energy.

At one point, such a chase did occur. A pack of long-haired, wolf-sized sharks with small elephant trunks came charging out from behind a cluster of dark, razor-leaved ferns, and the weary travelers were forced to stop and defend themselves. After a volley of well-aimed stunning casts, that particular threat was averted, but

Joel found himself feeling very winded and in desperate need of a rest. Felicity and Fireflower were both leaning over, looking as tired as he felt.

"Uh, how much...time do we have?" he gasped. Despite the ever-increasing chill in the air, he was sweating.

"Not...much," Fireflower panted, looking up at the Aura trail in the sky. "He cannot do anything until the shell is full, but it is nearly there."

"Wait, what?" Felicity said. "What do you mean by, 'he cannot do anything'?'"

"If he draws upon the power contained in the shell before it is done absorbing all of Spectraland's Aura, the process will be ruined. I do not think he wants to wait until the next Nadir."

"Um, so he'll be just as weak as us," Joel said.

"Possibly," Fireflower answered. "But I am sure that his own personal energy is stored up, rather than depleted, as ours is becoming."

"Okay, enough talking, more running," Felicity said.

Joel found himself admiring Felicity's fighting spirit as he followed after her. He wasn't sure if it was going to do them any good at this point, but it was inspirational enough to make him forget his fatigue and push on.

He had always been very future-oriented; everything he did was part of a grand vision that he saw in his mind and acted upon, trying to turn the vision into reality. And while this quality certainly helped him with his songwriting and other creative matters, it could also be very frustrating at times—if one part of the vision could not be realized, it would spoil the entire picture. At times, he was a perfectionist beyond reason, refusing to even begin a project out of fear that he would not be able to meet his own impossible standards for it.

His teachers and his mother would always tell him that sometimes you just have to take a chance. Sometimes it's best not to think so much. Take your best shot, even if it doesn't seem perfect, and more often than not, it will work out better than you expected. And if you fail, so what? You learn and move on.

And so it was that he continued to take one step after another as they hurtled headlong into the depths of the jungle, even as their big picture seemed increasingly hopeless. After all, wasn't that how they'd survived everything else up until this point?

CHAPTER 21: CROWNROCK

"I swear, if I see one more weird creature, I'm gonna scream," Felicity said as she struggled to catch her breath.

Encounters with several more groups of vicious hybrid animals had left them completely exhausted, and there was still no end in sight to the jungle. To make matters worse, the ribbon trail of Aura was growing lower in the sky, which made it harder for them to know which direction to go. It also meant that Marshall was almost done absorbing all the power he needed.

Searching for something positive to hang on to, Joel thought about how, despite the angler-mammoth and all of the other beasts, the Jungle of Darkness had not seemed nearly as bad as he had originally thought. That a non-Elder shaman and two offworld amateurs were able to make it this far, through a place where Elders had feared to tread, seemed to him to be a noteworthy accomplishment.

He opened his mouth to make this point, but shortness of breath and a last-second internal warning from the Uncle Dave Instinct put a quick end to that impulse.

Just as he was congratulating himself on his super-stitious self-restraint, however, Felicity spoke up.

"At least it hasn't been as bad as I expected," she said, before a look of regret immediately crossed her face. A heavy black mist began to filter out from between the surrounding trees and plants.

"Oh, of course," she muttered.

Joel prepared himself to run, but the mist quickly surrounded and enveloped them. He felt the crackling of electricity on his skin.

"A wraith," Fireflower said.

"VISITORS...IT HAS BEEN A WHILE...." echoed a low male voice that sounded like Darth Vader with a cold and a lot of reverb. "YOU SEEK THE ORIGIN?"

The three travelers looked at each other through the mist that swirled around them.

"The—origin?" Fireflower asked.

"OF THE AURA POWER," the voice replied wearily. "ON THE ISLAND IN THE WATER. THAT IS WHY ALL TRAVEL THROUGH HERE."

"Oh! Yes—yes, we do," Fireflower said.

"AS I THOUGHT," the voice said, before Fireflower could explain further. "WELL, I AM SORRY, BUT YOU MUST BE DESTROYED."

"Wait!" Fireflower shouted. "You do not under-stand—there is someone there. He is killing our island, and we need to stop him!"

"SOMEONE THERE? IMPOSSIBLE," the voice boomed, incredulous. "I HAVE GUARDED THE WAY TO THE ORIGIN FOR CENTURIES. ALL WHO PASS THROUGH HERE MUST BE DESTROYED, LEST THEY GAIN TOO MUCH POWER."

Joel thought this declaration to be a bit odd, seeing as how there was a nonsecret tunnel that easily bypassed the jungle. "Um, there's a tun—" he started to point out, before Felicity cut him off with a subtle shushing noise.

"That is precisely the problem," Fireflower continued. "An offworlder has gained possession of the Songshell, and has somehow managed to arrive at Crownrock—at the origin. He is attempting to steal all of Spectraland's Aura."

"IS THAT SO?" the voice said, before it paused for an uncomfortably long period of time. The black mist whipped back and forth several times, and Joel could feel tiny jolts coursing throughout his body.

Finally, it spoke up again. "WELL, THAT IS NOT MY CONCERN. I HAVE ASCERTAINED THAT YOU ARE TELLING THE TRUTH, YET I HAVE BUT ONE DUTY, AND THAT IS TO PREVENT PASSAGE THROUGH THE JUNGLE OF DARKNESS."

Perhaps an exception can be made, a calm, silky voice interjected.

Joel looked around. "Nineteen?" he said. Felicity and Fireflower both looked at him like he was crazy.

Hello, Nineteen's voice sounded in Joel's head. *It appears that your former companion is doing something...objectionable.*

"Um, you mean Marshall? Yeah—yeah, he is! Can you transport us to Crownrock? Or can you stop him?"

Unfortunately, I can do neither. I have some control over Aura fields in the surface layer, but not over physical objects. In fact, it is curious that I am able to communicate with you now. I suspect it has something to do with your former companion's removal of most of the island's Aura.

"Oh," Joel said, not fully understanding but feeling disappointed nonetheless.

"What's going on?" Felicity asked.

However, perhaps it is serendipitous that we find ourselves in contact once again. You see, the beings that you refer to as wraiths were actually creations of my people, before we were forced from the surface into the Prism Valley. We formed them to serve as guardians of the most important areas on the island.

Joel made himself ignore the details and questions that were forming in his head as he tried to get straight to the point. "Okay—so, um, can you help us?"

Somewhat, perhaps, Nineteen replied. *I will instruct the guardian to let you pass. Still, I am not sure you will make it in time. Even the fastest mounts would fall short.*

Joel's thoughts raced. Suddenly, an idea struck him. "Ever hear of the laws of aerodynamics?"

♪♪♪

It took Nineteen three seconds to absorb all of the details about aerodynamics that Joel had memorized. Shortly thereafter, the Jungle Wraith morphed into a dark vortex that lifted the three of them into the air and above the trees.

Good luck, Nineteen said. *It will carry you as far as its Aura power lasts.*

The vortex sped off, carrying them along like a horizontal tornado. As Joel stretched out his arms in classic superhero fashion, he looked down at the expansive stretch of jungle that lay before them and realized that Nineteen was right, they never would have made it on foot.

They were about a hundred feet above the ground, and the view was spectacular. Beyond the jungle, which was bracketed on each end by mountain ranges, Joel could make out a long stretch of beach, as well as the ocean behind it. Right off the shoreline, there was a smattering of small islets, one of which reminded Joel a little of Chinaman's Hat, but with a flat top. It was this islet that the remaining Aura ribbon appeared to be funneling down into. *That must be Crownrock*, he figured.

As they got closer, Joel could make out a figure standing atop the islet's plateau that he assumed was Marshall. He began to worry. Even if they were not too late, what would they actually do once they got there? Even though they outnumbered Marshall three to one, and their three included an experienced Wavemaker, what if Marshall had, as Fireflower said, stored up his personal Aura energy? They would have no chance.

Then something that someone once said to him popped into his mind. Something about worrying being a waste of time...

He shook his head to clear it of its thoughts and resolved to simply press on and let whatever would happen, happen.

The vortex began to lose speed as they neared the beach. It entered into a gradual dive as bits of black mist began to break off and float away, and Joel realized that its Aura energy was reaching its end. Fortunately, by the time it disintegrated completely, they were about five feet above the soft, gleaming white sand surface, upon which they were deposited. Joel rolled, stood up, and dusted himself off. The sound of a loud, steady hum like an alarm siren surrounded them. He looked up and saw the Aura ribbon leading directly to the top of the islet.

"That was incredible," Fireflower said as she ran up to Joel. "What was that called again?"

"Um, what was what called? You mean flying?" Joel replied.

Fireflower gave him a quizzical look. "There is no word for what you just said in my language. I suppose we will have to invent one."

They dashed across the beach and quickly waded through the shallow portion of the water, which was painfully cold. Joel's teeth were chattering as they climbed onto a section of reef that led to the base of the islet. Sammy started to run in circles around Joel's shoulders, squeaking animatedly.

"What—what's wrong?" Joel asked.

Just as they reached the islet, Sammy leaped off and scurried away so quickly that Joel lost sight of him.

"Hey!" Joel called. Suddenly, he had a splitting headache.

"There's a trail," Felicity said, grabbing his arm and motioning in the opposite direction of where Sammy had gone.

What looked like a man-made hiking trail spiraled its way up and around the islet's central cone. Apparently, despite the best efforts of the Jungle Guardian, Crownrock and its high concentration of Aura had been a popular and frequent destination of past travelers.

They ran up the trail as fast as they possibly could. Joel could feel his heart beating loudly in his chest, although oddly, he did not feel particularly nervous. His mind was distracted with trying to remember who had told him that line about not worrying—normally, details like that never escaped his memory, and the fact that this one was so evasive made him feel somewhat annoyed.

"So, what's the plan?" Felicity asked him as the humming sound grew louder.

"What?"

She moved closer to him and cupped her mouth with both hands near the side of his head. "I said, what's the plan?"

Her breath felt warm and comforting against his nearly frozen ear. Now he felt nervous, and not because he didn't have a plan. He stopped in his tracks and looked at her face, noticing how the light from the Aura ribbon reflected in her eyes. He paused for two awkward seconds before replying, wondering if this was one of "those" moments.

"Um—wing it, I guess."

"Great," she said, rolling her eyes.

And just like that, the moment was gone.

The trail ended about two feet below the edge of the plateau. Joel grabbed onto the well-worn dirt-and-grass surface and clambered up close to the top, where he was joined on either side by Felicity and Fireflower. Peering over the edge and between two piles of large rocks, he saw Marshall standing motionless near the Songshell, which was suspended in the air three feet in front of the Biledriver singer's face. Marshall's arms were crossed over his chest, and his eyes were closed. The shell pulsed with a brilliant pearl-white light as the Aura ribbon continued to flow into it.

Joel looked at Fireflower, who gave him a Spectra-land shrug. Thinking *oh, what the heck*, he pulled himself up onto the plateau, trying to stay as flat as possible in order to hide behind the rock pile. Fireflower and Felicity followed closely behind.

He crawled slowly on his stomach until he was facing Marshall's back. Then he got up into a half crouch and carefully approached, pausing and looking after every step like a stalking animal. He made up the plan in his head as he went along: once he got close enough, he would leap out and tackle Marshall, and—hopefully—one of the girls would grab the shell, and the other would use whatever Aura power they had left to stun Marshall—or something like that.

Perhaps they could have tried stunning him from a distance? That would have been riskier than going in at point-blank range, he rationalized, and it was too late for that now anyway. Joel learned years ago that you can't change the past, no matter how much you regretted things that you had or had not done.

Closer and closer they got, creeping along step by step. Marshall remained still as a statue. The humming noise was growing louder, and the end of the Aura ribbon was now only twenty feet above their heads.

Just a little closer...

A little more...

Joel tensed his body to jump.

And...

"Glad you folks could join me," Marshall said without turning around.

Joel quickly stood up, shocked but not altogether surprised. Felicity raised her wavebow and played it, but nothing happened outside of the sound of her chord getting drowned out by the hum. Fireflower and Joel then both attempted stunning casts of their own, only to end up with the same result.

"So, tell me," Marshall said, now barely looking over his shoulder, "how cool is this? So much power...incredible."

"But why?" Felicity asked as they all cautiously backed up a few steps. "Why do you need to do this?"

Marshall unfolded his arms and slowly turned around. "Hmm...bored, I suppose. I achieved my goals of rock stardom, and then I took over this—this crazy, miniature amusement park. I needed another challenge, something else to conquer. Being stagnant makes me sad."

"Uh, but what about helping young musicians achieve their dreams?" Joel said. "All that stuff you told us? Was that all a lie?"

Marshall chuckled. "No, honestly, that really was an idea I had. But once I found out about the Songshell, that mission seemed pitifully modest in comparison to, well, as the cliché goes—world domination. Thank goodness aliens really do exist, eh?"

"Okay, you're crazy," Felicity said. "You would wipe out an entire world—island, whatever—full of living creatures, just so that you could, what, I dunno, be able to make yourself invisible back home?"

Marshall laughed as he took a step towards them. "Seriously, love, are you really going to make me tell you all about my 'evil plans,' like some stereotypical, hackneyed movie villain? Tell you all about my troubled childhood, boo hoo, and how I'm going to get revenge on a cruel, cruel world that never appreciated my genius?

"The truth is, it's more than making myself invisible, or levitating things, or what have you. I already was a highly successful performer, an entertainer, so what makes you think I want to do that again?

"No, this is about—about, I don't know, entertaining myself, I suppose. With these powers, I can do anything I want. If I wake up one morning and feel like turning the sky purple, I can. If I'm a wee bit hacked off because my tea is cold, and so I feel like wiping out a small country— I can. No limits! Anything will be possible."

"Yeah, but where will it stop? Eventually, you'll just get bored again," Felicity snapped. "And what about everyone you'll be hurting? Don't you care about that?"

Marshall sighed. "Yes, it certainly is possible that I'll run out of things upon which to use all of this power. But with my creativity, I don't think that'll happen for quite a while.

"As for hurting people—or little green aliens, for that matter—I don't know, I just don't feel anything for them. People die every single day, and everyone expects us to be sad, to say 'oh, that's terrible,' or whatever. But I don't even know them! Who bloody cares, right? Empathy is a foreign concept to me—just like it is for you, my dear."

Joel looked at Felicity. Her face was a mixture of hurt and horror.

"I'm nothing like you!" she screamed. She lunged at Marshall in a sloppy rage, with none of the finesse or technique one would expect from a martial arts black belt. Marshall deftly raised his wavebow and played a short chord in one smooth motion. A red wave shot out and struck Felicity square in the midsection, sending her flying back a good six feet, almost to the edge of the plateau.

"No!" Joel yelled as he turned and ran to check on Felicity.

"She's fine," Marshall said impassively. "I want all of you to watch as I take the Songshell and travel through the Rift. It's quite a sight, believe me. Think of it as, I don't know, my final show for you."

Felicity grimaced as she sat up with Joel's help, who was kneeling at her side.

"Are you okay?" he asked.

"Sure, why not," she exhaled.

At that moment the Aura ribbon completely vanished into the Songshell, and the humming noise abruptly ceased. The ensuing silence seemed louder than the noise that preceded it. The shell's color changed from pearl white to a dimly glowing dark purple.

"Perfect timing," Marshall said, grinning. He reached out his hand to pluck the shell from the air. An instant before his fingers closed around it, however, a silver streak darted out from nowhere and knocked the shell away from his grasp and onto the ground, where it rolled several feet before coming to a stop.

"Sammy!" Joel shouted with a smile.

"Pesky little—" Marshall grumbled as he fired a short red wave at the silvertail. His aim was true, and with a painful squeal, Sammy went careening over the plateau's edge toward the reef and ocean below. Joel's mouth opened in shock.

Fireflower lunged for the shell, only to be met with a swift kick from Marshall that knocked her to the ground.

"Get the shell, I'll take him!" Felicity yelled, scrambling to her feet.

"No, wait—" Joel started to say, but it was too late. Marshall played a different note, generating an orange wave that enveloped Felicity like a throw net, freezing her in place. Fireflower stood up and was also immediately immobilized.

Marshall then turned his wavebow on Joel, but when he played the same note, nothing happened. He tried again several times, but still—nothing. He played different notes, chords and riffs, but the only things that came out were small, plinky sounds that were reminiscent of an out-of-tune ukulele.

Marshall cursed as he held out and looked at his wavebow as if it were roadkill.

"Um, out of energy," Joel observed as he stood up.

"Yes, I can see that. Sooner than I expected, I must say," Marshall muttered. He turned and took a few slow, purposeful steps forward. "No matter. The shell will give me back enough power."

Marshall bent over to retrieve the shell like a golfer picking his ball out of the hole. As soon as he touched it, however, he cried out in pain and recoiled.

Joel wasn't quite sure what had just happened, but sensing his opportunity, he ran and gave Marshall a flying kick to the hip, and both of them fell to the ground.

"What the—" Marshall sputtered, more surprised than hurt by Joel's offensive.

Joel got to his feet and assumed the ready stance that Felicity taught him back in Spearwave when she was still recovering from the bloomfish poisoning.

Marshall laughed derisively as he stood up as well. "You're joking, right? C'mon, Joel, I've seen you fight. You're pathetic."

"Not as pathetic as—um, not as—" Joel stammered, trying but failing to think of some witty retort.

Marshall laughed even harder. "Fancy yourself a hero, now, do you? Joel Suzuki, next in the long line of epic 'chosen ones' who save the world from the forces of evil and darkness? Well, I don't mean to shatter your fantastical adolescent bubble, but those stories are just a bunch of made-up fairy tales. As strange as it all seems, *this* is real life—and I don't know if you've noticed, but real life doesn't always have a happy ending."

Happy, Joel thought. *That reminds me of something. Something that has to do with that whole thing about worrying. Why can't I remember?*

"Right, then, I'll fight you," Marshall snickered, setting his wavebow aside. "Should be worth a good laugh or two."

Marshall threw a somewhat lackadaisical punch that Joel, furiously trying to recall everything that Felicity taught him, was able to easily block. Marshall threw a second, more forceful punch, which Joel then dodged.

"Not bad, I guess you—*ooof*," Marshall said, as Joel came back with a punch of his own to Marshall's exposed midsection.

"All right, you little git, it's on," Marshall growled, clutching his stomach.

They began to brawl as Felicity and Fireflower looked on in (literally) petrified horror. Thanks to Felicity's crash course, Joel was able to hold his own for a few minutes, but Marshall's size and strength advantages proved to be too much as he landed a couple of blows that had Joel reeling.

Still at least able to speak, Felicity shouted out instructions to Joel, but this ended up having the unintended effect of distracting him. A fist to the face left Joel dazed, with a bloody lip and nose, but still on his feet.

"I'll try not to knock you out completely," Marshall said as he reared back for one final, finishing blow. "I still want you to watch as I leave this little pond behind."

"Duck!" Felicity cried.

Joel ducked. Marshall's right hook hit air. Joel lunged forward, wrapped his arms around Marshall's waist, and pushed the larger man to the ground. With a loud, frustrated yell, Marshall lifted Joel off and threw him to the side. Joel rolled several feet, coming to a stop next to—

"Joel! The shell!" Felicity yelled.

Woozy, Joel raised his head. Indeed, the shell lay just a foot in front of his face, still with its dim purple glow. Summoning up an extra reserve of strength, Joel scrambled forward and grabbed the shell with both hands. It felt very warm. Currents of energy began to flow through his body.

"What? No!" Marshall shouted as he got to his feet. "How are you able to—?"

"You should have picked it up *before* you starting fighting, stupid," Felicity said to Marshall, laughing. "See? You *are* a stereotypical bad guy."

"Shut up!" Marshall barked. "He shouldn't be able to touch it—*I* couldn't, it's too hot—ugh, no matter. Joel—Joel, listen to me."

Joel pulled himself up with renewed vigor as the energy currents healed his wounds and restored his stamina. He clutched the shell to his chest. It vibrated like a video game controller. A steady humming sound droned in Joel's ears. He looked down at the shell.

"Joel," Marshall said again, this time in a much gentler tone, like the one he used when they first met on the street outside of Art's guitar shop.

Art's guitar shop...

"Stun him, or something!" Felicity yelled.

Marshall took several slow, cautious steps in Joel's direction. "Look at you. You—you have some kind of special power...not just the Sight, but you can *hold the shell*, with all of its energy. I could not! Think of—think about what this means! I'm sorry, you really are—are—I don't know what you are, but it is incredible..."

"Joel, the Aura—release the Aura," Fireflower said.

"I—I have a brilliant idea," Marshall continued, his eyes flashing. "We should team up—yes, team up, return together as—as conquering heroes, as the pioneers of a new age, discoverers of a new world, like—like, who was it? Ah, yes, Lewis and Clark, right?"

Joel continued to stand still while all of his tension drained away. He could hear Marshall talking, but the words were not quite registering with his brain.

"Or, no, no, no, not explorers—rock stars! Yes, of course! We could—we could be in a band together! After all, I was your idol, right? We could form a band—the greatest band the world has ever known!"

"Don't listen to him!" Felicity shouted.

"Yes, the biggest rock stars ever," Marshall continued seductively. "Bigger than Elvis. Bigger than the Beatles. Bigger than Nirvana."

Nirvana...they got into that feud with Guns 'N' Roses...Art's guitar shop...oh yeah! Now I remember—Art quoted Guns 'N' Roses, saying that worrying was a waste of time. Whew, what a relief.

"All of your problems will be solved," Marshall said, moving nearer and nearer to Joel. "Rock stardom—it's what you always wanted, right? And take it from me, it's as awesome as you think it is—no, no, even more so."

Joel continued staring at the shell, satisfied that he had finally answered the question that had been nagging at him. He noticed that the shell was expanding ever so slightly, and that tiny spiral patterns were developing under its surface. Also, its purple glow seemed to be getting brighter, stronger. And was the humming in his ears growing louder?

"All of your problems will be solved," Marshall repeated. "I promise, Joel—you *will* be happy. You will finally have found happiness."

That got Joel's attention. Was Marshall right? After all, happiness is what Joel had been after when he followed Marshall here in the first place.

"Don't do it!" Felicity yelled.

"Just...put the shell down, Joel," Marshall said. "Please. Remember—happiness. Right?"

Joel wrestled with his emotions for a second. Just then, however, pieces of a puzzle fell into place in his mind, and he recalled something else that Art had told him.

"Happiness...is a state of mind," he said calmly.

Smiling, Joel casually tossed the shell at Marshall, who was taken completely by surprise. Stuck in between wanting to catch the shell and not wanting to burn his hands off, Marshall juggled the shell like a potato before he realized that it was no longer as hot as he had expected. A look of malevolent glee spread across his face.

"What are you doing?" Felicity screamed at Joel.

Joel gave her a confident nod with an expression that said *don't worry*.

Marshall held the shell aloft in his left hand triumphantly, peering into its purple glow. "Brilliant—it cooled down on its own," he mused to himself. Then, to Joel, he said, "I suppose you're not so special after all. Consider my offer withdrawn."

"That's fine," Joel said. "There are some other people I'd rather play music with anyway. Um, by the way—I wouldn't keep holding that thing if I were you."

Marshall furrowed his brow and gave Joel a look of sneering contempt, which slowly morphed into an expression of intense agony. The purple glow of the shell was starting to spread like ink onto Marshall's arm, giving off tiny electrical sparks in the process. The humming sound had returned, now audible to all.

"What the—" Marshall shouted as his entire body began to convulse.

"Told you," Joel said as he shrugged, Spectraland-style. Then he ran, scooped Felicity up, and carried her behind the rocks near the edge. Marshall moved to give chase but appeared to be rooted to the spot where he stood.

"What's happening?" Felicity asked.

"Um, it's gonna blow."

"What? How do you—?"

He started to reply but just looked at her with widened eyes instead.

"Ah, right," she said, half smiling. "The Sight. Cool."

Joel set Felicity down on the ground and went back for Fireflower. The dark purple glow had now almost completely enveloped Marshall, who was spasming violently and giving off what looked like miniature lightning bolts. The humming sound continued its steady crescendo. Joel paused as he momentarily took in the gruesome scene.

"Joel?" Fireflower said.

"Oh—yeah, sorry," Joel said before he turned to carry her off toward the rocks.

"Do not be sorry. You have done very well. Thank you."

"Um, okay," Joel said as he laid her down on the ground next to Felicity. He barely had a chance to get down himself before the volume of the humming sound reached arena-rock levels, a huge explosion took place, and everything was momentarily lost in a brilliant flash of blinding white light.

CHAPTER 22: HEADSMOUTH

L
ike a lot of people his age, Joel didn't have much patience for philosophy. Even the morals and life lessons that were couched in the shiny packaging of modern kids' programming and literature tended to go over his head, lost amidst the fancy action, the snappy dialogue, and the bright colors. And so all of the strange quotes and sayings that Art would spout back at the store seemed to Joel like incomprehensible babble, the ramblings of an eccentric old (and to Joel, forty *was* old) man.

But now he got it. Or some of it, anyway. One thing in particular.

♪♪♪

Joel wasn't sure how long it was before the white light had finally faded away. It seemed like seconds, although it could have been hours, for all he knew. Somehow, during that time, he had gone from assuming a duck-and-cover position on top of the islet known as Crownrock to lying flat on his back on some very soft sand. He blinked several times and sat up. It was still night, but the luster and vibrancy of the landscape had been fully restored, making it seem more like dawn. A fountain of dazzling multicolored light was erupting like fireworks from a point off in the near distance. The warmth and humidity had also returned, much to Joel's relief.

Snapping back to full awareness, he quickly glanced around for Felicity and Fireflower. They were there, each several feet away on either side of him, apparently just having regained consciousness as well as their mobility.

"Ugh, I have the *worst* headache," Felicity said, rubbing her temples with her palms.

Joel's eyes followed the light fountain back to its source, which turned out to be the top of Crownrock. He realized that they were on the beach directly in front of the islet. Then another urgent thought popped into his head.

"Sammy," he blurted out, leaping to his feet.

"Wait, Joel—" Felicity said, but it was too late. Joel's heels kicked up sand as he charged down toward the shoreline.

Wading waist-deep through the now-warm water, Joel looked up and located the general area of the islet where he remembered seeing Sammy fall over the edge after Marshall's wavecast struck the little animal. Tracing the silvertail's probable path down with his eyes, Joel saw nothing until he noticed a glint of white among a section of reef jutting out from the water's surface.

"Oh no," he muttered to himself.

With a hollow feeling in the pit of his stomach, Joel made his way over and clambered onto the reef. Seven seconds later, he was crouching over the still, broken body of his little friend. There was no holding back the tears this time.

Felicity and Fireflower arrived by his side as he searched for signs of life in Sammy.

"Um, the Aura's back," he said to Fireflower, trying to regain his composure. "Is—is there anything that you can do?"

Fireflower looked from Sammy to Joel and then sadly shook her head no. "I am sorry," she whispered.

Joel nodded in grim acknowledgement as he gently lifted Sammy into his arms. He eased himself off of the reef and back into the water.

"Should we—uh, maybe go check on top of the plateau or something for—oh, um, I dunno," Felicity said, "you know—Marshall—maybe he's still—"

"He's not," Joel said, his eyes downcast. "Just like Sammy."

As Joel trudged back toward the beach, he heard some unusual whistling noises, like the sounds of a strong wind whipping through a tunnel. He looked around and noticed several thin streaks of light breaking off from the main fountain still emanating from the plateau. The streaks darted around like long-tailed dragonflies until one of them turned and headed straight for him.

He made to dodge it, but it was too fast and it struck Sammy's lifeless form. A moment later, the orb on the end of Sammy's tail lit up, and Joel could feel a little stirring within the animal's body. As Joel stared at Sammy's face in hopeful amazement, the stirring turned into shaking, and then Sammy opened his eyes.

"Um—Sammy?"

The silvertail chirped in response.

Joel blinked several times. "You're alive! Hey—" He turned his head toward Felicity and Fireflower and shouted ecstatically, "He's alive! He's alive!"

"What? Wonderful!" Fireflower exclaimed, her eyes wide with surprise.

"Oh, that is *so* corny," Felicity said under her breath through a half smile. A tear leaked out and trickled down her face, and she quickly wiped it away before anyone could see.

♪♪♪

They made their way back through the Jungle of Darkness, intent on rescuing the slimebacks. Although they faced a number of wild creatures along the way, the return of the warmth and the Aura made the journey seem like a gentle afternoon stroll when compared to their first time through. There was very little talking, as all of them were too overwhelmed with exhaustion and relief to even think of anything that they wanted to say.

Using a tracking cast, they were able to locate the slimebacks in relatively short order. (Joel noted that they could have saved a lot of time using the pathway that they were on now when they were originally headed to Crownrock, but oh well.) As Fireflower had thought, the Aura-sucking angler-mammoth was still safely out cold. The protective shield that she had given the slimebacks had dissipated, but fortunately, the mounts appeared to be unscathed and untouched, with the exception of a few small, cotton-tailed, pad-footed lizards (rabbit geckos?) that were crawling all over the slimebacks' bodies but being largely ignored.

"Destiny!" Joel called, rushing over to her side. "Oh, you're okay. Thank goodness. See, we came back, just like I promised."

"Where do you come up with the stuff you say, Epic 101?" Felicity said.

Joel gave her a sly grin without knowing what a sly grin was. "I read a lot," he said.

Fireflower brushed aside a few of the rabbit geckos before she started to play a lush, soothing melody on her wavebow. A golden layer of light settled onto the slime-backs, and five seconds later, they each slowly got to their feet, tentatively testing the strength of their healed legs by tapping several times on the ground. Destiny gave a happy-sounding croak. Dreamer seemed much less rambunctious than normal as she willingly let Felicity stroke her neck.

The remainder of the way was not without incident, and at one point Joel even endured a nasty gash across his cheek in a scuffle with some badger-clams, but Fireflower healed him up to the point where only a faint scar remained, and eventually, they all finally made it safely out of the Jungle.

Headsmouth village looked a little different than how Joel remembered it. The mushroom-shaped huts and tree houses were still there, in all of the same places, but they seemed to have gained an invisible veneer of restoration—like they had been washed, or polished, or something. Even the natives in the village had a different vibe about them; they all seemed more...*aware*, as opposed to when Joel first met them, when it was like they were walking about in some sort of haze. The village bustled and crackled with activity and lively conversation.

"They are free of the incantation," Fireflower explained. "The one that Marshall used to cloud their memories and turn them into dull, passive servants. You will see that we are actually a very vibrant people, full of life, energy, and brilliance."

"Very cool," Joel said, dodging an errant ball-like object thrown by a nearby child.

"Sorry," the child said in a chirpy, nasal voice as he ran off to chase the ball.

As they rode further into the village, an older, matronly looking female native that Joel did not recognize spotted them. With a look of shock, joy, and disbelief, the native dropped the basket she was carrying and rushed up to them. Joel saw Fireflower anxiously dismount her slimeback to meet the oncoming female with a warm embrace.

"Fireflower!" the native sobbed. "Oh—I—we—we thought you were dead! After the veil was lifted and we could see again, we remembered everything, and—and we..."

"I am here, Mother," Fireflower said through tears of her own. "It is over. The nightmare is over."

"But—but Chief Byle—and—and who are these—these offworlders?" Fireflower's mother said, cautiously looking over her daughter's shoulder at Joel and Felicity.

"They are my friends," Fireflower replied, smiling. "They have helped save us."

Joel and Felicity looked at each other and shrugged, Earth-style.

♪♪♪

Many explanations and reunions later, Joel and Felicity sat in the relative comfort of what was formerly Marshall's primary living quarters, a spacious hut at the base of the chieftain's tree house, sipping on hot, mushroom-flavored beverages. They had earlier refused a number of gracious invitations to remain in Spectraland, including a rather embarrassing offer to be the new Chieftain and Chieftess of Headsmouth ("They can't; they're Wave-makers," Fireflower had said, getting them off the hook).

In spite of Joel's newfound attitude toward worrying, he was still concerned about his mother and sister and was anxious to see them again.

Fireflower felt sure that the secrets to sending them back through the Rift could be found at the temple. So she traveled there, alone, despite Joel and Felicity's insistence that they accompany her; in truth, the two Earthlings were much too exhausted to go anywhere other than home at this point, and so they graciously accepted Fireflower's explanation that it would be much faster for her to go by herself.

"Do you think we'll have the—you know, *ability* when we get back?" Felicity asked absently, not looking up from her cup.

"Hmm, what?" Joel replied. He had been counting the number of concentric circles made by the rippling patterns in his drink.

"The ability...you know, to write...to write hit songs, basically."

"Oh—um, I...I dunno. I thought that was a lie. Mostly everything he told us was a lie."

"Yeah, I know," she said glumly. "I was just...I was really looking forward to that."

"To what?" Joel blinked.

Felicity made her usual expression that preceded biting sarcasm, but then she caught herself, and her features softened. "Music career...people loving me...happiness."

"Um," Joel said as Sammy darted across the floor, batting around a small polka-dotted fruit.

"It's gotta be true, right?" she said hopefully, looking up at Joel. "I mean, you hafta admit, his first two albums *did* suck. So something must've changed."

Joel was momentarily speechless, more so than usual. When he finally found his voice, he said defensively, "Well, no, they didn't—I don't think they sucked, really. I, uh, I actually thought they were pretty good. Really good, actually. I was a fan since the first album."

"The self-titled one? You gotta be kidding me," Felicity scoffed. "That thing was a mess! I mean, 'Hang On Darkness'—pfft, seriously?"

"I—that—oh, come on, that was a great song!" Joel protested. "The way it shifts time signatures every other measure, and then sounds so atonal right before going into the three-part vocal harmonies in the chorus, and then the second bridge being like the same notes as the main riff, just played in a different order, and—"

"Okay, okay, maestro," she interrupted. "Believe me, I understand all that. Yeah, all right, maybe that stuff was amazing for its sheer virtuosity. It's just that—I dunno, it didn't *move* me—emotionally. You know?"

Joel paused and sighed. "Yeah, you're right—I guess."

"You guess? No, dude, I *am* right."

They looked at each other for almost two full seconds before they both broke out laughing.

"I'm glad you spoke up for yourself, though," she said as Sammy jumped nimbly over her outstretched foot.

"It was just slightly harder than fighting an Aura-sucking angler mammoth." He grinned.

Outside, the light of day was starting to fade. The twin moons were already imprinting their massive, shining visages onto the landscape, which at the moment resembled a fluorescent ant farm filled with multicolored sand. Sammy decided that he had had enough of play and sunk his teeth into the tiny polka-dotted berry, splattering little squirts of juice onto Joel's leg. Joel laughed, wiped the juice off with his hand, and took a sip of his mushroom brew.

"Someone told me once, happiness is a state of mind," he said, carefully settling on each word in his head before saying it. His heart started beating faster for some reason.

"Yeah...isn't that what you said to Marshall before you gave him back the shell?" Felicity said, her brow furrowing.

"Yeah, um, I never understood it before. But then, at that moment, I realized what it meant—that happiness isn't being a rich rock star, or ruling a small island, or having a bunch of people loving you. It just means *being* happy. *Choosing* to be happy, and not putting a condition on it. Marshall was never gonna be happy because he was never satisfied. He always wanted something more. He would get it, realize that it didn't make him happy, and then he would try to get something else."

"Well, you can't always be happy. Sometimes sad stuff happens. Then you would just be faking it."

"Oh, no, I know—it's not like that. It's okay to be unhappy sometimes; that's just natural. But I think that after you get over it, like, you know—'this too shall pass,' or whatever, you realize that, well, life goes on, and you think of what you do have to be happy about, like, um, you—what's the word?"

"Appreciate?"

"Yeah, appreciate what you have. I guess, um, I guess I'm just saying that if things are fine, more or less, then you should just choose to be happy."

"Like a default state."

"Exactly! You're in control of your own emotions, so, you know, why make yourself unhappy when you don't have to. Right?"

Felicity paused for what seemed like a very long time (actually forty-four seconds, to be exact), apparently letting it all sink in. A ray of moonlight broke through one of the hut's open windows. Finally, she spoke.

"Being loved is still important, though. Don't you think?"

Joel gave her a puzzled look. "Um, well, yeah, of course."

"Not necessarily by a bunch of people," she said, raising her eyes. "But...at least by one."

Joel gulped. Another splash of berry juice hit his leg as Sammy scurried by.

"I have it!" a breathless Fireflower announced as she came charging through the hut's entrance. "But we need to hurry!"

♪♪♪

After changing back into their Earthly clothing and exchanging hasty goodbyes with various villagers, Joel and Felicity mounted their slimebacks and sped back toward Crownrock with Fireflower in the lead. Along the way, Fireflower explained that she had discovered and learned the incantation to send them back, and that because they had been in Spectraland for less than four cycles, she could return them to nearly the exact time they left Earth, as long as they did it before this current cycle ended. She also proudly displayed her new symbol, the forearm tattoo that would allow her to open the seal to Stonelight Tunnel.

"How did you get it?" Joel asked.

"I—I copied it out of a book," she admitted as Joel and Felicity laughed. "Normally forbidden, yes, but remember, after you leave, I will be the only remaining Wavemaker in Spectraland. The knowledge needs to start again from somewhere."

"Will you be training new Wavemakers?" Felicity asked as the wind whipped through her hair.

"Yes, I will. I will find those with the ability and we will rebuild our order. And we will see to it that nothing like the events of the recent past ever happen again."

They hurried through the tunnel, which seemed even mustier than Joel remembered it, and emerged at the beach amidst a thick grouping of yellow palms. Joel spotted Crownrock right away. The fountain of Aura energy was gone, but he could still perceive an intense concentration of power at the islet's summit. There was a hum in the air, different from when they were here before, but still nearly as powerful. The twin moons blazed high in the night sky, looking like enormous silver dinner plates.

"Hurry!" Fireflower said, leaping off of her slimeback. "The cycle is nearly over!"

Felicity sighed. "We always have to hurry," she grumbled.

They ran across the sand, through the water, and onto the reef. At that moment, Joel realized something.

"Wait—Sammy," he said to Fireflower as the silvertail moved from his left shoulder to his right. "What about Sammy?"

"I—I do not think he will be safe in your world," Fireflower said. "Even if you can keep him hidden, he needs the elements of Spectraland to thrive. I am sorry."

Joel glanced at Felicity, and then at Sammy's wide, dark eyes, and instinctively, he knew that Fireflower was right.

"I will take good care of him," Fireflower said. "Perhaps one day you can return and see us again."

"Okay, let me guess, no more time for sentiment, right?" Felicity said as she jumped from the reef to the base of the islet.

Without another word, they ran up the trail and arrived at the top. A misty sphere of silver light, eight feet in diameter, hung in the air just a few inches above the ground in the center of the plateau.

"Stand over there," Fireflower instructed, pointing at the sphere.

Joel and Felicity set their wavebows on the ground and walked forward. Sammy chittered in Joel's ear, jumped off, and then ran over to sit next to Fireflower.

They entered the silver light and were instantly engulfed by it. It felt warm and tingly all over.

"Well, um, that was fun, huh?" Joel said. His voice sounded like he was talking though an old telephone receiver.

"Yeah, way fun." Felicity smirked.

"Stand closer," Fireflower called out as she began to play a complex succession of notes and chords on her wavebow. The melody that she generated sounded perfectly in tune with the humming sound in the air.

Joel and Felicity edged closer together.

"Closer!" Fireflower shouted.

They moved closer until their arms were touching.

"Is this really necessary?" Felicity shouted back.

"No." Fireflower smiled.

The music swelled. Joel could feel the electrical currents coursing through his body. Or were they something else?

"So, yeah, look me up online, maybe we could, I dunno, get together to jam sometime," Felicity said, looking straight ahead.

"Um, I dunno, after seeing you every day for months, I might need a little break," Joel replied.

She hit him on the arm. He looked at her. She had a full smile on her face.

Then tiny colored streams of light danced before his eyes, and everything went dark.

EPILOGUE

Julio set his empty drink glass on the counter as he headed out of the club. Normally, he never walked out on bands midset, and especially not midsong, just out of courtesy to his fellow musicians. He knew, from over fifteen years of playing shows, making flyers, sending out emails, and recording demos, just how hard it was to "make it" in the music business. Now that he was *part* of that business—on the other side, so to speak—he wanted to remember his roots. And to help himself do that, he tried his best to never disrespect someone else's performance, no matter how lifeless or unlistenable it was.

But tonight was different. He hadn't been in a good mood to begin with, after fighting with his wife in the morning and getting chewed out by his boss in the afternoon, and it seemed like today was one of those days where he would have been better off just staying in bed. This band that he had come to see was well recommended by a trusted source, and the buzz on the street seemed genuine enough, but either they didn't have it at all tonight or Julio's source had misled him.

Discovering new bands to sign had always been a challenging job to begin with, and these days, with the Internet and the seemingly endless amount of new "talent" being churned out every day, ferreting out the diamonds from the garbage was an arduous, grueling task. It had been a long time since Julio had found a diamond, and the pressure was on him to perform; he couldn't coast on his track record forever, not when the label was losing so much money and good people were being let go left and right.

As he walked out the door, he took an absentminded glance at a colorful flyer plastered on the window that advertised a show for the following week. He wasn't sure why, among the dozens of other pieces of paper surrounding it, this particular example of self-promotion caught his attention; perhaps it was the unique computer-generated graphics, which depicted wild hybrid animals in a surreal-looking tropical landscape, or perhaps it was the sheer naiveté in its declaration of "FIRST SHOW!" He took note of what he assumed was the band name, printed near the top of the flyer in plain courier font:

Joel Suzuki and The Wavemakers

Quaint, Julio thought to himself as he stepped into the chilly, wet Seattle night. He thrust his hands deeper into the pockets of his leather jacket and headed back for his car, which was parked on a side street seven city blocks away (even though he could easily afford to park in a structure, one of his many quirks was a general refusal, on principle, to pay for parking).

As he walked down the street, he was momentarily startled by the sounds of a fight. Julio wasn't a big man, or a particularly brave one, and he usually went to great lengths to avoid conflict and keep himself out of trouble. With a technique honed to perfection during years on the road with his band, he looked around for the source of the sounds without making it obvious that he was looking; his eyes shifted left and right ever so slightly, and a casual turn of the head revealed what was happening without drawing attention to himself.

He saw two teenage boys, one fairly short and stocky, with a muscular build, and another, taller, lankier one, engaged in a very heated argument next to an even more overheated black, souped-up '65 Mustang, which was belching columns of black smoke from its engine.

"You stupid moron!" the short one yelled.

"Mitch, dude, it's not my fault!" the taller one shot back.

Julio appraised the situation, decided that it was neither a threat to him nor something that he should get involved in, and continued walking. *Stupid kids*, he thought to himself, moving to the other side of the street just in case.

Just as he reached his car, trying to decide whether to hit another club or go home and argue with his wife some more, a brief glint by the curb caught his eye as he crossed back over. Well-hidden under a landscaping bush was a compact disc, its presence revealed by the light of the nearby street lamp that struck its shiny surface at just the right angle. Normally Julio was a germaphobe and never touched anything that had been on the ground (he once threw away a Parker Premier fountain pen that his sister had given to him for his birthday because he had accidentally dropped it on the office bathroom floor), but for some reason, curiosity overrode caution tonight and he retrieved the disc.

He turned it over in his hand and felt a brief twinge of nostalgia. He hadn't seen, much less held, an actual compact disc in months. Everything was directly on the computer now. It had actually been that way for a while, but for older die-hards of an earlier era like Julio, it still took some getting used to. He had always preferred the physical nature of grabbing an album with your hands, looking at the art printed directly on the disc, thumbing through the glossy insert pages, straining to read the lyrics and the credits in tiny microtype. Back then, an album was an *album,* a collection of songs that were meant to hang together as a cohesive message from an artist at that point in their lives, a collection of songs that were meant to be listened to all together, in the order that the artist arranged them in, from start to finish, in a single sitting.

Julio stepped off of his internal soapbox and got into his car, which he noticed had been freshly keyed from hood to trunk. Sighing, he sat down in the driver's seat and fired up the ignition. He looked at the compact disc in his hand. It was a Maxell CD-RW, and it had been preprinted with the following information:

Art's Guitars - Buy, Trade, Sell
(206) 555-2789

Julio's heart sank. For some unknown reason, for a split second he had thought that perhaps the universe had just thrown him some kind of a bone, that maybe he had randomly stumbled onto the Next Big Thing, thrown away like a misread winning lottery ticket on the side of the road. It would have been one of those incredible, you-can't-make-this-stuff-up *Behind The Music* VH1 biography stories that you see only on television, or perhaps in books or movies.

But, sadly, this was real life, and real life was probably a blank disc that some two-bit local music store had used as a drink coaster. Since it was already halfway between his hand and his CD changer, Julio slipped it in and turned up the volume, expecting total silence. He released the parking brake and began to drive away. Then, he panicked for a brief moment. *Will this thing mess up my CD player?*

Before he could press "stop," the CD player recognized the single track that was present on the disc and began to play it.

Julio lost track of where he was driving. A combination of instinct and sheer luck prevented him from plowing into a coffee kiosk that had been long closed for the night.

"Oh my g—" he said to himself as he fired up his car phone.

Ring...

Ring...

Ring...

"C'mon, Larry, pick up, pick up," Julio muttered as the track played on in the background.

Ring...

"This is Larry," a gruff-sounding voice answered on the other end.

"Oh—Larry, dude, guess what—you are not gonna believe this. I just found the most *amazing* band I have ever heard...."

www.joelsuzuki.com

Made in the USA
Columbia, SC
12 April 2019